The Steeple Chase

Dave Biebel is the author of *The Radon Files,* book one in the
Rocky Mountain Dossier series, as well as several nonfiction
books. He and his family live in Colorado Springs, Colorado,
where he is communications director of the Christian Medical
and Dental Society. He is an ordained pastor with the
Evangelical Free Church.

The
Steeple Chase

DAVE BIEBEL

Fleming H. Revell
A Division of Baker Book House
Grand Rapids, Michigan 49516

© 1994 by Dave Biebel

Published by Fleming H. Revell
a division of Baker Book House Company
P.O. Box 6287, Grand Rapids, MI 49516-6287

Printed in the United States of America

This story is fictitious. Any resemblance, whether in name, setting, or event, to organizations past or present, or persons living or dead, is unintentional or by permission.

Library of Congress Cataloging-in Publication Data

Biebel, David B.
      The steeple chase : a novel / by Dave Biebel.
         p.   cm.—(The Rocky Mountain dossier ; bk. 2)
      ISBN 0-8007-5522-7
      1. Church—Rocky Mountains Region—Fiction. I. Title.
    II. Series: Biebel, David B. Rocky Mountain dossier ; bk. 2.
PS3552.I3436S74   1994
813'.54—dc20   94-3904

Unless otherwise noted, Scripture quotations are from the King James Version of the Bible.

Some Scripture quotations are taken from *Life Recovery Bible: The Living Bible* (Wheaton, Illinois: Tyndale House Publishers, 1992).

The readings in chapter 11 are taken from Gerald G. May, *Addiction & Grace: Love & Spirituality in the Healing of Addictions* (San Francisco: Harper San Francisco, 1988), page 5.

The quote by Rabbi Harold Kushner in chapter 21 is taken from Harold Kushner, *When Bad Things Happen to Good People* (New York: Avon Books, 1983), page 134.

To

**Tim and Diane
Ron and D. J.**

Friends when I needed some

1

The second thing Nate Freeman noticed as he retrieved the morning paper from his front porch was a small package, wrapped in plain brown paper, leaning against the post by the steps. The young minister dropped the cup of coffee he'd been holding, and dove back inside the house. After the recent bomb threats, he couldn't be too careful.

Freeman sat on the floor in the bathroom, his back against the old cast-iron tub for protection, and tried to collect his thoughts. His black labrador retriever, Rowdy, had followed Freeman into the small room. Rowdy sat directly in front of his master, waiting and wagging, anxious to play this new game.

"This ain't Belfast, Rowd," the preacher said, finally. "It's Raptor, Colorado."

He stood, walked back to the kitchen, poured himself another cup of coffee, then looked out the window at the parcel. The fact that the deer had nibbled the buds off his roses again—the first thing he'd noticed—had suddenly become unimportant compared to finding out what was in that package.

But as he stared at the bundle, a movement behind it caught his eye. Mocha, his favorite horse, was standing at the gate, as she did every morning, waiting for their after-breakfast ride. She whinnied, nodding her head up and down when she saw him.

"Yep," Freeman said out loud. "Still tryin' to scare us outta town—but we don't scare easy." He walked resolutely outside, picked up the box, and brought it indoors. His hands trembled slightly as he examined the container more closely.

Rowdy took one sniff of the wrapper and started to whine.

"You know somethin' I don't, pup?" Freeman asked.

Then he noticed the blood, just a small fleck of it on one corner of the paper, too deeply crimson to be paint or ink, or any type of spilled liquid. Pulling out the Buck pocketknife he'd won twenty years earlier in the youth division of bronc busting at the state rodeo, the cowboy preacher slit open the covering and laid the box on his kitchen table.

Inside, he found another tightly-wrapped bundle, perhaps three inches wide by four inches long, and quite flat. It was soft, yet firm, in a way only a piece of meat can be. Freeman unfolded the note taped to the parcel and read: "Keep your mouth shut. Or you'll never preach again."

He opened the inner wrapping slowly, until the freezer paper fell away, revealing the last few inches of . . . a tongue.

Freeman gasped and jumped back from the table. Despite the many animals he'd butchered, and the various ways he knew body parts could be used, the mountain minister wasn't prepared for the double impact of the note and the package's contents.

Freeman sat down again at the table, studying the tissue before him. He'd seen pig, goat, sheep, deer, elk, and

8

cow tongues often enough to know that this one didn't come from any of those animals. "C'mere, Rowd," he said, letting the dog lick his hand as he eyed its tongue. *Ain't dog, neither,* he thought, rising from the table and returning to the bathroom.

Anybody saw me now, he observed to himself as he faced the mirror and extended his own tongue, *they'd think I was plumb loco!*

The sardonic humor quickly gave way to horror, however, as Freeman finally let register in his brain what his intuition had been telling him all along. *Human!* Suddenly, it was all he could do to keep from losing his breakfast. *Who'd do such a thing? Who* could *do such a thing?*

He walked back into the kitchen and reached for the phone. "Hello, Chief Price? Nate Freeman. Sorry to bother you this early, but somebody left a little present on my porch you need to see."

"Another gag, Reverend?" Price replied. "I'm a busy man. I can't run over every time someone makes you feel unwelcome."

"But this time a law's been broke. I'm sure of it."

"Oh, really." Price's voice dripped with sarcasm. "Then I better come over, since I'm the only law around!"

Freeman nursed his coffee thoughtfully, eyeing the package as he waited for the policeman to arrive. *After callin' me paranoid last week, Price'll have to eat his words. Bad stuff's happenin', right under his nose.*

"Then again," he said to the dog, as he put down his cup and strode to the knife rack on the wall. "Then again, maybe bad things are happenin' right under his nose because he don't want to see 'em!"

With one swift motion of a meat cleaver, Freeman sliced a sliver of flesh from the organ on the table. He wrapped it tenderly in a clean linen handkerchief, enclosed it in a small plastic bag, and placed the packet in the refrigerator, just as the police car pulled up at the front porch.

"Mornin', Chief. Thanks for comin'," Freeman said, handing the lawman a steaming cup of coffee, along with the note.

Price glanced at the paper, turned it over, then looked at the minister rather disdainfully.

"Reverend," he started, deliberately. "I thought you said a law's been broke. I wouldn't call this note friendly, mind you, but you're overreacting again. Face it, Reverend, it's time to find another parish. You got only thirty people left now, and no building of your own to meet in. No people, no building—I'd say you're a man without a job."

Freeman stiffened just a bit, which still left him four inches shorter than the six-foot, two-hundred-fifty-pound lawman. The smaller man pulled nervously on his bushy mustache for a moment and then adjusted his wire-rim glasses before replying.

"I'll be outta work when *my Boss* says so. So far, all he's said is not to let his house become a den of thieves!"

"Den of thieves!" Price guffawed. "Ain't you seen that Steve Martin flick? The real thieves are robbing little old ladies in the name of the Lord!"

Again he laughed derisively, much louder than before. But when Freeman refused to be baited, the chief continued. "At least when they get done turning that church into the Cathedral Casino, gamblers'll get something back for their money. They're gonna put the biggest five-dollar slot machine in the world—Mephistopheles—right where the altar is now. All the symbols are magical. Can't wait to play it when they open on Halloween."

Freeman cringed inwardly at the blasphemy, but kept a poker face.

"Think of it positively, Reverend," Price continued. "Instead of people walking out of there feeling guilty, they could walk out with some big money without losing big bucks."

"Five million bucks, last month alone," Freeman replied. "That ain't big bucks?"

"Nope. Just a lot of people spending a little at a time. Only one person in town sees anything wrong with that."

"This town has been ruined," Freeman replied forcefully. "If I don't tell the truth about it, nobody ever will."

"Truth, Reverend? Seems the truth is, you were stupid enough to turn down a million bucks for that old building!"

"Only stupid decision *we* made was trustin' Skip Sanders. We didn't know the loan could be called anytime. Couldn't buy it, so they stole it instead."

"Banks don't steal churches, Reverend," Price chortled. "You're taking this way too personal."

"I ain't the only one," Freeman replied, gesturing for Price to follow him into the kitchen. "Ever since I started picketing, they been tryin' to scare me outta town. Evidently, they'll even *kill* to get their point across."

"Kill?" Price repeated. "You think this note is a death threat? You *are* paranoid."

"Maybe," Freeman said. "Maybe not. Look what came with it." He pointed to the package on the table.

Price walked over, took a quick look, and said, "Deer season, Reverend. Just another practical joke."

"Look closer."

11

Price leaned over, apparently examining the tissue in the box, then stood up and said, "Deer. No question about it." And before Freeman could do anything to stop him, the chief led the dog to the front door and tossed the object out onto the grass. Within seconds, Rowdy had pounced upon the piece of flesh, disappearing around the back of the barn to devour it in private.

Freeman stood in the doorway with his mouth hanging open. "I can't believe," he said, finally. "Can't believe you did that."

"Why not, Reverend?" the chief said over his shoulder as he got into the cruiser. "The dog'll make better use of it than you or me!"

Stunned, Nate Freeman watched the cruiser disappear down his driveway.

Before the dust settled, the preacher picked up his phone.

"Operator," he said, quietly, "I need yer help. I need to reach the police. No, not the local police. Sheriff? Maybe. State police? Sure. Could you say that number again, please? Thanks."

He paused, pondering the millions of dollars in new tax revenue pouring into the state's treasury as a result of the legalization of low-stakes gambling. Would a county or state law enforcement officer risk biting the hand that was feeding him?

"Is there anybody else?" he asked. "Federal Bureau of Investigation, Boulder? Right. Shoulda thought of that myself. Thank you, ma'am."

2

Bruce Davidson, bureau chief of the Boulder, Colorado, FBI office, tried to focus on the illuminated dial of the alarm clock next to his bed. *Eight o'clock!* he castigated himself. *Slept through it again. Today, of all days. That minister is supposed to be in my office in an hour.*

The forty-one-year-old agent rolled over and looked at his springer spaniel, Sandy, still curled up contentedly next to him on the queen-size bed they shared every night. He frowned at the empty Old Grand-Dad bottle on the nightstand, cursing his growing tolerance for hard liquor.

He'd been battling the bottle for years, but his current slide had begun in earnest seven months earlier after Clare Conroy had turned down his marriage proposal. The younger agent had only asked for time to think it over. But days turned into weeks, and weeks into months, until he required at least a quart of whiskey each night just to get to sleep and escape the pain, plus a double on the nightstand when he woke up, to jump-start the day.

The warm Coke and rum he'd mixed at midnight would have gagged him six months earlier; now he simply gulped it down, and stumbled toward the bathroom.

His hand was trembling as he tried to shave, as much from the alcohol as from his anxiety about being late again for work. The new razor helped a little, conforming to his face just as promised in the ads. But as the shaving cream gradually disappeared, Davidson found himself face-to-face with a person he hardly knew anymore. Maybe it was the still-blurred vision or the headache, but the feelings of condemnation and worthlessness that greeted him each morning had been getting worse. As the self-hatred increased, so did his longing to open another bottle.

The only thing keeping Davidson from capitulating was the slim hope that Conroy, who worked with him daily, might still change her mind. If, or when, that happened, he certainly wanted to be sober enough to realize it.

The fear that alcohol might put his position at risk never bothered the chief, however. He was counting on his best friend and assistant, Fred Billings, to cover for him. After all they'd been through together, Billings owed him that.

Dressing quickly, Davidson paused on his way out the front door to face the sixteen-by-twenty enlargement of the last photo ever taken of his wife, Ellen. "I'm sorry," he muttered as he did every time he passed that spot. Even after eleven years, he still felt totally responsible for her death from a car bomb intended for him. He shook his head, sadly, as he walked by.

"It went entirely according to plan," Leonard Price said to Stanley Hawkins. Price fanned the ten one-hundred-dollar bills Hawkins had just handed him. "Freeman is one scared rabbit, no doubt about it," Price continued. "When I tossed that tongue to his dog, I thought he was going to have a coronary. He really believed it was human."

"It *was*."

"You—You're kidding."

"Not at all. The guy's worked in a slaughterhouse," Hawkins said. "We knew the only way to impress him was with the real thing. That's why we told you to get rid of the evidence."

"I had no idea," Price said, quietly. "Are you crazy?"

Hawkins gently stroked the ugly scar on his left temple as he stared coldly at Price. "Use that word again in relation to me," Hawkins said, finally, "and you'll regret it."

Price tried to recover. "What I meant was, why risk the whole project by putting a body part on the guy's front porch? What if he tells somebody?"

"Because," Hawkins said, "then they'd be even more convinced he's lost his marbles."

Hawkins laughed, then looked directly at Price. "I'll worry about the small stuff, Chief, and you worry about the reason we brought you to Raptor. To get real blunt, we're not happy this preacher is still in town. He's here when the Cathedral Casino opens, there will be hell to pay. Am I making myself clear?"

"Yes," Price replied. "But how far do we go? Freeman sees himself as some kind of messiah."

"Does he have family?" Hawkins asked, narrowing his eyes and fondling his scar again.

"Nobody local," Price said. "Just a dog and some horses."

"Start with the dog," Hawkins said. "No, better yet— I'll take care of it."

At 9:25 A.M., Nate Freeman followed Bruce Davidson into the director's spacious office, its west-facing windows framing a panoramic view of the Rockies' front range. Fred

15

Billings joined them a few moments later, through a door in the north wall connecting his office with Davidson's.

After a few initial pleasantries, and some very strong and somewhat bitter coffee, Davidson immediately got to the point. "Reverend Freeman," he began, "our analysis of the tissue sample you brought in last week confirmed your suspicions. That is why we asked you to return."

Freeman leaned forward in the dark brown leather-upholstered chair; he placed the coffee cup on the glass table before him, and nodded his head. "Knew it," he said. "Had to be human. Sorry I couldn't bring the whole thing."

"You brought enough for DNA screening," Davidson replied. "We just got the results back from Washington."

"Really! You mean you know who it came from?"

"Not exactly," Davidson said. "But we know it was from a Caucasian female, probably twelve to sixteen years old, with brown hair." As he spoke, the bureau chief reached under his desk to activate a recording device. He also glanced toward the small one-way mirror in the office's south wall, through which he knew Agent Clare Conroy was observing.

"Must be a million girls fit that description," Freeman said.

"True," Davidson replied. "But how many of them have ever been in or near Raptor, Colorado?" He paused, carefully studying the slate-gray eyes of the wiry young clergyman before him, looking for any sign of anxiety. "And also knew you?"

When Freeman noticed how intently Davidson was watching him, he said, "You don't . . . you don't think I had somethin' to do with it."

"Not directly," Davidson answered immediately. "But

there has to be some reason this victim's body part ended up on your front porch instead of somewhere else."

The bureau chief nodded to Billings, who reached for the briefcase next to his chair, flipped it open, and retrieved a stack of file folders. He placed them on the table between Davidson and Freeman.

"So," Davidson continued, as he handed the top file to Freeman, "we pulled the files of missing persons who matched the profile and were also thought to be in our region. Maybe you'll recognize one of them."

Freeman opened the folder, glanced at the photo attached to the file's first page, closed it quickly and laid it next to the stack. "Not this one," he said, quietly. "But I had no idea there were so many."

"Thousands," Davidson replied. "Most of them simply disappear and are never heard from again."

Must be agony for the parents, Freeman thought, opening the second file. This time, he just shook his head, put the file on top of the first one, and reached for the third.

By the time he reached the fifteenth folder, there were tears in his eyes. But suddenly, as he opened that one, his face turned ashen, and he sucked in a long breath. Without a word, he jumped up, teeth clenched and fists tightened, and walked to the windows. He stared at the mountains, toward Raptor, for a full minute before saying, "I knew that one. We talked a couple of times . . . on the street, in front of my church."

Davidson reached for the folder, and read the name, "Stephanie Lockwood . . . runaway. She'd be sixteen."

"I was picketing," Freeman said, turning to face Davidson. "That's what I do every day, and sometimes all night, too. Can't sleep knowin' what they're doin' to the house

17

of God. Anyway, late one night, maybe two o'clock, this girl walks up and stands in front of me for the longest time, without sayin' a word."

He took his seat again as he continued, "She hardly blinked, like she was in a trance. And then, when we're the only people left on the street, she comes over and says the strangest thing. 'You are the light,' she says, 'and I am in darkness. Please, help me.'

"I didn't know what to say, at first," Freeman continued. "But then it came to me. 'Jesus is the light,' I said. 'And he loves you very much.' But when I said that name, she nearly had a fit, like a . . . a . . . ."

"Seizure?" Davidson interjected.

"Yup," Freeman replied. "I've seen it, couple times, y'know, epileptics. But this was differ'nt. All of a sudden, I hear another voice, deeper, but coming from her. 'Jesus is dead,' it says. 'Jesus is dead.'"

Wonder what they'd think if I told 'em I thought she was demon possessed? he thought. *Can't risk it. They'll think I'm a kook.*

"And then she just turns and wanders away, repeatin' those words, over and over," he continued. "I didn't expect to see her again," the pastor added, "but a week later she came back, 'bout the same time of night. And this time she was freer, more normal—I don't know how to describe it. We sat on the church steps, an' she talked non-stop, least two hours. Took her all that time to get to the point, but when she did, it was pretty gruesome—so gruesome, in fact, I thought maybe she was makin' it up."

"Please, be as specific as possible," Davidson said, checking under his desk to be sure the tape was still running. "We need to know everything you remember, even if it doesn't seem important. We'll sort it out later."

Shortly after Chief Price left Stanley Hawkins's office in the Settler's Bank building, the phone rang at the Kingsford estate, former home of gold magnate Cecil Kingsford, founder of Raptor. The spacious manor guarded the entrance of the inactive Kingsford Mine, located north of town, its access road at the bottom of Hawk Mountain Pass. In March 1993, the property had become home to Cynthia Stamford, a wealthy widow. She answered the phone.

"Hello, Mrs. Stamford?" Hawkins said. "Or do you like that other name better? What is it you call yourself? Aradia, isn't it?" Hawkins guffawed into the phone.

"Why don't you worry about your stuff and let me worry about mine?" Stamford replied.

"Right. Well we have a problem. Our preacher boy still didn't get the point and get out of town. And our New York friends are getting impatient."

"It's hard to believe Costellini's afraid of a two-bit hick who's shorter than me," the woman said.

"If you know what's good for you," Hawkins snapped, "you'll never connect that name with this town again. Or, for that matter," he added, "with the word *afraid*."

"Okay," she replied, "but if you guys are so tough, why don't you just do to Freeman what you do to everyone else who gets in your way?"

"We will," Hawkins growled, "if we have to. But people might ask the wrong questions if this punk just vanished, after picketing every day with a sandwich board claiming the bank stole his church."

19

"I thought all the tracks were covered."

"They are. Only Sanders knows what really happened."

"Why not just ignore Freeman, then, and let people think he's another fundamentalist nut?"

"They already do, and he doesn't care. So it's time to deliver a message he can't miss. I have another project for your group."

3

Well," Nate Freeman said to the two FBI agents, "if you want to know everythin', I'll begin at the beginning. My daddy was killed in a gunfight when I was four. After that, Mom worked as a barmaid, the only job she could find. But we kept movin', mostly in Texas and Oklahoma, 'cause after a few weeks in every little town the men would be hangin' round like a bunch of dogs, drinkin' and carousin' and fightin' over Mom. When she'd had enough, we'd up and move again.

"Eventually she married Lester, a professional rodeo rider, rough and tough and always movin', too. But at least Mom didn't have to work no more, till Lester got kicked by a bronc, and by then we was pretty well grown.

"When I was a teenager, I spent all my time ridin', ropin', shootin', and generally carryin' on with the boys, and never bothered with school. I didn't need no diploma to make my livin' in the rodeo, which was all I really cared about.

"Well, one day when I was seventeen, a tent meetin'

came to town, and Mom dragged me into it, even though she wasn't very religious. Guess she was desperate to keep me from wastin' my life. Anyway, during that meetin', God got ahold of me, and I just knew I was supposed to preach. It was a little late to finish high school, but I did finish my GED.

"The only school that would take me was Faith Bible Institute in Pueblo. During my second year there, I met a beautiful dark-haired, green-eyed girl named Annie at a church meetin', and we started datin'. Got married a year later. After I graduated, I applied all over Colorado, but the only church that would take me was Raptor Community. I never knew till later, I was the only applicant. Guess nobody else cared to deal with the feast or famine—summers crowded with tourists, winters a ghost town. But, far as I was concerned, I'd died and gone to heaven."

"Nobody's home," Randy Stebbins said to the two women in the metallic-blue Lumina van as he climbed back behind the wheel. One of the women slid the side door open and quickly stepped out, extending a doggy treat in the direction of Rowdy, Nate Freeman's black lab, who had been sniffing and wagging his way around the vehicle since it had pulled up in front of the parsonage.

"Here, doggy. Nice doggy," she said.

Rowdy wagged his way over and gratefully devoured the munchies, which were followed by more treats, until the dog was sitting on the ground, licking the dark-haired woman's hand. He never noticed the syringe in her other hand; he was so involved in enjoying this unexpected pleasure that he hardly felt the needle pierce his skin. When he lost consciousness thirty seconds later, he still had a Milk-Bone dog biscuit between his teeth. The second woman dislodged the food from Rowdy's mouth as she checked for a pulse. "Perfect," she said, pulling a scalpel from the small black leather pouch at her waist. Randy knelt beside her, holding a silver chalice covered with etchings, while the woman deftly sliced open the dog's jugular vein.

"Right after the town voted to legalize gambling," Nate Freeman continued his story, "Annie had this premonition. She started beggin' me to take her outta there. Even called the district superintendent herself, askin' him to send me someplace, anyplace, else.

"'What better place to be?' I said. 'We'll give people a place of refuge when they've cast all their money before the god of chance.'

"At first, Annie stuck with me. But one by one, the shop owners—most of them church members—sold out and left town. Before long, Annie began to argue with me. 'Can't you see what's happening, Nate?' she'd yell. 'Pretty soon, the church will be the only non-casino on Casino Boulevard. You think you can keep it going in the middle of all that sin?'

"Within a few months, her words came true, and there was an anonymous offer—a million bucks, cash, take it or leave it. They even offered me an 'incentive'—ten percent—to mediate the sale. I mediated, all right. I reminded the people about makin' deals with the devil, and what Jesus did when Satan offered him the whole world if he would only bow down.

"After a bitter debate, the vote was even, thirty-four to

thirty-four—that's all the people we had left. But I hadn't voted yet. I wanted it to be their decision, since the building had been built by their parents and grandparents. I looked at Annie, who handed me a little note. 'Your choice, Nate. I don't care about the money. But either leave town, with me . . . or stay in this God-forsaken place, without me.' I cast my vote, and before I could get home that night, Annie was packed and on her way back to Pueblo."

Davidson glanced at Billings, unable to hide his astonishment. "You chose *the church* over your own marriage?" he interrupted.

"You might say that," the minister replied, softly. "But as far as I was concerned, I couldn't violate my callin', for money or for love. Besides, I knew Annie wasn't thinkin' straight. She wanted a family, but the more I tried to save the town, the less I was home. And when I was home, I was so beat I was a zero fer romance. That vote was just the last straw."

"It's done," Cynthia Stamford said. It'll be interesting to see if our preacher boy gets the message this time."

"Thanks," Stanley Hawkins replied into the phone. "How about a wager, say a thousand bucks? He leaves, I win. He stays, you win."

"He leaves, we *both* win," Stamford responded. "How do I win if he stays?"

"Because, in that case you'll get rid of him," Hawkins said. "And of course we'll videotape it, like with the girl, and clear a hundred thousand, just in Europe. So we both win, either way. I'm just tryin' to make it more exciting. Low stakes gambling is definitely not my bag."

***

"Reverend Freeman," Fred Billings said, "we certainly hope you'll be able to work things out with your wife. But I'd like to hear more about the harassment, and how that might connect with the apparent death of Stephanie Lockwood."

"I'd like to know that part, too," Freeman replied. "But as far as the harassment—I call it persecution—goes, it started when I started picketing. And I started picketing right after they stole my church!"

Again the minister leaped up; he walked to the window and paced in front of it as he continued. "After that vote, half the people left. But we had no debt, and I never took my pay till all the bills was covered. So we had no money worries, until . . ." He paused, turning back to gaze toward the mountains. "Until Skip Sanders, former chairman of our church board, started pushin' for new pews and a pipe organ. We was gettin' along fine, as far as I was concerned. The church was filled every Sunday, mostly gamblers, broke, with nothin' else to do. I was sure we'd done the right thing, and that was all that mattered.

"But Sanders, last winter, started pushin' to renovate. 'If we're goin' to have so many visitors,' he said, 'we need a nicer atmosphere than old wooden pews and an out-of-tune piano.' And borrowin' forty thousand dollars was no problem, since he was president of the bank.

"Biggest mistake I ever made was listenin' to Sanders. Or maybe it was lettin' him handle everything." Again, he paused, thoughtfully. "No, my biggest mistake was comparin' my church to others in the district. I even hoped Annie would come back if she saw how good we was doin'.

"Then all of a sudden, the bank gets sold, and Sanders

25

up an' leaves town a millionaire—maybe multimillionaire, judgin' by the pictures I seen of his place in Acapulco.

"Next thing we know, we get this letter from the new bank statin' that since our ability to repay the loan is questionable, they're callin' in the loan. Gave us thirty days to come up with the cash or vacate the premises. Well, nobody still attendin', including me, had any money, so we had no choice. We been meetin' in the grade school since then, and I been picketing every night.

"About a month ago, Chief Price—that's our only policeman—comes by and warns me if I get in the way of the workers, he'll have to arrest me. The same week, the bomb threats started, then sugar in my gas tank, crushed glass in my horse feed, things like that. But I never expected to find a human body part on my front porch, I'll tell ya that!"

Freeman paused and looked at Davidson, then at Billings, shaking his head. He walked silently to the couch and took his seat again.

"Reverend Freeman," Davidson said, "I think we've heard enough for today . . . enough to warrant our getting involved. So, here's a proposal. Keep doing what you've been doing. Just keep your eyes and ears open. We'll send an agent up there undercover, as soon as possible, who will become known to you by using the words 'cathedral' and 'conspiracy' in the same sentence.

"In return," Davidson continued, "we'll ask some of our people to closely examine how your church was stolen. There's six weeks before Halloween. Maybe we can still keep the Cathedral Casino from opening."

Freeman leaped from his seat, smiling broadly, and

embraced Davidson. The agent was more surprised by the strength in the younger man's hands than by the hug itself.

"I would gladly lay down my life to save my church," Freeman exclaimed.

"We certainly wouldn't want it to come to that," Davidson answered. "But this obviously isn't cowboys and Indians, with rubber-tipped arrows. So circle the wagons, pardner. The cavalry is coming."

"Thanks," Freeman replied. "But circling the wagons ain't my style. I'd rather have a showdown on Main Street at high noon."

4

are bird, don't you think?" Clare Conroy asked Fred Billings, as she entered Davidson's office seconds after the chief had left to escort Nathan Freeman to the parking lot.

Billings, standing at the window, turned and nodded. Then he draped his left leg over the corner of Davidson's solid walnut desk. "Single-minded, that's for sure," he replied.

"Are they all that way?"

"All who?" Billings asked.

"Ministers."

"Can't say from my own experience," Billings said. "I've only known one, twenty years ago." *Degenerate that he was. All the demons of hell couldn't force me back inside the doors of any church after what he did to me.*

"Same for me," Clare said, "but much more recently—specifically, earlier this year. Being the personal assistant of the Reverend Dr. J. R. Jenner was a real test. You know, when you hear something—anything—often enough, it starts sounding true, even if you know it's a lie. And I hate to admit it, but I've never heard anyone speak with such authority."

"Did you . . . lose your professional objectivity?" Billings asked. As soon as the words left his lips, he apologized. "I'm sorry. You don't have to explain anything to me. It all worked out in the end."

"It's okay, Fred. I need to talk to somebody about this. If Bruce hadn't lost his objectivity about me, he would have asked me to unload afterward. Truthfully, I became more attached to Jenner than I should have."

Conroy blushed. Pushing back her short blonde hair, the twenty-seven-year-old agent walked over to the coffee-pot, poured herself a cup, then returned to the couch and sat down.

After letting Conroy compose herself, Billings looked into his colleague's sky-blue eyes. "Is that why you turned Bruce down?" he asked.

She hesitated, searching Fred's face. "He said I turned him down? I never said *no*; I just asked for time to think it over . . . and, since then, it hasn't come up again."

"And if it did?" Billings replied. Immediately, he corrected himself. "Sorry; I only ask because Bruce and I have become such good friends. I know how troubled he's been since that day."

"I've noticed," Clare replied. "But with losing the case and the reprimand from H.Q., it could have another source."

"Love does funny things to a person," Billings commented, turning back toward the window.

"I suppose so," Conroy replied, "though I can't speak from experience. Closest I've ever come was with Jenner, and I seriously doubt it was really love."

Without turning around, Billings said, "In certain less guarded moments, Bruce has confided how much he cares for you. What you do with that, of course, is between you and him.

"At the moment," he continued, "perhaps we should focus on how to handle the puzzling case of the Reverend Nathan Freeman."

"Maybe agent Conroy should spend a couple months in the mountains," Conroy said. "I'm not an office person. I need to get back into action. Besides, with the tension between Bruce and me, it's pretty hard for either of us to concentrate."

"It's not my call," Billings replied. "But Raptor is fairly near your last assignment. What if someone recognized you?"

"How could the worlds of J. R. Jenner and Nate Freeman possibly intersect?" Conroy replied, chuckling. "But it's a good point. So, here's a proposition. I'll be back in a few minutes, in disguise. If Bruce doesn't recognize me, you'll support my assignment to Raptor. If he does, I'll apply for a transfer."

She ducked through the door into Billings's office, as Davidson could be heard outside, talking with his secretary, Diane Peterson.

"Where's Clare?" Bruce asked, as he walked into the room.

"She said she needed to pick up something at the lab and she'd be right back," Billings lied.

"Strange," Davidson replied. "She knew I wanted her impression of Freeman."

"She believed him," Billings said. "Evidently you did, too."

"You didn't?"

30

"He seemed sincere enough," Billings replied. "But skepticism is my basic approach to anything religious. From a law enforcement point of view, this stuff is a Pandora's box, like when you assigned me to that case in Aurora. Produced more questions than answers, as far as I was concerned."

"I'm not sure I agree," Davidson responded, "but we've covered that ground before. The question here is, can we ignore this case just because it has religious components?"

"Not necessarily. All I'm asking is that we stick to facts—physical, not metaphysical, evidence. The latter is a black hole."

"Okay, Watson," Davidson said, trying to lighten things up a little. "Let's hear your analysis of the facts."

"We don't have enough facts, to start with, Sherlock," Billings replied. "If you'll pardon my Latin, we *non habeas corpus*. We don't even know if there is a corpus. Sure, we have a sliver of tissue, but that doesn't prove the girl is dead. And even if she is, we have only the word of a minister desperate to reclaim his soapbox."

"This guy is for real, I wager," Davidson replied. "Any man who would trade his marriage for a higher calling is trustworthy."

"Or maybe addicted," Billings said. "Watson's view is that zealots and druggies have a lot in common. One gets high on faith, the other on crack. Yet we applaud one and arrest the other."

Any time Nate Freeman could find an excuse to route his travels past Gerry's Gun Shop, west of Boulder, he did so. And he always packed "Black Bart," his .45-caliber

Colt single-action revolver, just to run another box of shells through it on the range behind the store.

"Howdy, padre," Gerry yelled from the other end of the showroom, almost as soon as Freeman had come through the door. "Back again so soon? I was just tellin' these boys, Andy and Jimmy, about you. See you brought Bart along," he added, nodding toward the gun in Freeman's holster. "Box of shells, on the house, if you'll give us a little demonstration."

"Fair enough," Freeman said, taking the cartridges from the three-hundred-pound proprietor. He noticed, but ignored, the money changing hands between Gerry and the two younger, rather rough-looking hombres, each wearing a gray Stetson and grasping a Coors Extra Gold. "Might as well have some fun," he muttered, as Gerry held the door open to the range.

As the cowboy preacher loaded the firearm, his host set a single empty beer can on the top of a fence post about twenty-five feet distant, then joined the others behind Freeman. "Anytime you're ready," Gerry said, pulling on a set of ear protectors to deaden the sound.

Freeman paused, flexed his knees slightly, then practiced drawing, twice, without firing at the target. The third time, in one motion, he pulled the Colt with his right hand and fired six quick shots at the can, fanning the gun's hammer with his left hand. The can spun high into the air, once, twice, three times, before dropping to the ground as the last three shots missed.

The preacher grinned at Gerry. "Rusty," he said. "Need to get down here more often."

"Not bad, though," Gerry replied, handing each of the

younger men a twenty-dollar bill. "Make it forty?" he asked.

"Still five out of six?" Andy replied.

"Yup."

"Yer on."

"You, too?" he asked Jimmy.

"Of course," he said. "You nuts?"

They put the eight twenties under a rock on the corner post of the split rail fence separating them from the range.

"Need another can," Freeman said, as he reloaded the six-shooter. Jimmy downed the beer he was holding, and handed Gerry the can.

This time when Black Bart spoke, the can spun upward on the first four shots before falling to the ground untouched by the last two.

"Sorry," Freeman said to Gerry.

"You kidding?" Gerry laughed as he handed the younger men their money. "Ain't another cowboy in Colorado could hit it even that many times!"

He paused, waiting for Andy to finish his beer. "Boys," he said. "I still think he can do it. Want to make it a hunnert?"

"Each?" Jimmy choked a little.

"Each. Just tryin' to get my sixty back."

Jimmy looked at Andy, who asked, "Five out of six?"

Gerry pulled on his gray beard just a little, then studied the gunman for ten seconds before pulling out his wallet, and fishing out two crisp one-hundred-dollar bills. Placing them under the same rock, he said, "Five out of six. Need another can."

The two younger men hesitated, then drew their wallets. "Loan me twenty?" Jimmy asked. Andy handed it to him, then put his own bills under the rock.

As much as he hated gambling, Nate Freeman always enjoyed playing this game with Gerry. After all, it was Gerry's money, not his, and it wasn't really a gamble, anyway. Five out of six was a piece of cake.

This time the gunman crouched a little lower, for dramatic effect. In his mind, for those few seconds, he was Wyatt Earp, Matt Dillon, and all his childhood heroes rolled into one. More than that, he was Nate Freeman, gunslinger, taking out, one by one, the men who had made him an orphan.

In one motion, he drew and fired, each bullet sending the spinning can still higher into the sky. At four, he paused, the can still in midair, holstered the gun and turned and winked at Jimmy and Andy. Then, when the target had reached eye level, he drew again and fired, the bullet sending it heavenward for the fifth straight time. Just for show, he flipped the gun to his left hand and plugged the can one more time before it hit the ground.

The two young cowboys stood frozen for a moment, their mouths open. Then without a word, they turned and walked back into the store, followed closely by Gerry.

"Boys, boys," he said with a laugh, fingering the stack of twenty-dollar bills. "Here's your money back, plus twenty for the fun. I seen him shoot before. Even seen him plug a silver dollar."

"Nobody can do that," Jimmy started to protest.

"Wanna bet?" Gerry laughed. "Come on."

He led them back to the range, where the gunslinger was still blasting bandits. "Padre," Gerry interrupted the next time Black Bart was empty. "Ready for the grand finale?"

"'Course," Freeman replied.

34

"My last silver dollar," the proprietor said. "Plug it, I'll throw in another box. Miss, you can use it to buy us Cokes."

"Let her fly."

Gerry tossed the coin skyward.

For effect, Freeman rolled on the ground, pulling the sidearm as he did so. The first shot struck the coin on one edge, spinning it high into the air, but not out of sight. The second shot hit its other edge, spinning it upward again. The third struck dead center, but at waist level, driving the coin directly into the post twenty-five feet in front of them.

Gerry grinned as the younger men ran out to confirm that their eyes had not deceived them. Jimmy was prying the coin from the wood when Gerry and Nate arrived.

"Mister," he said, the awe in his voice unmistakable. "Who taught you to shoot like that?"

"My daddy," Freeman replied, softly. *Who might still be alive today if he'd learned how to shoot, himself.*

"You got another box comin'," Gerry said as they turned toward the store.

"How about a box of blanks," Freeman said. "Got one of them bank robbery replays comin' up. Gotta keep the tourists happy, y'know. Besides, since I don't get paid much from the church, Lord knows I can use the extra hundred bucks." *Not to mention it gives me a chance to show off,* he thought.

5

Mr. Davidson," Diane Peterson's voice said over the intercom. "Sorry to disturb you, sir. But there's a Miss Rodriguez here, asking for you by name. Juanita Rodriguez. Says it's urgent, and she'll only talk to you. Something about a hotel in the Poconos, and the Costellini family. Shall I have her make an appointment?"

Bruce Davidson looked at Fred Billings, with whom he was still discussing the Raptor case. "I thought we struck out on that connection," he said.

"Not exactly," Billings replied. "The lone witness was a juvenile Jamaican, and other possible witnesses either disappeared or were uncooperative. Maybe this one finally decided to risk it."

Davidson activated the intercom. "Send her in," he said.

A moment later, the door flew open, and in rushed a Hispanic woman wearing a bright floor-length, floral-pattern dress. Her long black hair framed very high cheekbones accented with heavy makeup. Her dark eyes peeked through rose-tinted glasses. She was speaking rapidly in very broken English. "They make us do it," she said. "But, we must work, so we obey, and tell no one."

Davidson started to ask her what she had been forced to do, but the woman continued, without taking a breath. "But when Maria die, from drugs they say, I think I am killed, too. Can you help me?"

The woman slumped onto the couch and started to cry, covering her face.

Davidson looked away.

Billings just stared. Finally, he replied, "We can help you. Especially if you will help us. But you must tell us everything. Hold nothing back. If you will do this, we will ensure your safety."

"You will?" the woman said, jumping from the couch to hug the assistant director. "You make me safe? Maybe in the mountains? Maybe in Raptor, Colorado?" she said, dropping the accent and looking directly at Bruce, who had turned to face Conroy, his mouth wide open.

Clare laughed as she pulled off the wig and the glasses, and then removed the dark contact lenses. "Well, Dr. Davidson," she said. "Fred agreed, if I could fool you, he would support my assignment to the Raptor case. I need a change of venue."

"Conspirators!" Bruce protested, with a laugh. "You set me up. Fred, I can't believe it."

"What could I say?" Billings replied. "She was threatening to transfer." He stopped short.

Davidson glanced at Clare, who avoided his eyes, confirming Fred's slip. *Her father wants her in the CIA,* he thought. *If she goes with "The Company," I may never see her again.*

When Davidson didn't respond, Conroy jumped in.

"After Freeman first came in with that tissue specimen, I checked on what's happening around Raptor," Conroy said. "There's a dinner theater there, run by the Regis Hotel. A local troupe is preparing, as we speak, to perform a Spanish play, *Dracula's Mistress,* from September twenty-first to December twenty-first. I saw an ad for tryouts, and auditioned. The part is mine if I want it."

"Dracula, or the mistress?" Davidson chuckled.

"I vant to bite your neck," she said, flaring her arms and feigning an attack. "The mistress, of course. Nothing too cozy. It's a comedy. Got to keep the patrons happy, after all, so they'll leave all their money in the casino after the final act."

"I don't know," Davidson hesitated. "This case could turn ugly. If anything happened to you, I'd . . ."

"Never forgive yourself?" She completed the statement. He nodded.

"Hey, guys," Billings intervened. "Can you work out the personal stuff over dinner or something? I suggest this decision be made on another basis."

"Good idea," Clare said, looking past Billings to Davidson. "Bruce, if I don't get back into the action soon, I'll *have* to transfer, for my own sanity. That's not a threat. It's the God's honest truth."

"I understand," Davidson muttered. "And I'm sure you can handle it. As of tomorrow, you're assigned to Raptor, Colorado. Code name for this op is THE STEEPLE CHASE."

"You won't regret it," Conroy said.

"I hope not," Davidson answered. "But now that we've

dealt with your request, I have one for you. How about dinner tonight?"

"Fair enough," she replied.

Nathan Freeman was still a hundred yards up his driveway when he noticed the strange form lying on his porch. At first, it appeared to be a sack of potatoes, or perhaps a bag of laundry. But the closer he got, the more convinced he became that it was an animal of some type—minus its skin. Too small to be a deer, and larger than a lamb, the carcass was wedged tightly against his front door.

By this time, Rowdy should have been bouncing around the pickup, barking and whining and carrying on. But at the exact moment that Freeman realized how quiet it was, the hideous reality hit him. "Rowdy!" he shouted, jumping from the truck. "Rowdy . . . noooooo!"

Freeman rushed up the stairs, every step taking him deeper into shock. His constant companion for the past six years had been brutally murdered. Trying to collect his thoughts, Freeman stepped back and noticed two things. Curiously, there was no blood on or around the dog's body. But before he could focus on how the deed could have been done so cleanly, Freeman realized that the dog's genitalia had also been removed.

Nathan Freeman turned away, trying, too late, not to vomit. He could break any wild stallion, but nothing had prepared this preacher to stomach the spectacle of his best friend, butchered.

He dashed around the corner and threw up.

After he recovered, the mountain man walked slowly back to the front stairs and sat down. Hatred, pure and unadulterated, burst from his soul. They had stolen his town, his church, his wife. And now they had killed his dog. Overwhelmed, the preacher put his face in his hands and started to weep. At first, the tears came quietly, but gradually they became an uncontrollable torrent. Everything he had hoped for, everything he had loved, was gone—except—

"Mocha!" he cried, looking toward the meadow. *Are you dead, too?* But in the far corner of the pasture, Mocha was feeding quietly with the other horses. He whistled, and she immediately trotted toward the gate.

Freeman walked slowly to the barn, grabbed two empty grain sacks and some baling twine. "I'm sorry," he muttered, as he returned to the porch. He lifted Rowdy's still-warm body, and slid it inside the burlap. When he moved the dog, he noticed, first, the incision in its neck. Then he saw the message, scrawled in blood, across the parsonage threshold: "GET SMART. GET OUT."

He saddled Mocha, tied the dog's carcass and a small shovel behind the saddle, and headed for the ridge south of the barn. The horseman didn't have to touch the reins as Mocha climbed the well-worn trail to Vigilance Rock. She knew the way, since they rode there almost every day. From that precipice, Freeman could see the entire town of Raptor, which was the main reason he came there so often to pray that the sinister force threatening this village might somehow be turned back.

This time, however, his main issue wasn't with that force, but with his God. "Where were you, Lord?" he cried. "After all I been doin' for you, couldn't you even protect my dog? All he had to do was run away and hide. But, no, he was too friendly, too good, too trustin'. This ain't his fight. It's mine!"

Freeman untied the dog's body, and started digging a hole, continuing the monologue with every shovelful of dirt. "I been tryin' to do right," he continued. "I've sacrificed. Is this what I get for it? Maybe Annie was right: Leave the place to the devil and go somewhere else. If I'd only listened, we'd be together now, and Rowdy'd still be alive."

When the hole was deep enough to bury the dog, Freeman gently lowered the corpse and began to refill the cavity. The first shovelful was the hardest, the second a little less difficult. But as he was about to throw in the third, the minister paused, shovel in midair, and walked to the horse.

Resolutely, he retrieved a small New Testament, with Psalms and Proverbs included, with all its multicolored marginal notations of insights gained at this very spot. He flipped through the pages one last time before dropping the Book into the grave. Then he quickly filled the hole, walked back to the overlook, lay down on the moss, and stared up at the blue sky above, hands behind his head.

"Why, God?" he muttered. "Whose side you on, anyhow?"

Freeman closed his eyes, not so much to pray as to shut out the realities of the past few months. Warmed by the sun and drained by the grief, the heartbroken pastor quickly fell asleep.

At three in the afternoon, Fred Billings happened to walk past the still-open door of the observation room where Clare Conroy had monitored the interview that morning. Through the mirror, he could see his boss standing motionless next to his desk, as if pondering the intricacies of a difficult case.

Billings was about to close the door when he noticed, in Bruce's left hand, away from the mirror, a small metal flask. As the assistant director watched, Davidson lifted the vessel to his lips and took a long swallow. Even though the younger man had seen his mentor do this many times off-duty, he was shocked to see that the bottle had now made its way into his office.

When, a moment later, Davidson took another long draft before sitting down, Billings shook his head sadly. *Ninja,* he thought, using Bruce's nickname. *Five o'clock's coming way too early.*

6

Bruce Davidson checked the dining room table for the hundredth time since arriving home. The center-piece, created by the local florist, employed an autumn motif, with bright orange sugar maple leaves as a backdrop, surrounding multicolored chrysan-themums, all highlighting a ruffed grouse drumming on a moss-covered log.

Clare should love this, Davidson thought, setting crys-tal goblets on opposite sides of the table. A bottle of 1985 Dom Pérignon champagne nestled in the ice bucket, await-ing the young woman's arrival. Davidson was confident the *duck a l'orange* baking in the oven, stuffed with wild mushrooms set in a tureen of wild rice, would impress his guest. *She thinks she knows me, but she never dreamed I'm a great cook!* he assured himself as he walked back to the den. *Getting the Seville oranges was the real challenge. The rest was easy.*

Facing the well-stocked walnut liquor cabinet, he tried to settle which aperitif would be best.

Cognac—Remy Martin XO—ought to set the mood

nicely, he mused, pouring two ounces of the liquid into the glass he'd kept constantly resupplied for the past two hours. Next, he filled his bent billiard dunhill pipe with Borkum Riff tobacco, tamped and lit it, and propped his slippered feet on the glass table between the couch and fireplace. The aromatic smoke from the pipe mingled with the scent from the combination of red oak and apple logs already burning on the hearth. *Lots of women would give anything to share this with me night after night,* Davidson thought. *If only Clare Conroy were one of them.*

Mocha's whinny woke Nathan Freeman from a dream in which he had been Gideon, charging the Midianites in the darkness, shouting "The sword of the Lord, and of Gideon." His right fist was still extended toward the sky as the events of the day clambered back into his consciousness. In his hand, in the place of a sword, he held the Colt .45 he'd been wearing since he left Gerry's Gun Shop.

The cowboy preacher glanced toward his horse, hoping the newly-dug mound of dirt would not really be there—that Rowdy would come bouncing up any second, wagging and licking and acting like he hadn't seen his master in years. But the sight of the fresh-dug soil rekindled his hatred for whoever had killed his dog.

The sword of the Lord, he mused. *I wish I had one. I'd do to them what they did to Rowdy!* But as Freeman focused on avenging Rowdy, another thought took over. *The sword of the Lord . . . is the Word of God—what I just buried!*

He holstered the gun, turned on his side, and propped himself up with his left elbow on the moss-covered precipice. In Raptor, two miles away, he could see some of the streetlights already on as the sun set behind the western rim of the valley. Golden rays reflected off the gilded steeple of Community Church, like a lighthouse in the gathering night. On the street below, people scurried from one casino to another, trying to make their last quarter pay off.

Sheep without a shepherd, he thought. *And the real question is, am I a good shepherd, or just another hirelin' that sees the wolf and runs? No, I ain't runnin'. But I ain't stayin' any longer, neither.*

When Bruce Davidson opened the front door to Clare Conroy's knock, she glanced at the pipe, smiled, and said, "So, Sherlock has solved the case without me!"

"Why do you say that?"

"Force of habit, I suppose. Daddy's habit, to be specific. Whenever he unravels a difficult case, he reaches for the pipe."

"Sorry," Davidson said. "Maybe that's a CIA quirk. I picked it up during a stint at Scotland Yard, and just find it relaxing, that's all."

"No apology necessary," she said, as they walked toward the den. "Actually, I'm glad the case isn't solved. Besides, I rather enjoy the aroma. Borkum Riff?"

Davidson nodded, handing her a snifter of cognac.

She held it for a moment. "I hope you won't be offended," she said, "but I'd prefer something non-alcoholic."

"Perrier with lemon okay?"

"Perfect," she replied, before explaining. "My first year at Yale, I discovered that alcohol could drown out the pain of my parents' divorce. Pretty soon I was drinking more and studying less. Thankfully, some kids who cared about me put me in touch with A.A., and I got a handle on it before it was too late.

"They also got me involved in an InterVarsity group, and I discovered an answer I'd never heard about."

"A spiritual awakening?" he replied, fighting the haze created by two hours of constant cognac. "I'm familiar with the Twelve Steps. Guess I better stow the champagne for another time. That'll just make more room on the table for the *duck a l'orange.*"

"I wondered what that delicious smell was. But I didn't expect a catered meal," Conroy replied.

"Made it myself," Davidson said, with a twinkle in his eye. "Gourmet cooking's one of my hobbies. Took it up maybe five years ago. Make yourself comfortable," he continued, motioning to the couch before the fireplace. "I'll get everything ready."

Clare sat down, kicked off her shoes, and curled up in the corner of the black leather couch, her sporty but dignified tan-and-burgundy herringbone tweed jacket by L. L. Bean matching perfectly the natural decor of the den. Sandy, Bruce's English springer spaniel, hopped up on the couch, wagging her little tail happily.

Clare affectionately stroked the dog's ears. "It's okay, Bruce," she said, when Davidson started to shoo the dog. "I love dogs, especially springers."

Davidson stood there for a moment, taking one last draw on his pipe before heading for the kitchen. *They look so good together,* he thought. *We would be so good together. I have to risk it. Maybe this time she'll say yes.*

Nate Freeman's hands trembled so much as he tried to dial the number into the old rotary phone that he got two wrong numbers before his third attempt succeeded.

"Hello, Annie? It's me, Nate. Can we talk? I need to talk." He got no further before the emotions of the day caught up with him; he simply broke down and started to sob.

On the other end, Annie waited for her husband to regain control. "Nate?" she asked, finally. "Nate? What's wrong?"

"Everythin'. . . everythin' is going to heck, just like you said. We lost the church, and I been picketing, and they been tryin' to scare me outta town. They put glass in the horse feed, sugar in my gas tank, and even left a human body part on the porch, and then today, when I was gone for just a few hours, somebody. . . somebody killed Rowdy. I think they skinned him alive, and they cut off his privates, and . . . I don't think I can take this anymore."

"Nate. Nate. Slow down," Annie said. "I can't follow you. Who did all this? What are you talking about?"

The minister paused, realizing how strange this information must sound. "Annie," he stammered. "It's too hard to explain over the phone. Could I . . . I mean, would it be okay . . ." He stumbled for the right words. "Can I come see you?"

"When?"

"Now. Tonight. I can make it by one, maybe two. Or should I come tomorrow?"

"Tonight," she said after a moment. "I was starting to lose hope."

"Raptor is a strange town," Bruce Davidson said, sipping an after-dinner espresso as he and Clare Conroy sat together on the couch in front of the crackling fire.

"How so?" Clare replied.

"Well, for years we've heard rumors that Raptor is the center for some pretty weird stuff, including occult practices."

"Why haven't I seen reports, since I'm going up there tomorrow?"

"Because there *are* no reports. These groups very seldom leave tracks. When they do, unless some bizarre crime allows the whole thing to be chalked up to lunacy, written reports tend to ignore details that could only be occult-related."

"Well, then, give me your off-the-record opinion."

"Okay. I think there is some truth *and* some hype in most of it. But if only ten percent of the reports—mostly from former cult members—are true, cult crimes are increasing at an alarming rate."

"But," Clare started, then paused; she stood, walked to the fireplace, and took a seat on the hearth, her back to the fire. "Why didn't you bring this all out today, at the office, when we talked the case through with Fred?"

"Frankly, because he's rather skeptical about cult crimes. When he investigated that case in Aurora in 1988, where adolescents were mutilating animals, he was consistently willing to accept any other theory than their own explanation—that they were satanists. Maybe you've noticed, but every time religion comes up, he steers away from it, even though it's obviously a factor in this case."

"And, in this case, it's Freeman's guiding light."

"Maybe not just Freeman's. Suppose his adversaries are driven by something bigger than greed."

"Such as?"

"Power, for example. Maybe it's more important to them to control the town than to own every part of it."

She pondered his words for a moment, then replied,

"So their problem isn't Freeman himself, but what he represents?"

"Now *you're* lapsing into the metaphysical, my dear. I'm just suggesting there may be more going on in Raptor, Colorado, than meets the eye. I urge you not to let down your guard, even for an instant. Don't believe everything you see, and don't discount *anything* you hear. And keep in close contact about *everything* suspicious. I know it's only a few minutes by copter if we have to come, but with cult groups, the end can come in just a few minutes, as we learned with the Branch Davidians."

"So you're sending me on a witch-hunt."

"Possibly, but my main concern is that the hunter doesn't become the hunted before I can render assistance."

7

ehold, a reading from master Therion, founder of the Ordo Templi Orientis, prophet of truth and spokesman of the one true god, Baphomet," Lady Aradia began. She gazed momentarily at the seven women and three men standing in black robes before her in the mine shaft; a circle, etched deeply into the ground, surrounded the group. Behind Aradia stood a gold-plated altar, draped with a black satin cloth. An inverted pentagram, enclosing a goat's head stitched in gold, was embroidered on the altar cloth. Several candles were arranged on top of the altar, including one in the form of a naked woman. A silver chalice, a dagger, and a small silver tray were grouped in the center of the table. A human skull, with a red candle protruding from its crown, adorned the altar's right rear corner.

The witch began to read in a soft, feminine voice that gained force with each passing line from "The Altar of Artemis" by Aleister Crowley.

Where, in the coppice, oak and pine
With mystic yew and elm are found,

Sweeping the skies, that grow divine
With the dark wind's despairing sound,
The wind that roars from the profound,
And smites the mountain-tops, and calls
Mute spirits to black festivals,
And feasts in valleys iron-bound,
Desolate crags, and barren ground;—
There in the strong storm-shaken grove
Swings the pale censer-fire for love.

The foursquare altar, rightly hewn,
And overlaid with beaten gold,
Stands in the gloom; the stealthy tune
Of singing maidens overbold
Desires and mysteries untold,
With strange eyes kindling, as the fleet
Implacable untiring feet
Weave mystic figures manifold
That draw down angels to behold
The moving music, and the fire
Of their intolerable desire. . . .

***

For the past half hour, Bruce Davidson and Clare Conroy had been dancing in Bruce's living room, to the sounds of Bruce's CD collection, which featured artists from as far back as the fifties. Bruce was amazed that Clare knew every step, as well as most of the songs. *Not your typical baby boomer, that's for sure,* he thought, as Natalie Cole (thanks to modern technology), sang "Unforgettable" with her father, Nat "King" Cole. With each passing phrase, Bruce drew Clare a little closer, so that by the time the song was through, they were cheek to cheek, heart to heart, and both nearly breathless.

Clare, without pulling away, leaned her face back, invitingly, Bruce thought, so he kissed her. When she didn't resist, and even seemed to match his growing passion, he kissed her again, a long, lingering, intimate embrace. Then he grabbed her hands, stepped back at arm's length, and looked deeply into her blue eyes.

"Clare," he said, trying to catch his breath. "I don't know how else to say this, so I'll just say it. I love you. Since the moment you came into my life, I've found you attractive. And the longer we've worked together, the more that attraction has grown. A few months ago, I asked you to marry me, but you said you needed more time. Since then, I haven't been able to function. I go to sleep thinking about you, I wake up thinking about you, and when we're at work, I can't keep my mind on what I'm doing. So, tonight, I'm asking you again. Would you marry me?"

Clare didn't flinch, nor did she blink. With her hands in his, she replied. "You're very persuasive, Bruce," she began. "I didn't know what to say the first time. I'd never been out on a date in my whole life. So, it wouldn't have been fair to pretend that I was ready."

She hesitated, returning his gaze. "I must admit, I care more about you at this moment than any man I've ever known. But . . ." She stopped cold. "But . . ."

"I'm too old," he guessed.

"No, it's not that. What's fourteen years when you're eighty-four and I'm seventy?" she replied. "No, it's something else."

"Tell me," he pleaded.

"Okay," she said, after a long pause. "It's Ellen, your memory of Ellen, or something else. Maybe it's my imagination, but there just seems to be this lingering, unresolved . . . something. I don't know if it's love, or sadness, or both. Maybe you think that having me in your life could fill the emptiness. But truthfully, I don't know that I could do that, or even if I should try. Am I making any sense?"

Davidson, shocked as much by her frankness as by her insight, dropped her hands and turned away to keep Clare from seeing the tears welling in his eyes. *There is a hole,* he admitted to himself. *It started the moment the bomb exploded. And it's grown since then into a gaping, turbulent abyss. She's right. It's not fair to expect her to take Ellen's place. But I can't let her go, either. I can't let her go!*

"Clare," he said, ignoring the tears streaking down his face as he turned back to face her. "I'm sorry. What you said makes a lot of sense. But I think I—we—could work it out. We would be so good together."

"I think so, too, Bruce. But I don't want to be your therapist. The flow should go both ways, don't you think?"

Fighting his sense of desperation, Davidson made one last attempt to convince her. "I'll get down on my knees, Clare Conroy, if that will make any difference. I'll do anything you say. I'll get counseling. I'll work it out."

"Stop," she said, quietly. "Don't take yourself down any further. Groveling does not become you. I care too much about you to say no, but I also care too much about you, me—us—to say yes, at least for now. Can we leave the question on the table until I return from Raptor?"

"Who comes toward us? Why, our God, the Grand!" Lady Aradia howled as she neared the conclusion of her reading.

Our Baphomet! Come, baby, to the band:
Our God may kiss you—yes, he will spare you!
Fall down, my baby; worship him with me.
There, go; I give you to his monster kisses!
Take her, my God, my God, my infamy,
My love, my master! take the fruit of me!
—Shrieks every soul and every demon hisses!

"Baphomet has come," she cried, "to do our bidding. Take us, take us all!"

In the group, a low moan that had been building for the past few minutes suddenly erupted in a mixture of shrieks and ecstatic utterances, as two of the young women fell down, writhing on the floor.

Nice touch, girls, Aradia thought. *But let's not overdo it.*

"Come," she said. She took them by the hands, and led them to the altar. "Come and celebrate the mass. The blood of your victim is in the cup. Here, take the wafer, dip it in the blood, and repeat with me as we eat, 'This is the body and blood of our lord.' Then serve the others."

When all had eaten and drunk the liquid, laced with belladonna, Aradia opened the Book of Shadows, dipped the quill in Rowdy's blood, and wrote the name of Nathan Freeman. "Great lord of darkness," she said as she wrote, "only this man now stands in our way. We curse him, and beseech thee, in view of this sacrifice and solemn ceremony, to loose all the powers of the pit upon his person— fear and confusion, guilt and despair—until this man, and all others who dare oppose us, long only for death. So be it. Amen."

"Amen," they all said. They completed the ritual by repeating the Lord's Prayer in reverse.

***

On Interstate 25, just south of Colorado Springs, Nate Freeman was listening to soft inspirational music on a Christian radio station, when suddenly the radio went silent. As he waited for the sound to come back, the minister stared out at the darkness of the sky. As his thoughts wandered, the injustice of what had happened in the past twenty-four hours began to fill his mind.

An oppressive sense of gloom settled on his soul as he sped along toward Pueblo, at seventy-five miles per hour. He fought to focus on anything good, even the fact that Annie was still waiting for him, just a few miles away. But the further he went from Raptor, the more one thought bombarded his consciousness: *You failed, and now you run. You failed, and now you run.*

What difference does it make that I stayed? What difference does it make if I leave? he asked himself as his increasing tension forced the accelerator to the floor and he became totally oblivious to his speed. *What difference does it make that I was ever born? What difference would it make if I died?*

"No difference, none at all. No difference, none at all," he seemed to hear someone say, clearly enough that he sat bolt upright, gripping the steering wheel as if in a catatonic state as he rushed headlong toward the bridge abutment a thousand yards ahead.

But just as the truck's speedometer topped one hundred, the radio came back on, louder than before. The disc jockey was reading from the Scriptures, "The thief cometh not, but for to steal, and to kill, and to destroy: I am come that they might have life, and that they might have it more abundantly."

"Sorry, folks," he said. "We had a little power glitch.

But isn't it great that that never happens with God? Well, that's our verse for tonight. And now, another classic by the Imperials, 'He didn't take us this far, to leave us.'"

Clare Conroy gave Bruce Davidson a little peck on the cheek as she walked out his front door. Bruce closed the door, turned toward the den, and stopped in front of Ellen's picture. "You understand, don't you, dear?" he said out loud. "I mean, if it had been me, I would want you to be happy, and marry again if you found the right person."

Shaking his head sadly, he shut the lights off behind him as he went, until the only light in the house was coming from the fire slowly dying in the fireplace. He reached for a full bottle of Old Grand-Dad, sat down on the La-Z-Boy next to the couch, propped up his feet, and unscrewed the cap.

After filling the entire ten-ounce glass, he took a large gulp, then stared, somewhat blankly, at the glowing embers before him. "I wish it *had been me,*" Davidson said, as he took another gulp, followed by yet another, and another, until the bottle was empty, and he had passed out cold in the chair.

It was nearly 2 A.M. before Nate Freeman finally reached Annie's apartment, mostly because he'd spent a good half hour collecting his thoughts at a rest area just north of Pueblo.

As he stood at Annie's door, about to ring the doorbell, he suddenly realized that in his rush to get away from Raptor, he hadn't even brought along a toothbrush, much less a change of clothes. In fact, he was still wearing the dirty boots, jeans, and shirt he'd worn to Vigilance Rock that afternoon.

"Pickin' up right where I left off. Zero for romance," he muttered, as the door swung open and the only woman he'd ever loved stood before him, clad in the silk housecoat he'd bought her for their first anniversary.

"What was that?" she said, as she gently pulled him inside.

"Just talkin' to myself," he mumbled.

"Well, you can stop talking to yourself and start talking to me," Annie said, taking off his hat and tossing it on the chair as she kissed him. "But first, come sit by my fire and let me hold you. When you called, I was frightened. You sounded almost . . . almost crazy."

"I was," he said. "Crazy to let you go. Crazy to stay and fight 'em by myself. Crazy not to call you sooner. I'm sorry, Annie."

"Shhh," she said, tenderly stroking his oily hair. "You did what you had to do . . . and so did I. The only thing that matters is to pick up and go on from here. But that'll keep till tomorrow. For now, we have more important things to catch up on."

She drew him closer, at first softly and tenderly, as a mother comforts a hurting child. But as the smell of Chanel No. 5 filled Nathan's senses, compassion gave way to passion, and they each found in the other's arms what had been missing for much too long.

Love.

Bruce. Bruce, wake up."

Bruce Davidson slowly fought his way back to consciousness, but even with his eyes open, everything seemed so dark and blurred. He stared vaguely up at Fred Billings, who had been shaking him for nearly a minute.

"Boss," the younger man said, still shaking Davidson by the shoulders. "I don't mean to intrude, but I was afraid I'd find you like this. Clare called after she left tonight, worried. Practically begged me to call you. And when you didn't answer the phone, I thought I better see if you'd . . . if something had happened."

"Something, such as?" Bruce sat up in the chair, glanced at his watch to see it was 2 A.M.

"Such as . . . who knows?" Billings replied. "People do crazy things when they're despondent."

"Despondent? Did she say that?"

"No. No," he said quickly. "But she said you proposed again, and that she asked you to wait again, and I know how that affected you the first time."

"How so?" Bruce replied, instinctively reaching for the empty glass, and glancing toward the liquor cabinet.

"This, for instance," Billings said, taking the glass from Davidson's hand. "And this," he continued, holding up the empty whiskey bottle in his other hand.

"What I do in the privacy of my own home is not your concern," Davidson said, trying to regain some aspect of control.

"True," Billings said, "to a degree. But we're always on call, and getting stone-cold drunk is no way to be ready."

"Let me worry about that."

"I have been, so far," Billings replied, "mainly because you've been such a good friend to me. But here's my dilemma . . . *our* dilemma. If I'm going to be your good friend, I simply cannot stand by and watch you kill your-self, when help is available."

"I appreciate your concern, but I've got it under con-trol," Davidson replied, pushing himself from the chair into a rather wobbly stance. He turned his back to Billings, walked to the bar, and grabbed another glass. He began filling it with brandy, the bottle's neck rattling against the rim of the glass as his hands trembled.

Suddenly, Billings, who had followed Davidson to the bar, grabbed Davidson's right wrist from behind, pre-venting him from pouring any more liquid into the glass. Davidson, obviously surprised, resisted for a moment, then turned to face his protégé.

"It's *not* under control, boss," the younger man said, quietly but firmly. "It's *out* of control."

"I'll be the judge of that," Davidson replied, walking back toward the couch and taking a seat.

"Sorry, but you've disqualified yourself."

"What? How dare you!"

Billings put the brandy bottle down, and picked up the silver-plated flask he'd seen Davidson drink from in the office.

"It's not a matter of daring, but caring," he replied. "I've seen you drink from this at the office. I've seen you drink in bars, and here in your den. Over the past few months, I've seen you put down three times as much as should make anybody tipsy, without it fazing you. And tonight I find you stone-cold drunk in your chair, a pool of vomit on the floor, and an empty whiskey bottle on the table. I don't have to be an FBI agent to figure out my best friend's in trouble. But because *I am* an FBI agent, and you are, too, I have no other choice but to intervene."

"If it doesn't faze me, what's the problem?" Davidson protested, still trying to recapture the lead.

"The word's *habituation*," Billings replied, facing Davidson, but not moving back from the bar. "As Bruce Davidson, Ph.D. in psychology, knows . . . except when it's happening to him. You've been coming in later and later. You've been forgetting things. You've been drinking at work. I can't cover for you any more without violating the code."

"That so? Sounds to me like you're more concerned with yourself than anything else," Davidson said. As he spoke, he reached under the end table and produced a .25-caliber Walther PPK/S with a short silencer attached to its four-inch barrel.

"Now," he continued, waving the handgun in the general direction of Billings. "Isn't it time for you to get out of *my* house?"

"I'm not sure," the younger man said, stiffening just a

60

little, but without moving or showing any emotion. "I can't leave if you're acting irrationally."

"Irrationally!" Davidson shouted, as he slowly raised the gun and fired.

The first place Leonard Price went when he got back to Raptor after tailing Nathan Freeman all the way to Colorado Springs was to the office of Stanley Hawkins, on the top floor of the Settler's Bank building. Although it was 2:30 A.M., Hawkins's light was still on.

"Maybe the preacher finally got the message," Price announced.

"Really," Hawkins replied, flatly, thinking of the thousand-dollar bet he'd made earlier that day with Florence Bradley. "Are you sure?"

"Sure as I can be. Followed him beyond the Springs. Figured if he went that far, he wasn't coming back here tonight."

"Know where he's headed?"

"Not really, though the postmaster told me once he got a letter postmarked in Pueblo."

"From?"

"Who knows? Did you expect me to open it? It's a federal crime."

"Funny time to worry about that now, Chief," Hawkins said. "Find out where he went, who he's with, what he's doing, and if he's planning to come back."

The police chief's mouth dropped open. "You think I'm a one-man FBI or something?"

"I think we pay you to do whatever I say, and I say I want to know where he went, who he's with, what he's doing, and if he's planning to come back. How you do it is your own business."

Fred Billings had lunged behind the La-Z-Boy at the first movement of Bruce Davidson's hand. The younger agent knelt in his friend's vomit as the first two bullets shattered the glass doors of the liquor cabinet. Instinctively he reached for the snub-nosed .38 in the holster in the small of his back, his own mind reeling with the possibility that he might have to kill his own mentor before this confrontation was over.

As he pondered his options, however, he heard Davidson talking, not to him, but to the bottles arranged along the wall. "I'll show you irrational," Bruce muttered, as the PPK/S spat another round and the bottle of Remy Martin XO cognac burst. "Ninety-eight dollars . . . that's irrational," Davidson said, taking a bead on a bottle of wine one shelf higher. As it disintegrated, he said, "Pichon-Longueville, 1989 . . . seventy-six dollars. That's irrational."

Billings crouched behind the chair, as the nearly silent firearm disintegrated bottle after bottle; Davidson narrated the carnage, "Heitz Cellars, Cabernet Sauvignon—ninety bucks. Opus One, 1987, sixty-six bucks. Chivas Royal-Salute, ninety-six bucks. Jack Daniels, Korbel, Christian Brothers, Baccardi, Ron Rico, Gilbey's, Myers." Finally only one bottle remained.

"See that bottle, Agent Billings?" he said. "Dom Pérignon champagne, 1986. Handpicked by Mr. Davidson for tonight's engagement celebration with Clare Conroy. A hundred bucks. What a waste, don't you think?" he said, as he squeezed the trigger and the bottle exploded.

Then, with a slight grin on his face, Davidson turned to

face Billings, who was peeking around the side of the chair. "Come on out, Mr. G-man," he said, pointing the gun toward the younger man again. "But place your weapon on that chair, just so we know who's still in charge here."

"Boss," Billings started to protest. Seeing the determined look in Bruce's eyes, however, he complied.

"Good. You've said your piece, now I'll say mine," Davidson said. "And I'll keep it brief. You've been gunning for my job ever since you started here, and now you think you're going to get it by turning me in."

"Not true," Billings began, but his words were cut off by Davidson, who motioned him to sit on the couch.

"I'll say what's true and what's not at this particular moment, thank you. And you—maybe you and Clare, for all I know—have conspired against me, to ruin my reputation and end my career. But I promise you, I'm not about to let that happen."

"Nobody knows but us, Bruce. I swear. But now I don't have any choice. It's not a question of loyalty anymore, but love. I really do care about you," he said, quietly, a tear forming in his left eye, "and because I care, I simply cannot let you drink yourself to death."

"As you can see, Dr. Watson," Davidson replied, "that would be impossible, unless I got down on my knees and lapped up all that booze. Be tough on the tongue, don't you think? How about I promise to stay on the wagon, and you forget what you know?"

"Promises are easy to make, easy to break, especially if you never find the cause and deal with it."

"Since when did you become such an expert?"

"Since I talked it over with Dr. Oberly, who says you can get the help you need at the Hope Center. They specialize in treating professionals. It's in the mountains," he added quickly. "You'll like it there."

"You said nobody knows," Davidson said fiercely. "But you've been talking to someone at a treatment center."

"At least I haven't talked to headquarters."

"Well, you won't have to," Bruce exclaimed, "because Bruce Davidson is not about to go through detox with common . . . common . . ."

As he spoke, he swung the gun up to his temple. "I'd rather die first. I *will* die first!"

In Pueblo, Nathan and Annie Freeman were still talking, though it was well past 3 A.M. After several months of separation, they had more than passion to catch up on.

"I've gotten back into doing physical therapy," Annie said. "Since May I've been working with handicapped kids at a place called the King's Kollege. Mostly kids with Down's syndrome, cerebral palsy, and other brain injuries. I don't think I've ever been so fulfilled in my life."

"I'm happy for ya," Nathan said, rolling over on the bearskin rug where they had been lying in front of the fireplace; he added another log to the fire. "I expect livin' with me was pretty good preparation for understandin' them." He chuckled, as he pulled the goose down comforter over them again and then pulled Annie closer.

"True, but maybe not in the way you mean it," she replied. "We're all disabled in some ways, including me. And we all have special needs—especially to be loved. But sometimes I think the real therapy is in what they do for me, instead of what I can do for them."

"How so?"

"It's hard to say, but the thing I always come back to is

64

their simple joy in just about any achievement. Like saying a word right, or throwing a ball, running in a race . . . or riding a horse."

"Ridin' a horse?"

"Not like you ride, of course. They need two helpers to walk alongside and another to lead the animal. But, believe me, it's one of the best therapies for these kids I've ever seen. It's called hippotherapy."

"No kiddin'. This I gotta see."

"I hoped you'd say that, because tomorrow we go out to Liberty Riding Center. Will you come and watch?"

He shrugged. "Got nothin' else to do. Nothin' else I'd rather do."

Annie turned and kissed Nate's stubbly cheek, then walked her fingers down inside his open shirt to his waist and started to tickle him. Even when he was distracted, tired, or just plain ornery, this had always been her little signal that she wanted to play, if he cared to participate.

He did.

Fred Billings dove headlong toward Davidson, trying desperately to knock the gun from his friend's hand before Bruce's brains became the finishing touch in an already hideous scene. Billings had tried to count the shots, waiting for fifteen, the gun's maximum capacity. But in the confusion, he had lost track. "Bruce, don't!" he shouted, as Davidson pulled the trigger one more time.

The firing pin struck air, with a merciful metallic "click."

Bruce stared at the gun for a moment, then at Billings who was now standing at his side. The younger agent pried the weapon from Bruce's rigid fingers, one by one, and then dropped it on the floor. Then Fred wrapped his long arms around Davidson, who had begun to sob like a baby.

As he held his mentor in a bear hug, Billings glanced quickly toward the hallway, where he could see the red indicator light of his camcorder still on, assuring him the entire interchange had been videotaped. He had brought the camera partly for his own protection, but mostly as an ace in the hole, should Bruce ever claim he didn't really need help. But as Fred considered what might have been electronically preserved forever had Bruce's cabinet contained one less bottle, he began to tremble, too. He pulled the remote out of his pocket, and shut the camera off.

After what seemed like ages, he heard Bruce say, "It's over, isn't it? My life is over."

"Not necessarily," Billings replied. "Maybe just beginning again. But, whatever happens, boss, we're in this together. You can count on that."

on't worry about Sandy," Fred Billings said, referring to Bruce's dog. "The boys will take good care of her. Four weeks'll go by like a shot, you'll see."

"I don't know, Fred," Bruce replied, as he peered out the passenger-side window of Fred's Jeep Cherokee. "I don't know if this is the right thing. Maybe I should just resign and let you take over. Then I wouldn't have to answer to anyone but me."

For the past two hours, as they drove toward the Hope Center, Billings had been fielding Bruce's objections, one after the other.

"True," Billings replied. "And if that's what you really want, we can turn around right here and go back. The program is voluntary, even if H.Q. is picking up the tab. Complete it, and you can come back with nothing on your record. As far as Beatty's concerned, you're on medical leave. But bail out, and your FBI career really will be over."

As Billings spoke, he pulled into a rest area, a small outcropping at the highest point of Highway 57, which snaked its way from Boulder up through the front range and then out onto an expansive meadow. From this vantage point, the snowcapped Rockies were clearly visible to the west. The golden foliage of the aspens on their high meadows adorned the distant peaks like a gold sash on a regal blue garment of some colossal collection of kings crowned in white.

The two friends stood, silently surveying the panorama for several minutes before Bruce spoke.

"I can't go through with it. I won't go through with it. I'm not an alcoholic. I can stop any time I want to. This is ridiculous. Take me home. I'll just forget the FBI and stick to teaching at the university."

"Your call, Bruce. Like I said," Billings replied, nervously fingering the videotape in his pocket. "But what about Clare? Leave under these circumstances, and you might as well write her off."

"Already wrote her off," Davidson replied. "Look what she's done to me."

"I don't think she would have called me last night if she didn't care."

"Either way, I couldn't care less," Davidson said, his voice quavering slightly. "She's nearly been the death of me."

"I think there's more to it," Billings said firmly. "Blaming her isn't the way to overcome this."

"Overcome what?"

"Your dependence on the bottle to dull the pain."

"What do you know about it?"

"Enough, considering the thousands of hours we've spent together, on and off duty, over the past seven years," Billings replied. "There's something deeper going on."

"So. Everybody's got some baggage. That's no secret. Since when did you get to be a shrink?"

"Not a shrink, just a friend who longs to see his friend find a way out of the sadness. You know," he said, after pausing to consider the risk, "in all those years, I've never seen you smile, or laugh . . . unless you were at least half-tanked."

Stunned, Bruce walked away from Billings a few steps. Then, staring at him from twenty feet away, and fighting tears, he said, "Life stinks, and then you die." Then he turned away again.

Billings walked up next to Davidson and put his arm around his shoulder, half-expecting his mentor to pull away. When he didn't, the younger man said, "I'm not your judge, Bruce. Nobody's your judge. But not everybody sees life that way.

"If Judy died the way Ellen did, or if something happened to my boys, I don't know how I'd survive. But the reason I came over last night, and the reason I've gotten you into this program when there's a waiting list a mile long, is that more than anything else, I want you to beat this. We all want you to beat this. We believe in you. We want you to win."

Bruce pulled away again, then simply turned to face Billings. "I can win without your help," he said. "Take me home."

Billings said nothing for a full minute, nor did he move. Finally, desperate to change Bruce's mind, he played his final card. "Fine," he said, turning toward the car. Over his shoulder, he continued, "Then I guess you'll never find George Perelli again, so you'll never know for sure who killed Ellen."

Bruce's mouth dropped open at the mere mention of the hit man's name. For six months after Ellen's death, Davidson had trailed Perelli, as the evidence gradually made it clear that this man had at least built the car bomb that had killed Ellen.

Perelli had gotten away then, and he had escaped again during the commando raid on the New World Institute in early 1993. More than anything in life, Bruce Davidson wanted to interrogate Perelli, to find out the truth. But if he should leave the FBI, no one would pursue the case further. There were simply too many other crooks to deal with.

"Okay," he said, finally. "You win. I'll do it. But only you and I know the real reason why."

Nathan Freeman stared through the split rail fence of the riding ring at Liberty Riding Center. In his years around the rodeo, he'd seen some amazing feats of riding strength and agility, but he'd never seen anyone transformed by riding a horse. No other word came close to describing what he'd seen happen to child after disabled child, hour after hour, all morning long.

If you'd told him that a paraplegic, blind six-year-old would be able not only to ride around the ring, but bareback, with her arms raised triumphantly in the air, the cowboy preacher would have laughed you out of the room.

But such was the work Annie was doing, and it was obvious why she found so much satisfaction in it. She was perfect for the job, smiling at him every time she passed the place where he stood. One thing he knew for sure as he watched: He'd never appreciated her more than he did at that moment.

"You know Annie?" A male voice sliced into Nathan's musings as Annie walked past again, a few feet away. He turned to see that a large man, perhaps six-foot-four and two-hundred-eighty pounds, had joined him at the fence.

"You might say that," he replied. "We been married four years."

"Then you must be Nate," the man said. "Glad to finally meet you. I'm Big Jim, founder, president, chief fund-raiser and primary manure-shoveler of Liberty Riding Center." He stuck out his big hand, and they shook. "Whaddya think?" Jim asked.

"Never seen anything like it in my life," Nate replied. "And I seen a lot of ridin'."

"So I've heard. Like to take a horse out when the kids are done?"

"Sounds great. You, too?"

"Not today. But Annie goes out every Saturday afternoon for lunch. Rides up on that butte over yonder. She's become a real rider."

Again Nathan was shocked. "No kiddin'. Since when? She's never even ridden with me. Didn't know how. You teach her?"

"Well, yes and no," Jim replied. "Just part of the deal. We needed a physical therapist, but didn't have any funds to pay her. For a while, she just did it for free, but the more she saw the benefits to the kids, the more she wanted to get up there herself. I could just see it. So, my wife, Jenny—she's the primary instructor—taught her how to ride, and now we can't keep her off that black stallion over there when she's done working with the kids every week. Rides like the wind, too. Bareback."

Clare Conroy pulled to the side of the road, checking her makeup in the mirror and adjusting her black wig one last time before descending the serpentine highway leading from Hawk Mountain Pass into Raptor, Colorado. She stepped out of the standard government-issue light gray Dodge Shadow to survey the little town in the distance.

Her first impression, when she saw how small the village actually was, was to wonder if she'd made some mistake. *How could such a dinky town be the center of anything at all?* she wondered. But as car after car sped by from both directions, it became increasingly obvious that something was going on down there, a lot more than met the eye.

In preparation, she had read everything about Raptor that she could find in the local library. The small mining town had certainly had its ups and downs in its one-hundred-three-year history, including two major fires and a boom or bust economy that seemed to go in cycles.

The earlier cycles were controlled by the total output of Raptor's gold mines, which reached their peak production around 1938 when five hundred thousand tons of ore were mined and shipped by rail from the Kingsford Mine. During those days, when only the best ore was considered worth refining, the rest was used to pave Main Street, making Raptor the only town in the world whose main street was literally paved with gold. At the zenith of Raptor's success, trolleys had provided transportation in town, and a special railway had been constructed to connect with the Denver and Rio Grande at Northfork.

Legends abounded, including stories of how the various claims were made. One entrepreneur, having just arrived by stage, went to the edge of the canyon, tossed his top hat from the brink, and started digging to find one of the richest lodes in the valley.

Most, of course, had not been nearly as fortunate, coming to Raptor to seek their fortune only to leave penniless, not because they couldn't make it on a miner's pay, but because they spent everything, every time, gambling, drinking, or buying some comfort from the women of Second Avenue.

Other legends had survived, too, stories attributed to the Haitian laborers imported by Cecil Kingsford toward the end of his mine's productivity. Tales of black magic, voodoo rituals, child sacrifice, cannibalism, and midnight meetings in the cemetery were rampant, but the historians all agreed that these reflected prejudicial attitudes toward the most convenient scapegoats as the town's economy began to decline.

One particular case, however, had captured Clare's attention as she scanned the historical documents in Colorado University's library archives. In 1932, a witchcraft trial had been held in Raptor Community Church, since it was the only public building large enough to handle the crowds clamoring to attend.

The mutilated body of Cecil Kingsford's six-year-old daughter had been found buried in the mine shaft behind the estate. Throughout the trial, which lasted an entire week, the girl's parents demonstrated almost no emotion as the evidence implicated their daughter's nanny, a Haitian named Elyse Morais, who had arrived along with the mine workers. In the end, the woman had been hanged from scaffolding attached to the church's steeple, but only after proclaiming, as the rope was placed around her neck, that the Kingsfords had sacrificed the girl to Lucifer in exchange for six more years of prosperity for their mine. With her dying breath, the woman, who never denied being a witch, had placed a curse on the town. Within ten years, Raptor had become a ghost town once again.

As she drove slowly down Main Street toward the Regis Hotel, Clare paused briefly in front of the former Raptor Community Church, half expecting to see Nathan Freeman standing on the building's marble steps wearing a sandwich board proclaiming his grievances. When she saw instead that a large weekend crowd of gamblers was already filling the sidewalks and spilling out into the road, she decided she should find her room and then try to locate Freeman on foot.

"Miss Rodriguez," the desk clerk said. "Welcome to Raptor. We trust your accommodations are satisfactory." Motioning for the bellboy to carry Clare's bags upstairs, the clerk handed her a book of coupons for free drinks in all the casinos, and a heavy roll of silver dollars to use in the slot machines. "These work especially well downstairs, immediately following any performance," the clerk said with a wink. "A little perk."

Conroy followed the bellboy up three flights of stairs, and then down a winding, narrow hallway to a ten-by-twelve-foot corner room, set just under the north eave. The slopes of the roof reduced the usable dimensions of the room to slightly more than the size of the four-poster solid mahogany double bed, which boasted a silk canopy to match the lace on each bay window. The room's Victorian style was accented perfectly by solid brass fixtures in the bathroom, and brass andirons on the hearth. A brocaded reproduction of a Rubens painting decorated the room's west wall. As far as she could tell without scraping it, the frame was plated with gold.

The hotel's turret, of which the room was the highest

74

point, provided an unobstructed view north and south along Main Street, and east down Second Avenue.

"Perfect," she muttered, as she unpacked her suitcase, careful to conceal her compact binoculars and a .32-caliber Beretta beneath her clothing in the antique mahogany dresser. The room had a mysterious, almost magical feel about it, so much so that Conroy even tried to wiggle several of the granite bricks to see if there might not be some secret passage, or at least a concealed compartment built into the wall.

Couldn't have picked a better observation point myself. The air had a slightly musty smell, as if the room hadn't been used for several months. So she unlatched and opened the east windows, and stepped out on the small balcony to see if Nathan Freeman was anywhere to be seen.

"Let's race," Annie said, giving her black stallion a little nudge with her heels. The animal shot off in the direction of the butte a mile away. No matter how hard he spurred his horse, Nate Freeman simply could not catch his wife. She reached the foot of the butte a full ten seconds before he did.

"Where'd you learn to ride like that?" he said, dismounting and trying to catch his breath.

"Jenny taught me," she said, laughing, as she hopped down. "Always wanted to learn, but didn't think you had the time to show me. I did it for me . . . but mostly for us. Just don't ask me to learn to shoot, too.

"This is my favorite spot. There's a little trail to the top. Come on, tie your horse to this scrub oak, and I'll show you."

Annie had nearly reached the top of the hundred-foot

precipice before Nate had scaled twenty feet, mostly because she was wearing sneakers and his leather-soled cowboy boots kept slipping in the gravel. He arrived at the peak to find a picnic lunch spread out on a soft blanket, and Annie lying on it as if she'd been there for hours.

"Nice view," he commented, taking a seat next to her and looking west toward the Sangre de Cristo range about fifty miles distant. Behind them, but blocked from view by the very top of the rock formation, was the rest of Liberty Ranch. Toward the north and south, several hundred cattle grazed contentedly in a pasture stretching as far as he could see.

"I wanted to share it with you," she said, taking his hand as he reached with his other hand for a sandwich and lay back on the blanket. "But I was afraid . . ."

She stopped, tears coming into her eyes.

"When you didn't write, and didn't call, I just figured you were so angry with me for leaving that I might never see you again."

With that, she lost control and really started to cry, quietly at first and then, as he held her, in unabashed sobs until she had no more tears to cry.

"Nate," she said, finally. "I've found my niche here. And there's a place for you here, too. Jim and Jenny want to start a residential center for handicapped kids, and use riding as their primary therapy. I could run the program, but we need somebody who really knows horses, and someone who knows hearts—the families have such deep hurts."

She pulled back from Nathan just a bit and looked into his eyes. "It could be so good, Nate. For both of us."

"I'd love to stay," he said, pulling her back into his embrace. "I want to stay. But . . ."

She pulled away again. "But? It's perfect. How could it be any better? It *couldn't* be any better!"

"It's the church," he said. "Just gettin' away like this feels so good. Bein' with you feels so good. But somethin's pushing me . . . or somethin's pullin' me. The FBI's sendin' help. There's still a chance to save the church, but only eight weeks to do it. I don't expect anybody to understand, but I *can't* stay. I *have* to go back."

"Nate," Annie said quietly. "I understand, but it feels like that church has displaced me. I won't beg you to stay now, or to come back later. You can invest your life here or throw it away there. Your choice. But remember—every time you choose, you choose for both of us. I'll wait two more months, but after that, your new mistress may become your wife."

She stopped again, then reached out and pulled him close. "Now, before you go, let me show you one more time what you'll be missing."

10

Glancing quickly around the small circle, Bruce David-son's first impression of his first group meeting was that the four other men and three women sitting there had all had lobotomies. They were simply too happy, too relaxed for residents—he preferred the term "inmates"—in an alcoholic rehabilitation center. *Fred dropped me at a loony bin by mistake,* he mused, as Doris, the group leader, got things going.

"Harold asked to speak first," she said, nodding to a middle-aged man to Davidson's left.

"Morning, everyone," he began. "My name is Harold, and I'm an alcoholic. But," he added, "because of this program, and Dr. Oberly's help, I've finally reached step five. My only regret is that it took me so long to admit to God, to myself, and to another human being the exact nature of my wrongs."

Everyone except Bruce clapped, as if on cue, as Harold continued. "I must admit, finishing step four—a search-ing and fearless moral inventory of myself—was more challenging than anything I'd done since my first day in medical school, when we had to start cutting the skin off our cadaver. It was Anatomy 101 again, only this time I was the one being cut apart, piece by piece."

Tears started running down Harold's face, but (oddly, it seemed to Bruce), the doctor didn't seem embarrassed. More oddly, the men sitting on either side of the physician reached toward him, simultaneously. One put his arm around Harold's shoulder briefly as he continued talking. The other patted him on the back.

Holy cow, Bruce thought. *What gives here?*

"I lost my marriage, my kids, and almost lost my medical license before I realized that the only way I could really be a good doctor was to become a good patient first. A couple more weeks, and I think I'll be ready to face life, maybe for the first time, without having to view it through an alcoholic haze."

Now everyone clapped, even Davidson, though listening to Harold increased his own longing for a full bottle of Old Grand-Dad. Yet, even as he fantasized about that bottle, and every cell in his body cried out for a fix, the other members of the group began introducing themselves to him, one by one.

"I'm Jerry, and I'm an alcoholic."

"I'm Sandra, and I'm an alcoholic."

"I'm David, and I'm an alcoholic."

"I'm Doris," the group leader said, "and my story's a lot like Harold's, except that I've been in recovery for about eight years, and working here as an addictionist for six."

A woman. How is she supposed to help me? Fred set me up! Davidson thought. But his ambivalence was quickly overwhelmed by a greater concern—specifically, what he was going to say when it finally came his turn to speak.

"I'm Bruce," he mumbled, his mouth drier than he could recall it ever being. "And, truthfully, I don't know why I'm here."

"Welcome, Bruce," Dr. Oberly said. "You've come to the right place."

Three hours after leaving Annie in Pueblo, the Reverend Nathan Freeman slowly paced back and forth on the granite steps of the former Community Church, reading his Bible to himself. "For the eyes of the Lord are over the righteous, and his ears are open to their prayers: but the face of the Lord is against them that do evil."

The minister paused, listening to the carpenters working inside the church building. Looking through the window, he could see that the entire sanctuary had been gutted, except for the altar, still in place. *Strange,* he thought. *Why're they workin' around that, instead of turnin' it to kindlin'?*

The choir loft above and behind the altar had been enlarged, and a wide spiral staircase was being installed at the right front where the platform had been. A gold embossed sign proclaimed: "The Upper Room—Poker with a Heavenly Twist."

"If your face is against 'em," he continued his part of the dialogue, "how can you watch 'em turn a place of praise into a poker hall?" Freeman turned sadly back to his vigil.

"If ye suffer for righteousness' sake," he read, "happy are ye: and be not afraid of their terror, neither be troubled."

Shaking his head, he said, "Your idea of happy and mine seem a million miles apart. I ain't afraid of 'em, but how can I *not* be troubled by what they're doin' to the house of God?"

***

Stanley Hawkins stalked around his corner office on the top floor of the Settler's Bank building, accenting each expletive by pounding on the desk. "Look!" he shouted, commanding Leonard Price to the window overlooking Main Street.

"You said he was gone!"

"He was," the police chief replied, quietly. "You want me to track him everywhere he goes, I'll need more people. I've got to sleep sometime."

"Stuff your excuses, pal. Just get him off my street."

Your street? Price thought. *How about we meet on it sometime and have it out, old west style?*

"On what basis?" he replied. "He's not even wearing the sandwich board this time. Just walking back and forth, dressed in his clerical robe, reading his Bible."

"Just do it," Hawkins growled.

On the street below, Nathan Freeman was still walking and reading. "Ye have heard that it hath been said, Thou shalt love thy neighbour, and hate thine enemy. But I say unto you, Love your enemies, bless them that curse you, do good to them that hate you, and pray for them which despitefully use you, and persecute you; that ye may be the children of your Father which is in heaven: for he maketh his sun to rise on the evil and on the good, and sendeth rain on the just and on the unjust."

Freeman was about to fire another question heavenward, when he felt a hand on his shoulder.

"Reverend Freeman," the policeman said. "You are under arrest. You have a right to remain silent, but anything you say can and will be used against you in a court of law."

"On what charge?"

"Disorderly conduct."

"Talkin' to God is disorderly?" Freeman replied, glancing around to see if anyone was on his side.

"If I say so," Price answered. "But since you and him are on talkin' terms, you might inquire why you're going to spend tonight in jail."

"You ain't serious."

"If you come along now, without making a scene, it may only be *one* night."

Clare Conroy, playing the dollar slots near the front door of the Regis Casino, watched, disbelieving, as Price led Freeman toward the police car, parked nearly in front of her. Every law enforcement cell in her FBI body urged her to intervene, to call the lawman's bluff. Her fingers tightened on the handle of the one-armed bandit, dropping in five dollars before she realized what she had done. As Freeman walked by, their eyes met, but his serene expression so defied logic that Clare wanted to shake him back to reality, or at least let him know that help had arrived. At almost the same instant, she caught a glimpse of her own image, reflected in the plate glass window that separated them, and she wondered for a moment who the dark-haired woman was, staring back at her.

Remembering with a start, she quickly pulled the lever, hoping no one had noticed her interest in what was happening outside.

Upstairs, in the control room monitoring every area of the casino, an employee moved his right knee slightly, nudging a button on the underside of the station where he was sitting.

The three rows of symbols on Clare's slot machine slowed and stopped, one after the other, sevens on each payline. Suddenly, silver dollars were falling loudly into the stainless steel bib affixed to the bottom of the machine, and a red light mounted on its top began to flash.

"Did I win something?" she said in a thick Spanish accent, pretending not to know that the one-armed bandit would vomit five hundred coins for that single spin.

"Something?" one short, balding bystander replied, as he knelt next to Clare, scooping up the heavy coins spilling onto the floor. "I started with five hundred last night, and only got five dollars left," he continued. "You walk in and win five hundred on the first try. Figures!"

"Thank you, sir," another voice interrupted, announcing the arrival of one of the casino's stewards. "Please place the lady's winnings in this bucket here."

"Wait," Clare said, as the last of the coins fell out and into the container and most of the nearby customers had already turned to their machines with renewed enthusiasm. She motioned for the helpful bystander to stay.

"Here," she said, reaching two handfuls of coins in his direction. "To say thank you." Before he could resist, she had filled his tattered tweed jacket pockets with cash.

The steward started to protest, but Clare immediately silenced him with a shrug. "Easy go, easy come," she laughed. "Maybe they be lucky coins!"

"Why, thank you, ma'am," the fellow replied. "I don't know what else to say."

"Nothing to say," she replied. "Just play, play, play!"

She got up from the stool in front of the recently benevolent machine, and motioned for him to sit.

"But, ma'am, you just hit. Odds are against me, a million to one. They never pay twice in a row."

She laughed, and said, "Just try. You see."

Eddie Hazard looked at Clare, then at the steward, who still waited to carry Clare's cache to the teller.

"Okay," he said, slipping a dollar in the slot and grabbing for the handle.

"One only?" she asked.

He reached into his pocket and reluctantly fed his nemesis two more coins. And before Clare could urge any further waste of his newfound treasure, Eddie pulled the handle.

This time, the man in the control room chuckled out loud as he hit the switch. "This'll glue him to that machine," he said to the screen as the machine whirred to a stop, sevens across again, another jackpot.

As the coins poured onto the floor, and the steward scrambled for another bucket, Eddie turned and looked at Clare, his mouth open in surprise. "I've wasted every paycheck in this town for the past three months," he said. "Never went home with more than a buck in my pocket. You must be lady luck," he said. "No doubt about it. You are lady luck."

"Lady luck?" Clare replied, again feigning ignorance. "I am Dracula's mistress. I don't know lady luck."

As she turned to follow the steward to the cashier, she urged Eddie. "You come, too?"

The gambler started to follow her, then noticed five people waiting to play his machine.

"Sorry, folks," he announced. "I ain't done yet. Got to play her while she's hot."

84

With that, he turned, jacked five quick dollars in the slot, and yanked the lever.

When Clare walked past fifteen minutes later, the gambler was still sitting in place, his supply of coins slowly dwindling as he lost five for every two the machine spit back at him.

Clare paused at the door, noticing for the first time the sheer racket in the place, and the heavy smoke, even though the evening crowd had not yet arrived. There were at least five hundred machines in the casino, most of them in use, each beckoning players with a different twist, from baseball to mining to progressive poker. And, every few seconds, it seemed, one station or another announced another winner, its flashing light and siren exhorting discouraged players not to lose hope until they had pumped in every last coin.

She glanced toward the blackjack tables, only one of which was in use at the moment, and then upward toward the poker hall. *Have to try my luck with cards next time,* she mused. *Like to know if they can rig them as easily as slots. The gaming commission will be very interested, I'm sure.*

At ten o'clock, Nathan Freeman still sat on the bunk in his cell, dressed in his clerical robe, his Bible in his hands. After spending the past few hours reading it, looking for an answer to why he should be locked up like a common criminal, he finally laid the Book aside, stretched out on the bed, and stared at the single bare lightbulb hanging from the ceiling.

The Chronicle *will have a heyday with this! I'll be the laughin' stock of the entire town. Maybe I already* am *the laughin' stock of the entire town!*

He walked over to the barred window and gazed out into the rapidly falling darkness, the distant heavens seemingly indifferent to the unfair imprisonment of a two-bit pastor in a puny village in the middle of nowhere.

Suddenly, behind him, a voice said, "He has surrendered. No rage, no hatred. He is dead inside. We have won."

The minister whirled to see who had entered his cell, but when he saw no one, he fought through his mounting fear and asked, "Who are you?"

"We are the angels of the curse. Raptor is ours, and all who oppose us are doomed."

Desperately, Freeman lunged for his Bible, like a drowning man for a life ring. He shouted as he opened its pages, "In the name of the Lord Jesus, Son of God, my Savior, I command you to leave me now!"

For a moment, he thought he heard laughter; but only silence greeted him as he continued praying, "I need your power, Lord. I cannot do this by myself. Help me, please."

The Book's pages fell open to Isaiah, and the preacher's eyes fell on these words: "The Spirit of the Lord GOD is upon me; because the LORD . . . hath sent me to bind up the brokenhearted, to proclaim liberty to the captives, and the opening of the prison to them that are bound. . . ."

"Okay," he said out loud, glancing heavenward. "But how am I supposed to proclaim liberty when I got no audience?" He closed the Book, laid it tenderly under his pillow, climbed onto the hardwood bunk, pulled the wool blanket over himself, and quickly fell asleep.

Four hours later, Nate Freeman awoke with a start. Outside in the street, a car door had just slammed, and there was a lot of shouting going on.

"It was fixed, I swear! I seen a lady win five hundred, and then I hit for three. But after that it just played with me, back and forth, till it stole it all back."

"Eddie, Eddie," Leonard Price said. "We go through this every Saturday night. It doesn't matter which casino— you always make a scene and then I have to throw you in here so you can cool off."

"You'd be hot, too," Eddie Hazard shouted, "if you lost everything to a crooked machine."

"You been watching too many old movies. These slots are monitored by the federal gaming commission. They're set so sometimes you win, sometimes you lose."

"Not me," Hazard replied, somewhat more subdued as they stepped through the front door. "I always lose."

"Maybe that's because you don't quit while you're ahead. You said yourself you were ahead. But you didn't quit. Right?"

"I was on a hot machine. How could I quit then?"

"You could've quit when you started to lose."

"I had to try to make it back."

"Well, you got nobody to blame but yourself, like I tell you every week," Price said, as he locked the gambler in the cell adjacent to Freeman's.

"At least tonight you got some company," the chief said, turning on his heel. "See you in the morning."

Eddie Hazard walked slowly to the bars separating him from the preacher. "Hey," he said, "what're *you* doing in here?"

Sitting up on his bunk, the minister replied, "Disturbin' the peace."

"Duke it out with the constable?" Hazard laughed.

"Nope. Readin' my Bible and prayin' on the steps of my church."

"The Cathedral Casino," Hazard replied. "Can't wait till it opens. It'll have the biggest slot machine in the world."

"Ain't gonna open."

"Yeah. Who says? You?" Again he laughed.

"The Lord. His house cannot become a den of thieves, where you can squander your children's inheritance."

Suddenly, the gambler became silent. He turned away, walked to the other side of the cell, and sat down on the bunk, facing Freeman. After several minutes, he said, "You ever gambled, preacher?"

"Can't say that I have."

"Then, as my daddy used to say, 'Judge not that you be not judged.'"

"Your family religious?"

"Maybe. What difference does it make?"

"'Cause faith is the key to set the captive free."

"Who's a captive?" Again Hazard laughed, but not as derisively this time. "Let's face it, padre, we're both captives at the moment."

"But I'm a captive by choice."

"Then I must be a captive by chance."

"No such thing as chance, least the way you mean it. But there is choice. You can choose to be free again."

Freeman reached for his Bible. "I'll show you how, if you really want to know."

11

hief Price! I don't have to gamble anymore. I'm a free man!" Eddie Hazard shouted as Chief Price entered the jailhouse.

"Don't look too free to me," Price replied, taking the keys off his belt as he walked toward Hazard's jail cell.

"But I am. Jesus set me free. The pastor said so, and now I got to tell everybody."

"Look," Price replied. "Tell anybody you like, once you get home. Cause another scene in Raptor, your next stay will be more than just overnight. Your best bet is to take the 9 A.M. bus outta here, and never come back."

"Can't. Sorry," Hazard replied. "I promised Reverend Freeman I'd go to church with him and give a testimony. And then I got to get baptized. After that, I got to tell the rest of the boys."

Price stopped halfway across the floor and stared at Freeman. "You have no right to mess up this guy, just because he happens to spend the night in the cell next to you."

"Mess him up?" Freeman said, standing to his feet and walking toward Price. "Eddie ain't never been as straight as he is at this present moment, all thanks to you. And I thank ya, too, fer lockin' me up so we could meet."

"You're *thanking* me?"

"Of course. I know you meant it fer evil, but God meant it fer good," he said, handing Price the cash-filled envelope that had been tossed through the bars of his cell at 3 A.M. "Bail," he said with a smile. "Five hunnert, right?"

"You said you didn't have any money. Why else would you spend the night instead of payin' your way out?"

"When I checked into this hotel, I was flat broke. But in the middle of the night, this money came flyin' through my window."

Price stared at Freeman, then opened his cell door. "Can't argue with greenbacks," he said. He opened Hazard's cell. "You two stay outta trouble today. Go to church, get baptized, whatever religious types do. But make a scene in my town, and you'll be back in here faster'n you can spit."

"I stay outta trouble with you, I get in trouble with him," Freeman replied, nodding toward heaven. "I'll take my chances with you."

"There's good news and bad news," Doris Oberly said, as she scanned the lab report lying on the office desk between herself and Bruce Davidson. "Which do you want first?"

"Good news, naturally," Bruce Davidson replied, shifting in his chair more nervously than he wanted to admit.

"Okay," the addictionist replied. "First of all, you're probably not going to die of a heart attack, or AIDS. Your cholesterol looks great, and you're not HIV-positive."

"I could have told you that," Bruce replied. "You do an HIV screen on everybody?"

"Confidentially, of course," she said. "Since a lot of drug addicts share needles, it's something they usually want to know—and so do we. It's always better to know than not know, whether we're talking HIV infection, or simply knowing ourselves, don't you think?"

"I suppose," Bruce said. "But that sounded like a rhetorical question. What's the bad news?"

"The bad news, Dr. Davidson, is your liver's in trouble. GGTP, 459; SGOT, 124; SGPT, 111."

"Translation, please."

"One, you've been hitting the bottle pretty hard over a fairly long period of time. Two, if you don't find a way to stop, you'll die within five years."

"I can stop anytime," he replied. "I just haven't had enough incentive."

"What would it take?"

"Being threatened with the loss of my job if I don't complete this program, for starters," he said.

"You resent being here," she followed up, "even though you know you can leave anytime you like."

"Sure!" he shot back, surprised by his own bitterness.

"You could do something else. You're an educator. That would be fulfilling."

"True, but I can't leave the FBI quite yet. Too many loose ends."

"Such as?"

"Incomplete investigations."

"Please tell me about them."

"In the FBI, we use a phrase—need to know—about sensitive information. People who don't need to know, don't." He stopped, staring icily at the doctor for a moment, then said, "In this case, that includes you."

"Of course," she replied evenly, with a little smile. "I don't need to know—or want to know—any classified details. On the other hand, if I'm going to help you, I need to know *everything* about anything that may have contributed to your addiction."

"Addiction? The only addict in this room is you, by your own admission. I've never been addicted to anything."

"I *am* an addict," she said, "on the road to recovery, the first step of which was to admit I was powerless before the substances I used to dull my pain, and that as a result my life had become unmanageable—"

"I know the twelve steps," he interrupted, growing increasingly agitated. "They may work for basket cases. But if I had a real problem, I would simply lick it on my own."

"Like you've been doing with every problem since you were nine?"

"What?"

"More specifically, since your father died and left you the man of the house?"

Bruce, surprised by the connection Doris had made, sat silently, struggling to hold back the tears. Finally, he said, "Even then I had enough willpower to make something of myself. Is there something wrong with that?"

"Not exactly," she replied, more gently, "for without it, who knows what would have become of little Bruce? But," she hesitated, reaching for a book on the shelf behind her desk, "your story is so similar to Dr. Gerald May's. Let me read you a little from his book, *Addiction and Grace*. Just sit back, relax, and listen."

Bruce Davidson was about as far from relaxed as he could possibly be, but he wasn't about to let her know that, so he sat back in the comfortable leather lounge and closed his eyes.

"As with all children," she read, "the earliest years of my life were 'simply religious.' In the innocent wonder and awe of early childhood awareness, everything just *is* spiritual. My religious education had given me a name for God, but I hardly needed it. I prayed easily; God was a friend."

Suddenly, Bruce Davidson was a little boy again, walking hand in hand with his father across an open meadow toward the river behind their farm, each carrying a fishing pole over his outside shoulder. It was late afternoon of an early spring day in southern Texas. The mayflies would be hatching, setting off a feeding frenzy among the bass. Unlike most of the other fishermen in Hague County, who flailed away with poppers, spinners, and crawlers regardless of what was happening on the surface of Misty River, T. Bob Davidson knew exactly how to match the hatch, and had taught his son to do the same. Lay the fly out gently, and you could catch a fish on nearly every cast. As father and son peered through the underbrush at the river's edge, a hundred circles on the usually still surface promised action enough to make a kid's arm ache. Just the anticipation of this daily ritual each April was as close to sheer pleasure as any nine-year-old ever knew. The homemade fly on his line was laid out thirty feet over the bass-filled eddy, drifting lazily toward the water when the memory screen went blank as Dr. Oberly read on.

"I expected God to somehow keep me in touch with my father after his death. I prayed for this, but of course it did not happen. As a result, something hurt and angry, something deeper than my consciousness, chose to dispense with God. I would take care of myself; I would go it alone. My wanting—my love—had caused me to be hurt, and something in me decided not to want so much. I repressed my longing. Just as my father faded from my awareness, so did God, and so did my desire for God."

Davidson, his eyes still closed, fought the fading of the image with such intensity that his whole body went rigid in the chair and both hands grabbed hold of its arms until his knuckles were white.

"During college," the reading continued, "I fell in love with literature and philosophy. In retrospect, I think this was my desire for God surfacing again, as a search for beauty and truth. I even tried to go to church on occasion, but I wasn't consciously looking for God. By then I was searching for something that I could use to develop a sense of mastery over my life, something that would help me go it alone."

"I found it in the CIA," she added, "and then, later, in the FBI."

Startled, Bruce Davidson opened his eyes. "What? Nobody would put that in a book."

"A little interpolation," she replied, handing him the book. "Based on information provided by your good friend, Mr. Billings."

"So, I can't have any secrets."

"You can have all the secrets you please," she replied. "This stuff was just out there on the surface, for any trained eye to see."

At that moment, Bruce Davidson wished he could escape the analysis and dive back into the dream. More

94

than that, he longed to get out of Hope Center and into the nearest tavern. After all, what could this woman possibly understand about the struggles he'd faced, not only as a boy but later as a CIA agent in Vietnam and then in his career with the FBI?

"What else do you know about me?" he asked.

"Enough to believe I can help you," she said. "But you'll have to let me inside the pain if I'm to be your companion on the journey."

"Journey toward what?"

"Sobriety, sanity, serenity . . . wholeness," she said. "Call it whatever you choose. But the power only comes through admitting we're powerless on our own. The freedom only comes from surrender to your true Master. The joy only comes from embracing his way with us."

"I didn't know this was a religious program. Can't we stick to science and leave the God stuff out?"

"We could try," she said, "as you've been doing. In fact, I tried, when I first started. But I discovered that all the lasting recoveries made by my patients came from the inside out. When I analyzed it further, I realized that the same thing was true for me. Now I believe that every important issue in every addict's life is spiritual in some way."

"I'm *not* an addict," Davidson exploded. "I told you that already."

"Please," she said. "Read me the first three full sentences on page four of that book in your hand. If you don't believe me, you might believe him."

He fumbled to find the right spot, then read, "We are all addicts in every sense of the word. Moreover, our addictions are our own worst enemies. They enslave us with chains that are of our own making and yet that, paradoxically, are virtually beyond our control."

He stopped reading and looked at her. "Are there any other therapists? I can't believe this approach is acceptable to the Bureau."

"Any approach that works is acceptable," Dr. Oberly said. "And the only method that really works must be personalized. Before you arrived, we studied your files and agreed that I should work with you. You may be surprised to find how much we have in common. So, before we make a change, I wish you would read the first two chapters in that book and come to our next session prepared to discuss them. After that, if you still insist on changing therapists, we'll do our best to accommodate you."

Reverend Nathan Freeman looked out over his congregation, sitting in three rows of folding seats in the gymnasium of Raptor Elementary School. He picked up his guitar and slung it over his shoulder, strumming a few chords as if to lead the praise singing they began with each week. Instead, as he played softly, he said, "You probably saw the *Chronicle* this mornin', and the story about me spendin' last night in jail. Well, I'd like to set the record straight. I got arrested fer prayin' and readin' my Bible, that's all. But instead of borin' you with the details, let me sing you the song I wrote about it:

> I started to run, though my work wasn't done
> When the Lord whispered into my soul,
> 'You got to let go, don't fight 'em no more,
> Just be still and know who I am.
> For I am exalted, I will be exalted,
> Over them, over all the earth
> Over them, over all the earth.'

I tried to obey, but was greatly dismayed
As the workmen kept wreckin' his house.
But instead of objectin', I did some reflectin'
On lovin' and hatin', cursin' and blessin'
Like him on the cross when they spit in his face
'Father, forgive them,' he prayed.
'For they know not what they do
They know not what they do.'

Now, strange it may sound, soon as I turned around
I'm sittin' in jail just for prayin',
And layin' there worried what people will say
When the gossip mill starts the next day.
But then God clearly tells me,
Yes God clearly tells me,
To open the prison to them that are bound,
To open the prison, for them that are bound.

What more could I ask, than to have such a task
And to know there's a purpose in livin'.
I don't have to win, just need to stay in
His will for my life, which is givin'
The key to believin', a way of receivin'
The One who's the source of the hope that is in me;
The One who's the source of the hope that is in me."

After the song, Freeman gently laid down the guitar. "I never been in jail before," he said, "but—this will sound funny—I'm glad it happened, 'cause in the middle of the night two miracles happened, one right after t'other. First, Eddie here ends up in the next cell . . . captive audience, I guess. But I'll just let him tell you, hisself."

Freeman sat down and Eddie Hazard, obviously very nervous, walked to the podium. "I've been here in Raptor every weekend for the past four months," he began, "and lost my paycheck every time. They call it low stakes gambling, but I promise you, in less than an hour you can lose everything you made in the last forty, one quarter at a time. They call it gaming, but it ain't no game, least not for guys like me who are hooked. When you have to do something, and you can't stop, no matter what, it ain't a game but an addiction.

"Well, last night, I lost everything in the Regis Casino after I got suckered into playing the dollar slots. What made it worse was I actually won—three hundred dollars—on my first pull. And I should've quit while I was ahead. That was what the lady said to do. I called her lady luck, because she won just before me and then gave me two pockets full of money . . ."

He stopped in mid-sentence as he caught sight of Clare Conroy, disguised as Juanita Rodriguez, who had slipped in and was now sitting in the back row. Flushing with embarrassment and confusion, Eddie nearly choked. But then he continued. "The lady urged me to cash out, but I wouldn't listen. Instead, I pumped everything I had into that machine, still hoping to hit the jackpot again. Then, when I ran out of money, and the steward told me to vacate the machine if I wasn't going to play anymore, I grabbed him by the lapels and started yelling that I'd been set up.

"So I ended up in jail, with a set of bars between me and Reverend Freeman. Next thing I know, he's telling me that by myself I would never beat gamblin'. But if I would admit to God that I couldn't do it, he would give me the power. I had nothing to lose and everything to gain, so I did what the Reverend said and I'm here to say I've been delivered!"

He stopped, tears in his eyes, as Freeman embraced him

and the congregation clapped. After a moment, Nathan asked him, "And what are you going to do before you go back to your wife and kids?"

"Get baptized in Tinker's Creek."

"And you're all invited," Freeman said to the group. "Two o'clock, at the old swimming hole."

He stopped, staring at Clare for just a moment, sure that he'd seen her before, but unable to remember where.

"But," he continued, "there was a second miracle last night. As soon as Eddie got saved, a plain white envelope with five hundred dollars in it came flyin' through the window of my cell—the exact amount I needed to make bail!"

12

Unknown to Nathan Freeman, Eddie Hazard had come prepared for his baptism in more ways than one. Not only was he ready to say why he was about to allow himself to be immersed in the waters of Tinker's Creek, but anticipating the icy bath, Hazard had wrapped each limb in plastic sealed with duct tape, with one large bag over his torso for good measure. None of it showed, however, as the new convert made his way to the riverbank, since he was also wearing a black choir robe provided by the pastor.

News of the outdoor baptismal service had spread through Raptor like the fire of 1913. By 2 P.M., onlookers eager to see "the dunking" had lined both stream banks five deep, for several hundred feet north and south of the swimming hole.

Nate Freeman tossed a silent prayer skyward as he made his way to the pool's sandy bank. He, too, was wearing a robe—his clerical robe—and carrying a Bible in his left hand as he strode to the water's edge. Then he slowly turned full circle, acknowledging the people in every direction. Eddie Hazard stood barefoot beside the water, awaiting the signal to step forward to make his speech.

Freeman held up his hand in a relatively futile gesture for quiet. As he waited for the chatter to diminish, he wondered how Jesus would have handled this rowdy crowd who had come as mockers rather than as witnesses. *Tell the truth. He always told the truth,* Freeman thought, *and let the chips fall where they may.*

"Ladies and gentlemen," he began, at the top of his voice. "You are about to witness one of the oldest traditions of the Christian church—believer's baptism. Going beneath the water symbolizes death—death to sin, the old self, the old way of livin'—burial, and resurrection to a new life. Today, Mr. Eddie Hazard of Denver will be baptized as a public testimony. But before we proceed, he has a few words to share."

Eddie stepped forward, shivering from the coolness of the afternoon and from nervousness; a number of his former drinking and gambling buddies had turned out to see if the rumors were true.

"As many of you know," he began, staring directly into the eyes of first one then another of those men, "over the past few months I've become a regular on Main Street."

"Not to mention Second Avenue!" a male voice shouted across the water, followed by a chorus of loud guffaws.

Hazard nodded, blushed, looked down at the sand in embarrassment, then continued, tears streaming down his face. "I started coming up this spring when the casinos first opened, just to find a good time and drop a few bucks in the slots. But gradually the gambling bug got under my skin. When I got my paycheck, I was on the next bus to Raptor, only to lose it all in just a few hours."

When several men in the crowd nodded knowingly, Hazard continued, with greater enthusiasm. "And that's the way this weekend started out, too—that is, until I hit a little jackpot and thought my luck had finally changed."

The former gambler glanced toward a disguised Clare Conroy, who was standing in the shadows of the bridge about twenty feet distant.

"And it had, though not in the way I thought. After I gave the one-armed bandit all its money back, I got thrown in jail, where I met Reverend Nathan Freeman; he got thrown in there for praying and reading his Bible on the steps of his old church building.

"Anyway, Reverend Freeman told me I didn't *have* to gamble, or get drunk, or do anything wrong, because God could change me from the inside out. And that's what happened!"

He was shouting now, and waving his arms in the air for emphasis. "I'm a free man, for the first time in my life. Free! And you can be too, Jimmy, Joey, Sammy," he yelled, reaching imploringly toward certain men in the crowd. "It ain't just for me. It's for anybody who's a slave to slots, or blackjack, or poker, or even Second Avenue. Only believe, and it'll happen for you, too."

The minister reached over and took the born-again gambler by the arm and led him slowly out into the frigid water. When they had reached waist depth, both men turned to face the shore. As they did so, Freeman noticed that Leonard Price was videotaping the event through the open window of his cruiser, parked on the bridge.

"Edward George Hazard, the third," Freeman said loudly and directly toward the camera's lens, smiling defiantly. "Because of your faith and your willingness to testify before these witnesses, I do hereby baptize thee in the waters of repentance, forgiveness, and new life."

The minister leaned Hazard backward into the water, expecting his body to submerge of its own accord and then resurface with a little help. But the air trapped in the plastic under Hazard's robe made the man as buoyant as an inflated tube. Instead of going under, he popped upward and then floated on the surface as Freeman held on, not quite sure what to do. In the end, in order to achieve total immersion, the minister had to lean all his body weight on the other man, after which the newly baptized believer popped up again with a sheepish grin and clambered ashore.

The bystanders, even members of Freeman's parish, chuckled quietly as the minister struggled to get his new disciple under. But by the time the men had reached the beach, the crowd's laughter was totally unrestrained.

"Sorry," Hazard whispered. "Didn't want to catch pneumonia."

"It's okay," Freeman replied. "Just wish I'd known." *'Cause now I* am *the laughingstock of the whole town!*

As he faced the laughing crowd, however, Nathan Freeman smiled broadly and said, "Bet that was the best slam dunk this here town's ever seen!"

When Clare Conroy had noticed Price videotaping the whole affair, she had retreated under the bridge, not wanting to be part of anybody's permanent record of this, or any other, event in Raptor, even if she was in disguise.

Conroy had also noticed Nathan Freeman leave a pile of towels there, and she chose that position to finally connect with him. After the service that morning, instead of revealing her mission in a setting where she might be overheard, she had slipped out the back.

But as the afternoon crowd quickly dispersed and Freeman stepped around the abutment, she handed him the towels, in which she had wrapped a balcony seat ticket to Tuesday night's performance of *Dracula's Mistress*.

"Why, thank you, Miss Rodriguez," he said, as he took the towels.

"How you know me?" she asked, careful to retain the Spanish accent.

He nodded. "From the ads in the paper." He paused, then asked, "Are you a believer? I saw you in church."

"Sí," she replied. "But in my family, we usually attend the cathedral, unless a conspiracy has shut its doors."

Freeman looked directly into Clare's dark eyes. "I thought you were an actress."

"I am, of course, but I am also come to help you. We cannot talk here. In your towel is a ticket to Tuesday night's show. Stay late in that seat, and I will find you."

Freeman unwrapped the towel's top layer and found the ticket. "I ain't much partial to plays."

"But you are an excellent actor," she chuckled. "Perhaps you will even enjoy it!"

Leonard Price was laughing so hard as the videotape concluded, he fumbled with the remote control to switch it off.

"Give me that thing," Stanley Hawkins roared. "How can you make a joke of it when they're multiplying like flies?"

"They made the joke, not me."

"Maybe. Maybe not. The preacher recovered pretty good. Why'd you let him out of the can in the first place?"

104

"He made bail," Leonard Price replied. "Don't ask me how. Didn't have a cent on him when I locked him up, but he handed me five hundred the next morning. Claimed it arrived airmail, through the window."

"You believe that, I got part of a New York bridge for sale," Hawkins said. "You must've missed it."

"Not a chance."

"Then the gambler brought it in."

"You believe that, I got some Florida swampland for sale!"

"You aren't careful, you'll end up underneath it," Hawkins replied, staring icily at the lawman.

Try it, pal. Anytime, Price thought, as he turned away and walked over to the window in Hawkins's office and gazed blankly outside. "I got a plan," he said, without turning around.

"It's about time. What?"

"Friday. High noon. The robbery reenactment. Once a month, Freeman tries to rob the bank and I chase him outta town. You've seen it often enough."

Hawkins nodded.

"Well," the lawman continued, "suppose a couple real bullets get into the good guy's chamber?"

"Dead meat on Main Street!" Hawkins laughed at his own poetry.

"Too many witnesses," Price said. "With all the camcorders running, I'd spend the next month explainin' how such a horrible mistake could happen."

"That's your problem."

"I figured. So let me do it my way. Come Friday, the preacher's in for the surprise of his life, I promise. But, he don't get the message this time, he'll eat lead October twenty-ninth. Either way, he won't be there for the grand opening."

"Okay," Hawkins replied. He paused, as if still troubled, then added, "And the gambler? Run him outta town?"

"The guy's a loser. Let him flap his gums for awhile, then slip him a couple rolls of five-buck tokens. He'll self-destruct faster than you can say Mephistopheles, and take the preacher down with him."

Hand him a bottle, he'd fall off the wagon as slick as snot, Bruce Davidson thought, as Steven S. droned on about his bruised and broken psyche and his attempts to bury the pain with booze.

"When I was a child," Steven said, "I thought and spoke and acted as a child. Now that I'm a man, I want to put away childish things. But I'm still a little child inside. . . ."

Group, group, group, Davidson mused, as the Native American continued. His mind wandered again. *Three times a day. Worse than church when I was a kid and Mom used to drag me in there three times a week!*

Growing up in Texas, Bruce had heard a lot of testimonies, many of them like Steven's. Get abused, wander, fall into depravity, find God at the bottom, and then live happily ever after. The problem was, the older he got, the more little Brucie observed that a lot of these conversions didn't "take," and the ones that did often produced the biggest bores in the congregation, because they had exchanged one fixation for the other—from booze to bragging about how much they'd changed.

After his father's death, Bruce had gone through the motions to keep Mommy happy. As a result, he was already

106

twenty-five before his skepticism met authentic Christianity head-on in the Mennonite pacifists he spied on during the Vietnam War.

Later, Ellen had dismantled the rest of his duplicity with the simplicity of her trust, not only in him but in God. She made faith so real, you either had to believe or walk away. He had chosen the former, at least until the God Ellen trusted allowed her to be fried not fifty feet from her own front door.

"A lot of good it did you," he muttered, unaware that he was speaking aloud.

"Steven," Dr. Oberly interrupted. "Bruce seems to have a question."

Startled by Oberly's intrusion into his daydream, Davidson was horrified to find that not only had Steven stopped, but he was waiting, a smile on his face, for Bruce to speak. Everyone else in the group was waiting, too. There was no way to escape without explaining.

"Sorry," Bruce mumbled. "Something you said started me thinking . . . thinking . . . about nothing in particular."

He nearly choked on the lie. In the subculture in which he had become temporarily trapped, the only unbreakable rule seemed to be that if you spoke—which nobody forced you to do—you had to tell the truth. They wouldn't let you lie, to them or to yourself. Based on the friendly confrontations he'd already witnessed in the group that day, trying to hide behind such a fabrication was the equivalent of climbing into a cage of hungry lions, expecting them not to have you for lunch.

He waited, his pulse pounding in his ears and the sweat beading on his brow, for the inquisition to begin. But before it could do so, he heard himself say, "No, that's not exactly true. I was thinking about something, some things, very important to me. Sorry, Steven. I'm having trouble concentrating. But I shouldn't have interrupted."

"It's okay, Bruce," Steven answered. "Sorry to bore you. Sometimes going in circles is the only way I can get to the center, like peeling an onion."

Davidson opened his mouth, and tried to say, "You didn't bore me." But since that, too, would have been a lie, he just sat there with his mouth open, hoping no one could see his hands trembling. He glanced at Dr. Oberly, as if asking to be rescued, suddenly realizing she had created this crisis, probably by design.

As that realization hit home, his emotions finally found a focus: rage. He was a victim, here, as everywhere else. Doris Oberly could not be trusted, either.

And as the bitterness captured his imagination, Dr. Oberly began to take on the form of a vial of the finest cognac money could buy. Slowly he lifted her high and drained every delicious drop until, intoxicated with delight, he set the bottle back down where she had been sitting.

"Bruce," the bottle said. "Is there anything else you want to say?"

"No," he replied. "At least, not right now." And this time it was the truth.

13

Seated in the darkened balcony of the Regis Theater, Nate Freeman was still shaking his head. Only minutes before, Dracula had simply vanished from the stage below in a puff of smoke. Then the image of a bat had flown into the heart of a full moon projected on the back of the set as Juanita Rodriguez cried furtively after it, "Come back, darling. Come back!"

Behind Freeman in the dark, the door opened, then shut quickly as the actress slipped into the seat next to the minister.

"How'd you do that?" he asked, staring at her neck to see if it still bore any wounds.

"There's a hidden passage between my dressing room and this box."

"No, how did they make Dracula just disappear?"

"Trade secret. But here's a hint. Next time, look for the trap door under his feet."

"Next time?"

"It's a good place to meet, and I have to be here every night. Anybody asks, you can say you got hooked on theater. Nothing wrong with that. And if we're seen together, well, we're just together. Actresses have to keep the fans happy."

"Some of my parishioners might blow a cork," he said. *Not to mention what Annie might think if she could see me now.* "But just like you got to perform, I got to picket. How about, if you got somethin' for me, you get me a ticket somehow. And if I got somethin' for you, I'll just show up."

"Okay," Conroy replied, leaning toward him just a bit in the darkness as she activated her miniature tape recorder. "But just to get me started, please tell me everything you remember about Stephanie Lockwood. I want to find out what really happened to her."

"Well," Freeman said, sucking in a long breath. "Like I told the other agents before, me and Stephanie only talked twice. So we weren't really best buddies. But the second time, she really spilled her guts. Said she was a witch."

He paused, reviewing the conversation in his mind.

"Tell me," Conroy said, "every gory detail."

"Okay. She said she'd run away with her boyfriend, an older guy into drugs, sex, motorcycles, and worshipin' Satan. One night he picks her up and they head for Las Vegas, where he's supposed to marry her. But when they get there, he moves her into an apartment with a bunch of his friends, and before she knows it she's high on drugs most of the time, workin' as a prostitute.

"The bum takes off after a few months, leaving her penniless. But her new friends said she could stay, if she would become their *brood mare!* After fifteen years of raisin' horses, I knew what that meant, but never heard it used about people."

"What could she possibly mean?"

"I'll get to that," he said, "but first I need to tell you that when she said those words, all of a sudden she jumped up, like a wild woman, wavin' her arms around like she was gettin' stung by hornets. But this time she didn't run away like before. It's like she'd made up her mind to talk. She confessed that in the last four years, she had given birth to three babies, all conceived specifically to be used as sacrifices!"

"What?" Conroy exclaimed.

"That's what she said. You think I'd make it up? Anyway, after the third baby, she ran away from that group and came to Raptor, tryin' to start over as a cocktail waitress.

"But here's the craziest thing. She's in town two months and she finds another satanic group."

"Maybe they found her."

"Works out the same. She thought she was trapped, least till she saw my picture in the *Chronicle*. I was talkin' about how evil was takin' over this town, and maybe she figured I was her only hope. She asked me to help her escape, or find her a place to hide."

The preacher's voice broke, then he grabbed his face with both hands and started to weep. "I didn't know what to think, much less what to do. I offered to call her parents to see if they'd like to have her come home. But she said, 'No way. They're better off thinking I'm dead than knowing what's really happening to their little girl. They couldn't understand, and they never would forgive me.'

"Nothing is beyond forgiveness," I said.

"When she spoke again, it was that voice I'd heard before—deeper, raspy, without feeling. 'She gave her

111

children to the lord of darkness,' it said. 'She is the bride of Satan. She has cursed God and renounced the name of Jesus. She is ours.'"

He paused, studying Conroy's face for a moment before continuing. "Any idea what makes a person talk like that?"

"Multiple personality disorder, maybe," Conroy replied. "MPD for short. She'd been through a lot, even if only half of it was true. What do you think?"

"I'd heard of this before, from missionaries. They called it demon possession."

"Didn't demons go out with the dark ages?" she replied. "We have more scientific names for it now."

"Don't matter what you call it. Matters what it *is*," he replied. "In any case, I never saw her again. Did she die because she talked to me? Why?"

"Not just why, but who? When? Where? How?" Clare responded. "We have a lot of work to do, that's for sure. But if we're going to get anywhere, we have to stick to facts, not phantasms."

"Then you do think I'm nuts."

"No, you may be right. But even if you are, we need evidence that'll stand up in court—names, dates, places, motives, and means. Did she ever say anything else that might help?"

"Only one thing. There's a meetin' every full moon at midnight in North Face Cemetery at the grave of Elyse Morais."

"The Haitian witch that cursed Raptor just before she was hanged."

"You know about that?"

"I did my homework."

"And you think it's just superstition?"

"I never said that. But what hanged a witch in 1932 would be thrown out of court today as religious bigotry."

"Bigotry?"

"There's a tax-exempt Church of Satan in California, and open witchcraft in Rhode Island. Attending midnight ceremonies, even in a cemetery, is not a crime. But interfering is."

"So, we're the bad guys and they're the good guys?"

"Justice is blind, or so they say. The trick will be observing without them even knowing we're there. The crucial question is, when's the next full moon?" she asked, pulling out her purse to look at the calendar. "September thirtieth—a week from Thursday. I can get the stuff in time."

"That makes the last full moon . . ."

"September first. Why?"

"Last time I saw Stephanie was August thirty-first. I wonder. . . ."

"What?"

"If that's when she died. They have to have some kind of sacrifice every full moon."

"How do you know that?"

"After the first time I met Stephanie, I studied everything I could find about modern satanism. The deeper you go, the scarier it gets. But it does accomplish one good thing; it forces you to decide if you really believe there's a war going on between good and evil."

At the stroke of midnight, Aradia carried the victim to the altar, accompanied by the moans and gyrations of the group gathered in the Kingsford Mine. The six-week-old puppy made no effort to resist as the witch felt for its carotid pulse with her left hand, while holding high the athame, the ceremonial dagger, in her right hand. For a moment, the only sound in the cavern was the animal's pathetic whining for its mother.

The witch brought the dagger down, dramatically, until its needle-sharp point pierced the animal's skin and a trickle of blood began to flow, collecting in a small channel around the altar's lip and then down the front of the black marble slab where another woman knelt to catch it in a silver chalice.

"Baphomet, lord of darkness, prince of princes and ruler of the unseen world," she intoned. "Accept this sacrifice as a token of our devotion. For we long to do your will, to purge this place of every foe. We curse them. We curse them all, for we know that with your help we shall win, we must win. And they must die."

The blood stopped flowing as she spoke the final words and reached for the Book of Shadows. As if by command, the woman who had knelt to catch the blood presented the witch the chalice, a wisp of steam rising from it as the warm moisture met the chilly underground air.

Aradia took a long quill from its holder, dipped it in the blood, and wrote in the book: *We curse you, Edward George Hazard, III, and commit you into the hands of lust. You are her slave forever, and nothing shall deliver you.*

She paused for a moment, scanning the document; then she read aloud the name of Nathan Freeman. "And, Baphomet," she prayed, "we doubly curse this man. May he drown in doubt, surrender to fear, yield to pride until he is broken beyond repair. And then may he die a horrible death, he and all who dare oppose your will. So be it."

"So be it," they all said, in unison, as they passed the

114

chalice around, each taking a drink until the blood of the sacrifice had been consumed.

Bruce Davidson sat bolt upright in his bed, wondering if anyone else had heard the scream. In a dream he had been standing by his father's open coffin, right next to his head, just like always when this particular memory replayed itself in his unconscious mind.

As usual, friends and family and other well-wishers had filed by slowly, paying their last respects to T. Bob Davidson, each with some kind word to say to brave little Brucie.

The nine-year-old tried to tell them, one after another, how sorry he was, how awful he felt. But they just patted him on the head and walked away, shaking their heads sadly.

Whenever he had this dream, he tried to call them back, to make them return, to make them listen. But when he opened his mouth, nothing came out.

Until tonight.

This time, after all the people left and his mother was pulling him away from the casket so the undertaker could close it, Bruce Davidson had glanced one more time at his father's face, only to discover he was looking at himself, forty-one-year-old Bruce Robert Davidson. Amazed, he looked up at his mother for an explanation, only to find that she had become Doris Oberly, and she was pushing him—no, she was pouring him—into the casket just as it slammed shut.

In the darkness of that container, as he became himself, a thirty-two-year-long scream filled the space, filled every space, until it became so intense he couldn't stand it any more. He awoke with a start.

Shaking, the FBI agent stood up and wandered to the washroom, wondering if he had finally fallen over the edge of sanity. *But if I were insane,* he tried to reassure himself, *I wouldn't be wondering about it.*

But the person staring back at him in the washroom mirror was a stranger, too. Three days without a drink had changed something, though he couldn't be sure what. One thing he was sure of, however. He was feeling a lot more pain than he had felt in a long, long time. *Fred said this was a healing place,* he thought. *But if that's true—and I'm not convinced it is—why does it hurt so much to get healed? And if it hurts this much after only three days, four weeks will be torture. It can't be worth it. It isn't worth it! I have to take myself out of here.*

He wiped his hands and headed back to his room, down a hallway that seemed to have gotten much longer in just the past few minutes. Every couple feet there was another bulletin board, peppered with A.A. principles, helpful platitudes, a few smiley faces with the exhortation to have a good day, and an occasional Bible verse.

Davidson shut himself into his room, and started to pace, as he had done each night at the Hope Center. As his body longed for sleep, his brain raced wildly, producing neurotransmitters as it had every night for months to counteract the alcohol's sedative effect; it had no way of knowing that tonight there would be no sedative. And even though Dr. Oberly had warned him it would take a few days for his body to establish a new equilibrium, the withdrawal period had been a struggle, every minute of it.

As he paced restlessly, an impression wedged itself into

his psyche. *You're a loser, Davidson. A failure. Always were, always will be. Failed your father. Failed your mother. Failed Ellen. Failed the Bureau. And now you've failed yourself, stuck in a rehab center with a bunch of other failures. Your whole life has been a lie, and now everyone will know. Stay here, they're going to find out. They won't stop until they find out. Leave, and everybody else will know. Your career is over. Your life is worthless. You might as well get it over with.*

He continued pacing, but now he had a goal; find something, anything, with which to kill himself. A short piece of rope, even strong twine would do. He searched the dresser. Nothing. He explored the closet. Nothing. Then he had an idea.

He took down one of the heavy metal hangers, twisted it until it broke, then retrieved an emery board from his shaving kit. *If I can make it sharp enough,* he thought as he began sanding it, *maybe it will work. Not the heart . . . too much bone. Wrist might work if I hit it on the first shot. Jugular maybe. The ear! Take a straight shot right into the brain. Let's see . . . four centimeters should be long enough. The rest I'll bend over to make a handle.*

Once he knew what he was going to do, he worked methodically, first sharpening the instrument to a needle point. Then he wrapped the triply-bent remainder with Scotch tape. Finally, he opened the bed stand drawer and pulled out the paperback *Life Recovery Bible* inside it. With one motion, he shoved the instrument through the cover and deep into the text. When it penetrated easily, he was satisfied that it would work and that it was time.

But just as he reached to put the Bible back where it belonged, his bedroom door opened behind him. Quickly he slipped the killing instrument into the book he was holding, and turned to see who might be so intrusive.

"Good evening, Dr. Davidson," the attendant said, rather casually. "You seemed to be having trouble sleeping, so I've brought you some medication—Trazodone, one-hundred-fifty milligrams—just for tonight. Don't worry, it's not addictive. You'll feel much better in the morning."

The young man came toward Bruce, holding in one hand a tablet and in the other a water-filled cup. "I see you've been reading the Bible," he said. "Good choice. Here, let me hold that while you take these."

Trapped, Bruce followed the instructions. But when the attendant took the Bible from him, the homemade weapon fell out noisily onto the floor, bounced a couple of times, then came to rest at Bruce's feet.

"Interesting bookmark," the nurse commented, picking up the object before Bruce could react. "Certainly not something we would want in the hands of some of our patients, especially those who are a danger to themselves."

He pocketed the device as he spoke these words, and when he said the last phrase, he simply stared intently into Bruce's eyes.

Simultaneously, Bruce Davidson realized two rather disconcerting things. First, he had come within seconds of being a dead man, for the second time in a week. Second, the attendant's arrival at that precise moment could not have been coincidental. *They've been monitoring me. There must be a hidden camera in here somewhere!*

"No lie," he replied, trying to recover. "Thanks for bringing that medication. I haven't had more than a couple hours' sleep ever since I came here."

After Davidson had downed the tablet, the attendant handed the Bible back to him, turned, and left without another word. Davidson walked back to his bed and sat down, as the Book fell open to the last page not penetrated by the device—Psalm 56. He started reading at verse eight: "You have seen me tossing and turning through the night. You have collected all my tears and preserved them in your bottle! You have recorded every one in your book."

His eyes then settled on a phrase that seemed to jump off the page. "This one thing I know," it said. "God is for me!"

Is this the answer Clare was talking about? he wondered. *I never gave her a chance to say.*

Bruce Davidson's eyes filled with tears, from a mixture of sadness and gratitude—sadness that Clare had put him off again; gratitude that a person whose name he didn't even know had just cared enough to save his life. He lay back on the bed and said, "Thank you," whether to the eye in the ceiling or the eye in the heavens, he didn't really know.

14

Hello, Fred? I need some equipment up here ASAP," Clare Conroy said into her Motorola MicroTac Ultra Lite cellular phone. "Night vision binocs, nightscope with camera mount, and some good electronic ears."

"No problem," Fred Billings responded. "Sounds like you're making some progress."

"I am," she said. "I connected with Freeman. We're attending a graveyard ceremony next Thursday at midnight—from a quarter-mile out."

"Is it worth the risk? Don't go chasing ghouls and goblins and blow your cover."

"Stephanie was involved with this group. It's the only solid lead I've got. I'll be careful." She paused, wondering if someone might be listening in the hallway outside her room. "I've uncovered some other stuff, too," she added in a whisper. "Rigged slot machines, for instance, and prostitution."

"Predictable," he said. "Get what you can, but stay focused on THE STEEPLE CHASE. We're making some progress with the financials, turning up some interesting connections. Maybe some big players."

"Such as?"

"Eagle Corporation. Maybe this time we can nail them."

"Anything I can do?"

"Keep an eye on the bank. They're handling millions of dollars every month, some of which is still going to Skip Sanders."

"Anything else?"

"Eagle Corporation funded an interesting purchase this spring—the Kingsford estate, including the mine and mansion. Why should they care about that place?"

"Maybe they needed a gold mine. Who knows?"

"And," Billings added, "there is one other thing. This op is ours to win or lose. Bruce is out of the loop for a while. I finally convinced him to get some help, so he's spending some time at a treatment center."

"How'd you convince him?"

"Made him an offer he couldn't refuse," Billings replied. "Hardest thing I've ever done. Had to pry a gun out of his hand to do it, too. I never thought it would come to that. I hope it was worth it."

"He aimed a gun at you?" Clare replied. "That's hard to imagine."

"No. At his own right temple."

Conroy tried to respond but no words would come. Instead, a deep anguish that she hadn't felt since her parents' separation suddenly burst through her usual defenses, and she began to weep.

Billings, shocked, waited a full fifteen seconds before continuing. "The gun was empty, Clare," he said, softly.

"Bruce wasn't in his right mind. He drank a whole bottle of whiskey after you left."

"Maybe I drove him to it," she replied. "I had no right to bring up Ellen. But when I realized how much he needed me, instead of feeling valued, I felt something else—fear, to be honest."

"Clare," Billings said, with a level voice. "Like I said the other day, love does funny things to a person, and female FBI agents are no exception. Regardless, Bruce still needs you to solve this case. And so do I, since I promised H.Q. there was nothing happening we couldn't handle while Bruce was gone."

"When I read to you from *Addiction and Grace* the other day, you seemed to go somewhere," Doris Oberly said to Bruce Davidson. "I could see it in your face. If it's not classified, I'd love to hear about it."

"Just went fishing."

"Last week, or last year? Or a long time ago?"

"A long time ago, before . . ." He hesitated. "Before part of me died."

"Fishing with your dad?"

He nodded, wanting to look away, to escape somewhere. But there was no use trying to hide from this benevolent bloodhound.

"Bass," he said, finally.

"Sounds exciting. Bait, plugs, or lures?"

"Flies," he replied. *What difference could it possibly make to you?*

"Largemouths on flies? Pretty rare approach, I expect."

"That's for sure," he replied, becoming more animated. "Everybody else was beating Misty River to a froth. But

Daddy taught me to tie—and to fish—the blue-tailed darter. Invented the pattern himself. It was the best . . . the best . . ."

"Period of your life?"

"Well, yes," he replied. "Until I met Ellen. Then, for a couple of years, I was happy again."

"But since she died?"

"Never, except maybe with the help of my best buddy, Old Grand-Dad," he blurted out, wishing he hadn't said it, even though it was true.

She just nodded, waiting for him to continue. He did.

"But you want to take away my only friend, and replace him with what?"

"Reality, I hope," she replied. "Not to mention sanity, serenity, and joy . . . and more reliable friends."

I prefer Old Grand-Dad, he mused. *At least he doesn't intrude.* "Sanity? You think I'm *insane?*"

"Not in the usual sense of the word, but as the opposite of sane, meaning healthy, free from hurt or disease."

"I'm as healthy as most guys my age. I jog, work out, climb mountains, hunt, and fish whenever I can."

"But are you really at ease, even then? When was the last time you relaxed without some sort of chemical crutch?"

Davidson stared at the floor, his back muscles tightening even as he tried to recall *ever* relaxing since Ellen had died. "June 6, 1982," he said, quietly. "The day before the bomb. We went on a picnic, just sat and talked. Caught some trout, roasted them over a campfire, and made love under the stars."

"But the next day, another part of you died?"

He nodded, trying to keep the image of that burning car

out of his consciousness. But the more he tried not to remember, the more intense the memory became, like trying not to think of something once you'd been told not to think about it.

"The *rest* of me died," he said, quietly. "Do we have to dig this up?"

"You could keep it buried for a while longer, maybe a long while, on one level."

"So? It's working, but you still think you have to fix it."

"Every effort to mask the pain simply keeps it alive that much longer. In the end, the truth finally catches up to every addict."

"And what's the truth about Bruce Davidson, alleged addict, and the pain he's trying to escape?"

"He has to go through it in order to get beyond it, just like everybody else," she replied.

"Including you?"

She nodded. "Essentially, a new you must be born. Fight the contractions, or maybe pretend they're not happening, and you only damage yourself. But move with the pain and both the person you are and the person you're becoming will emerge healthier and happier."

"You're speaking in riddles."

"Okay, I'll illustrate, though I very seldom share the gory details of my own journey with . . ."

"Boozers like me?"

"Professional clients like you," she said, "terrified by the mere thought of trusting anyone other than themselves."

Terrified? he thought as he glared at Oberly. *I've killed people twice your size with my bare hands.* "Maybe that's because most people aren't trustworthy," he said.

"Because they sometimes let you down?"

124

"*Always* would be a better word."

"And have you always failed yourself, as well?"

This time he just nodded.

"I understand," she said. "Let me tell you why."

"Eddie," Nathan Freeman said, as the former gambler dragged a suitcase up the steps of the Cathedral Casino, where Freeman was picketing. "What are you doing back in Raptor? I thought you went home to your wife and kids."

"It's a long story, pastor," Hazard replied. "Karen was pretty happy to hear I wasn't gamblin' anymore. But when she heard how it happened, by gettin' born again, she got angry. Called me a holy roller, fanatic, and a bunch of other names I ain't going to repeat to a preacher. Said I just traded one addiction for another. I tried to defend myself. Actually, I tried to defend you—and God—and prove to her it was real."

"God don't need defenders. He can take care of himself," Freeman said, pausing a moment to reflect on how hard it was to apply this advice to himself.

"Should've known better," Hazard said. "But the more I tried to convince her, the madder she got. The real kicker was when I told her I'd been baptized. See, we both were raised Catholic, and the kids go to catechism every week. I guess she thought gettin' baptized made me a Baptist. Anyway, the bottom line is, she kicked me out. On top of that, I got fired from my job yesterday, for trying to evangelize my co-workers. They called it religious harassment. Since I had nothing else to do, I hopped the next bus here, to help you."

Thanks, but no thanks, the preacher thought. *All we*

need is Eddie Hazard messin' things up. But before Freeman could figure out a way to decline the offer, his new disciple was talking about where he should stay. "Can't stay at the Short Stop, like I've been doing, though it would be a good way to witness to the other guys. For one thing, I don't have any money. For another, they'd sure as shootin' try to drag me back into the old habits, and I'm afraid I might not be able to resist."

"Just bein' here at all will tempt ya," Freeman said, wishing Eddie would get back on the bus to Denver, while at the same time chastising himself for not giving his most recent convert the benefit of the doubt.

"You got an empty room?" Hazard asked, looking the clergyman directly in the eyes. "I could help with chores. I'm even a pretty good cook," he added.

"I have an empty *house,*" Freeman replied. "But . . ." He hesitated, pondering the increasingly shabby state of the parsonage since Annie had left and he had become totally focused on his crusade. "But it's been getting pretty run-down. I could use some help, now that I think about it. Toss your bag in the back of my pickup, and we'll go on home and rustle up some lunch."

"My parents were killed in a plane crash when I was ten," Doris Oberly told Bruce Davidson. "On their way home from their second honeymoon. I figured they'd gone to get away from me, so naturally I figured it was my fault that they died.

"For about a year I got passed from one relative to another until, finally, Aunt Mabel and Uncle Charlie Stemmler agreed to take me permanently. They were churchgoing, respectable citizens, who treated me well

126

enough, except they forced me to attend a church that was obsessed with self-reproach as the only route to personal holiness.

"Jason, my fourteen-year-old cousin, played the piety game pretty well, until we got behind closed doors. From the time I arrived, until the time I finally told somebody three years later, he was always after me. He'd walk around the house with nothing on, leave ripped-out pages from *Playboy* magazine under my pillow, and sometimes try to spy on me when I was in the bathroom. But when he tried to climb into bed with me one night, I figured it was time to blow the whistle, or my days as a virgin were numbered. So I asked my doctor, Dr. Winslow, for advice. I figured she'd understand.

"To make a long story short, I found out that blood flows thicker than water, and dear Unc and Auntie threw me out. The whole family got into such an uproar about it that in the end nobody wanted anything to do with the trouble-maker. At fourteen, I had no place to go.

"I might still be on the street if it hadn't been for Dr. Winslow. She invited me to live with her, maybe because she knew I wanted to be a doctor, too. Living with her, and making house calls, sometimes helping with home deliveries, cemented that goal and I became obsessed with getting into medical school. My first, but not my last, addiction."

"At least it was a healthy one."

"No addiction is healthy, long-term. I had to be first in my class. Nothing else would do. It took years to realize I was trying to fill a hole in my psyche created by my parents' death, and deepened by living with the Stemmlers.

Becoming a doctor seemed like a good way to give 'such a worm as I' some significance and self-respect."

"It didn't work?" he asked, leaning toward the doctor, intrigued by her story but also relieved; as long as he could keep her talking, he wouldn't have to talk about himself.

"No, it did work—too well, in fact. I began to respect only myself. I became self-reliant, self-sufficient, self-sustaining . . . and self-abusing—anorexic, promiscuous, and a recreational user of freebase cocaine.

"That's how I met Dave, a plastic surgeon who loved cocaine and very strong, very thin women. We had two kids right away because it seemed the thing to do. For a while we continued to be party animals, but as the girls got older, I began drinking more and doing cocaine less. Somehow drinking at home just seemed more respectable than doing cocaine there, and I certainly didn't want to set a bad example for the kids.

"The problem was, to dull the pain, I had to drink myself unconscious every night. The more I did that, the less I liked myself, so the void I was trying to fill just kept getting deeper and the pain more intense. I began to seriously consider suicide as the only way out, but the thought of leaving the girls alone kept me from doing it. When I began to fantasize about ways to kill them and me at the same time, I finally realized I was in trouble. Thankfully, I was still coherent enough to call my old friend, Dr. Winslow, who drove me up here, eight years ago this July. I've been here ever since, no thanks to David, who abandoned me and the girls rather than stay married to a 'drunk.'

"There," she said. "Now you know my life story, and maybe why our staff decided I might be able to connect with Bruce Davidson, Ph.D."

"I don't know what to say," he replied. "We certainly have more in common than I ever dreamed. Maybe I've been too hard on you."

"That's not the issue. The issue is whether or not you're willing to risk trusting me."

"With what, specifically?"

"With your broken dreams, your failures, and your fears . . . all the hurt, all the pain you've been pushing down all these years. To stretch my analogy, you're pregnant with pain and you need a midwife to help you release it so the real you can live, care, even love again."

"You make it sound like I'm a basket case or something. But to use your own metaphor, if I wait long enough, it'll all take care of itself. Maybe I don't need you as much as you think."

Doris Oberly reached into the solid walnut desk behind which she had been sitting during the entire session, producing a videocassette and the weapon Davidson had fashioned the night before.

"I didn't want to do this," she said. "But you leave me no choice. In my left hand is a videocassette made early on the morning of September 18, 1993, at the home of FBI Bureau Chief Bruce Davidson, by his good friend, Agent Fred Billings. It begins with Fred waking his boss from an alcoholic stupor, and concludes after Dr. Davidson has emptied his handgun and is threatening to end his life. Shall I cue the tape?"

"Don't need to," Bruce murmured, reeling from the realization that he was trapped. Still, he longed for a way out.

"Then there's this little device," she said, firmly, "fashioned by the same Bruce Davidson just last night in the privacy of his room here at the Hope Center. An interesting creation, depending on how you look at it. From this angle, it resembles a miniature dagger, don't you think?"

When he just stared blankly at the floor, the addictionist continued. "On the other hand, if you turn it around, it's nearly a copy of a first-century crucifix."

"What?" He lifted his gaze and took the object from her outstretched hand. The wire form was plated in silver and adorned with jewels.

"Silversmithing is one of my hobbies," Dr. Oberly explained. "And collecting gems is another. Those are beryl, amethyst, and topaz. A handsome combination, if I say so myself.

"Strange, isn't it, how a symbol of death can be transformed into a symbol of new life? Correct me if I'm wrong, but I believe you made this in order to kill yourself with it."

"Maybe I should have," he muttered, still turning the silver-plated cross over in his hands. "What difference would it make?"

"Because your life is worthless?"

"Practically."

"Because you let Ellen die?"

"Not only that," he said. "I let my father die, because I couldn't . . . I couldn't . . ." As he said this, his voice broke and he began to sob, not in quiet whimpers, but in a great heaving, agony of grief.

She waited, not moving or saying a word, until the sobs turned to groans and then died away to nothing.

"Because you couldn't . . ."

"Hold him up any more. He'd fallen down the riverbank, hitting his head on the way so that by the time I jumped in to try to help, he was already under water. I tried to pull him out, to hold him up. But he was too heavy, and I was only nine. It was only a matter of time before it was either him or me, or both of us. Maybe it would have been better to die with him."

"Which is exactly what you've been trying to accomplish all these years. You've been recreating the dynamics in an unconscious attempt to somehow change the past. But you never grieved it out, until now, which is the first step in actually achieving what you long to do."

"Change the past? Impossible."

"I've found a way, but we'll work on it another time. But I want you to keep that cross as a symbol that apparent failures can be transformed into success."

"You trust me with this? What's to stop me from using it to achieve my original intention?"

"You'll stop *yourself* . . . tonight, just like last night. Just like last Saturday night. When you were with the CIA in Vietnam, you must have killed people in more ways than most people can imagine."

"True."

"But when it came to killing yourself, you bumbled it so badly, others had time to intervene, which is exactly what you wanted, deep inside. Somebody to help you. Somebody to forgive you. Somebody to give you permission to live again, which is what all of us want to do, if you'll let us."

"What choice do I have?" he said, looking her straight in the eye for the first time that night. "I've made a total mess of it by myself."

"You've reached the first step in your liberation, a paradox of sorts. Only by admitting your inability can you be enabled. Now if you will plug into the real power source, you'll reach step two."

"You can't force me to believe."

"I don't have to. You already believe, but you don't trust God. That's the main problem."

"Based on the evidence, I'd say it's pretty logical."

"True enough. But faith is not primarily logical. It's relational. And any relationship can be restored, even when it's been severely damaged."

15

Clare Conroy had spent the entire morning searching her room, inch by inch. If there was a hidden passage from the VIP balcony box to her dressing room, there might be such passages in the hotel, too. After all, both had been designed and built to the specifications of Cecil Kingsford, whose reputation as a Casanova was legendary, as was his wife's outrage at the rumors she could never prove.

This would be the perfect room for a tryst, if old Cecil could get here without being seen, Conroy mused. *There must be a door somewhere.*

But after four hours of fruitless searching, it was time for the agent to become Juanita Rodriguez again in preparation for the afternoon show. The Westminster chimes in the church tower next door were striking noon, and the actress was carefully fitting her second dark contact in place when gunfire suddenly erupted on the street below.

"What!" she exclaimed, the lens falling off the tip of her right pinkie as she flinched; she rushed over and threw open the balcony windows to see what was going on.

Across the street, Nathan Freeman, dressed in black and wearing a black hat, was crouched on the veranda of Settler's Bank, a moneybag slung over his left shoulder, and a six-gun in his right hand. Fanning the gun's hammer, the bandit fired three quick shots toward targets on Conroy's side of the street before scaling the post by the bank's front door, as the good guys took their turn shooting at him.

Blanks, she said to herself. *Have to be. Lots of noise and smoke, but no glass breaking or splinters flying. Very realistic, though!*

Freeman returned their fire as he clambered along the porch roof and then up a downspout to the bank's roof. With the lawmen in hot pursuit, the thief vaulted the narrow alley between the bank and the flat roof of the Red Lion Casino, one building north of Clare's position, and at her eye level. For a fleeting moment, Freeman looked directly at her and winked, before diving for cover behind the lion-shaped red-and-gold plywood sign over the casino's front door.

The crowd gathered in the street behind the barricades to the south of the robbery reenactment and cheered, even as Chief Price and the security men doubling as his deputies dashed into the street to pursue the robber.

For the next ten minutes they battled, Freeman moving north, rooftop to rooftop, dodging and feinting his way along the facades of one casino after another as he tried to reach the edge of town where his horse was tied to the hitching post at North Star Tavern, the last building on the block. The lawmen followed him door-to-door on the street below, ducking when Freeman fired, in an obviously well-rehearsed routine.

"Nice show, Nate," Conroy muttered as she watched. "You should be making movies."

The drama reached its climax as Freeman, apparently trapped, grabbed a rope dangling down the west face of North Star Tavern. He holstered his gun and swung down to the side of his horse away from his pursuers. Throwing the money sack behind the saddle, he grabbed the reins, mounted, and began riding away at full speed, using the horse as a shield from the others, who dashed after him on foot.

Clare's mouth was dry, and her heart pounding as she watched the escape. "Perfect ending," Clare said, reaching to close the windows as the crowd applauded and the lawmen fired one final, desperate volley.

At that instant, the horse suddenly stumbled badly and went to her knees. Freeman, who had just raised his hat in his hand in a farewell gesture to the crowd, was launched full tilt over Mocha's neck. He tumbled to a stop twelve feet from the animal.

It's part of the act, Conroy tried desperately to believe. *Great acting, but now you can get up.* She wanted to shout, *Get up, Nate, get up!*

She dashed quickly to the nightstand, grabbed her binoculars, and then focused them on the preacher's body, lying motionless a hundred yards distant, his chin wedged awkwardly against his chest.

"God," she prayed. "Is he dead? Don't let him die! He's too . . . too good," she muttered as the whisper became a whimper and tears fogged her lenses.

There was only silence now on the street below as the people pressed hard against the barriers, curious to see what would happen next. Chief Price, who seemed the only

135

person on the street not totally shocked, ordered the security guards to keep the crowd back. He barked commands into his radio as he ran toward Nate Freeman.

Within seconds a siren sounded, and within a minute a rescue vehicle screamed to a stop next to the preacher. Conroy stared, unblinking, through the binoculars, trying to determine Freeman's condition from the way the medics worked, wishing with every passing moment that she could help him somehow.

The first clue he was alive was the crew's deliberateness. Very slowly they braced his neck, then strapped him to a backboard. By the time this was finished, the crew chief was talking to the preacher, whose eyes had finally opened. He was struggling against the restraints as he regained consciousness. The attendant, it seemed, was trying to make him lie still.

Then, as if responding to a question, the attendant pointed toward Freeman's horse, standing on three legs just a few feet away. Her left foreleg dangled from the knee by a piece of skin, its bone protruding slightly.

Freeman, his face skyward, could not see the animal. But when he whistled, the horse slowly limped to his side, and nuzzled his face with her whiskers. Then, as the attendants lifted the right side of the backboard so the horseman could see his horse's injury, agony twisted his face, and he screamed.

Freeman's voice echoed down Main Street for a split second, then drifted off into oblivion with him, as he passed out again.

"They shoot horses, don't they?" Bruce Davidson said to the group. "I guess that's what I've been doing to myself for years, but with little shots, mostly whiskey, but some-times rum, vodka, brandy, or anything that would put me out of my misery."

He paused, glancing around the circle, searching every face for hints of boredom, disapproval, or even surprise with his story, which he had just shared with a group for the first time in his life. But all he could detect was accep-tance, affirmation, validation, and compassion—attitudes he had longed for, but could not recall receiving, since his father's death. Instead of mocking him, in fact, the other addicts began to applaud.

This totally unexpected response caught Davidson so off guard that he wanted to laugh and cry all at the same time, which he did. Yet, even when he expressed himself in this totally uncharacteristic way, the men on his right and left simply turned and hugged him.

"It's okay, Bruce," Harold said, his hand still resting on Davidson's shoulder. "When I stopped fighting it, I found out that my capacity for pain was an indicator of my poten-tial for joy. It seems strange in the beginning, but it's part of becoming real."

"I've cried more tears in the last twenty-four hours than in the last thirty-two years," Bruce replied. "It's like we were drilling for water and struck a geyser, only its source is a giant pressurized cesspool, and all I'm doing is stink-ing up the place for everybody else."

"Don't worry about us," the psychiatrist/addict replied. "We're familiar with the stench. But let it flow long enough, and gradually it'll become fresh and clean instead of stag-nant. And then not only you, but everyone around you, will be refreshed and renewed, instead of defiled by it."

"Interesting analogy, Harold," Doris Oberly commented from across the room.

"As a young man, I was a fairly good poet," the man responded. "I saw beauty and analogy and deeper meaning everywhere I looked. But my mother insisted that I pursue gainful employment instead. If another great depression should happen, poets and philosophers might starve, but there would always be work for doctors.

"So, I created my own personal depression, instead, maybe just to prove her wrong. When I came in here, I just wanted to blame her, and everybody else, for creating the void I tried to fill with Demerol. But now that I've forgiven her, them, and even myself for simply being human, the poetic side has kicked in again. The real me is coming out, I guess.

"I was just encouraging Bruce to let it keep coming, now that it's started, even if it gets worse before it gets better."

"That's beautiful," Dr. Oberly replied, tears welling in her eyes. "I don't believe I've ever heard the process put that poetically before."

"Harold," Bruce said. "How deep did you have to go?"

"Deeper than my most gut-wrenching memory, my wildest fears, my vilest bitterness, my worst nightmares. But in the process I discovered, as Doris is fond of saying, that 'no pit is so deep that God's grace is not deeper still.'"

"That's not original with me," Dr. Oberly replied. "Betsy ten Boom said it, as she was dying in a Nazi prison camp, to her sister, to protect her from becoming a double prisoner—a prisoner, not only to her human captors, but to hate, as well. I've always loved that phrase, because it captures an idea so important, so key to my own recovery. No matter how deep our own stuff is, underneath it all there's a safety net; call it grace, call it your higher power, call it whatever you like—the result is the same. We never have to worry about falling through, because God won't let us."

16

Juanita," Count Dracula said to Clare Conroy as they waited for the curtain to rise. "I never noticed this before. I've never *seen* anything like it. Your eyes are different colors, one blue and the other black."

Great job, babe, Conroy thought. *Too distracted by Nate's accident. I have to find that other contact. But how do I weasel out of this?*

"I wearing contacts," she stammered, pointing to her right eye as she grabbed her compact from her purse and turned away from him.

"I sorry. I forget the other one. But I'm just wanting to be more beautiful for you, dear!" she said, throwing her arms playfully around his neck and giving him a little kiss.

"You're beautiful enough to drive me nuts by December," Miguel Ortiz replied, flaring his cape as he displayed his fangs. "I vant to bite your neck more and more, every time we're together. Actually, I vant to bite more than that, you know what I mean?"

"I maybe bite you first, you not be careful!" she said, laughing. *No wonder the Hollywood types end up with new lovers every time they play a different role,* she thought. *A kiss is still a kiss, for business or pleasure. But considering my total lack of romance so far in life, it's kind of fun to have somebody slobber over me twice a day. I just have to get one of those silver crosses in case this vampire decides to fly through my balcony window uninvited.*

"You really nailed the preacher this afternoon," Stanley Hawkins said to Leonard Price. "Anybody suspect foul play?"

"Not that I know of. Rescue people had their hands full with Freeman. And the vet never said a thing—just took the extra five hundred and put the horse down. I stood there while he buried her, so there ain't goin' to be any problems from him."

"And Freeman?"

"Concussion. Thought for a minute I solved the problem permanently. But from the look on his face when he saw that horse's leg, I'll be surprised if we ever see him again."

"I hope you're right," Hawkins replied, "because after surviving this tragedy, he may become more of a folk hero than he already is."

He walked, deep in thought, to the window. Suddenly he stiffened and then turned back toward Price. "Come here," he hissed. "You predicted we'd seen the last of that one, too."

Price walked over next to Hawkins, who was pointing to Eddie Hazard, pacing back and forth on the steps of Community Church, shouting through a megaphone.

"Get down there," Hawkins ordered. "And get that scum out of my face."

"No problem, boss," Price replied. "Time for Plan B."

"Okay," Hawkins said. "But it better work."

"It'll work," Price said, picking up the phone and dialing. "Hello, Charlotte," he said. "Remember that special project we discussed for one of the girls? Well, Eddie the loser's back in town, makin' trouble on the old church steps. Send anybody you like, just make sure he gets an offer he can't refuse."

Clare Conroy stared at the full-length mirror mounted flush against the wall next to her wardrobe, reviewing the day's events and wondering how much time she and Freeman were going to lose as a result of his injury.

But as she dabbed away the vestiges of makeup from the evening's show, she noticed a strange imperfection in her own reflection, as if the mirror's back side had been altered somehow. "Well, Alice," she muttered. "Maybe it's time we go through the looking glass and discover more of Cecil's secrets."

Quickly washing off the rest of her makeup, and removing the rest of her disguise, Conroy decided Juanita Rodriguez would be best left out of this adventure. If someone should see her, Clare Conroy could disappear into the night and still stay in town as her alter ego.

It took her ten minutes to figure out how to trigger the mechanism. When Clare simultaneously pushed on two small gilded maidens engraved into the lower corners of the mirror, the door swung open noisily. It creaked on its hinges as if it hadn't been used in years, revealing a small staircase, similar to the one she had already found in the theater, with oil lamps mounted every ten feet or so. Built into the staircase, just inside the mirrored entry, was a plush upholstered seat.

Conroy stroked the rich fabric with her left hand as she reached for her lighter with her right and swung the door shut behind herself. For a moment, while she was in total darkness, she glanced back toward her room, suddenly understanding more about Cecil Kingsford than any of his biographers had ever revealed.

Cece, she mused as she looked through the two-way mirror. *You old dog. Maybe you weren't such a Don Juan as you wanted everyone to think! Had your own private peep show, even if the lady wasn't cooperative. Wonder how you decided who should stay in this room?*

Before the satisfaction set in, however, Conroy was struck with another, far more sobering question. *Who decided I should stay up here?* she wondered. *And what if they know about this staircase, too? Or did Cecil take his secrets to the grave with him?*

"I certainly hope so," she said out loud, as she slipped on her gloves and lit the first lamp. She took two steps down the stairs and stopped cold. In the lamp's light, the tread marks from the lightweight, sponge-soled, black canvas Israeli commando boots she was wearing were clearly visible in the dust.

Solves one problem, she thought. *Creates another. If anybody uses these stairs, it'll show. But the same thing applies to me. What now?* she pondered. She didn't dare take another step, but steadying herself with the help of the polished brass handrails on both sides of the narrow staircase, she studied her options until she had a plan.

She lifted herself off the stairs, as she had so often on the parallel bars in gymnastics at Miss Porter's school as

143

an adolescent. Then, without touching the floor again, she swung her feet out, planted them, one on each railing, and brought herself to a crouch position all in one motion.

Only a 9.2, she chuckled. *But I think it'll work, with a little practice. Good thing these boots are as good as advertised. I'm not slipping in the least.*

She stuck a penlight between her teeth and snuffed out the lamp. For the next half hour, she inched her way down the staircase, balancing herself with each new step by running her gloved fingers along the upper seam of the ceiling on each side, where the evidence of human passage would be less noticeable.

However, the spiders, which had claimed this hallway as their own, were not at all pleased at the intrusion. By the time she had descended perhaps thirty feet below her starting point, the intruder was fighting to survive the reactivation of her childhood arachnophobia. Spiders crawled in her hair, up her pant legs, on her face, and occasionally into her mouth, no matter how hard she bit down on the penlight. The only thing keeping them from crawling down her neck was the lightweight Dacron turtleneck she wore.

Whenever she tried to brush the insects off, however, she nearly lost her balance and fell off her perch. When she reached the lowest point of the stairs, she simply couldn't take it any more. She wanted to scream. She wanted to run. But all she could do was hop down onto the landing, and smash every spider she could find.

Having accomplished this, she found herself standing on a small platform, perhaps three feet square. The staircase she was following ascended into the darkness directly in front of her, a darkness inhabited by thousands more spiders. Now her feet felt like lead. How was she going to climb those stairs? For that matter, how was she going to make it back to her room?

Get a grip on it, babe. This could be important. Got to make the most of it. Got to find another way, she screamed internally as another spider, perhaps an inch across, climbed out of her hair, *or I'll go stark raving mad!*

She grabbed the insect and threw it against the wall, as hard as she could. But then, as she stared at the legs sticking out from the blob on the wall, she got an idea.

This time, instead of standing on the brass railings, which were about two feet apart, she knelt on them, pulling her body ahead with her hands while the sponge soles kept her from sliding backward. It was harder going, much harder, but at least this way she was far below most of the webs. In just a few minutes she had reached another landing, this one perhaps a floor lower than her room.

Kneeling on the railing, she listened closely for any telltale sounds, though not really expecting to hear much at this hour. In the distance, but seemingly overhead, the church tower chimes rang two o'clock. *I'm in the church,* she realized.

She pulled off her gloves and dropped them to the floor, then swung herself down on tiptoe, careful not to step off the leather doormat. Then she slowly turned the handle and pushed against the door, which squeaked loudly, even though she tried to open it a millimeter at a time. She leaned over and placed her eye as close to the one-inch crack as possible.

About three feet ahead, in the semi-darkness, she could barely make out some sort of grating, covered with a fine wire mesh. *A window? Who would put a window screen inside a church? Then again, who would connect a labyrinth of secret passages with a church?*

Then suddenly, remembering her own upbringing, she realized that she was looking out from the inside of a confessional booth. *Of course. One of the historians mentioned how, long before the days of ecumenism, the church had served both Catholics and Protestants after Kingsford converted to Catholicism. Perfect cover,* she said to herself. *Everybody thinks you've turned religious. But every time you go to confession, you end up with more to confess!*

Now she was confident that even if the place wasn't totally deserted, nobody would know she was there because every confessional was constructed to keep a barrier between penitent and priest. Cautiously, she pushed the door open wide enough to slip through, and found herself standing in a two-foot-square cubicle, with a view of a nearly-completed poker hall.

To her left, she could just make out a wide circular staircase leading to the street level, and a sign welcoming gamblers to the "Upper Room."

They're leaving this in for ambience, she realized. *Of course. Every cathedral needs a confessional. But with me in here, they might end up confessing to somebody who just can't keep a secret!*

17

Forgive me, Father, for I have sinned," Eddie Hazard said as he knelt beside the hospital bed of Nathan Freeman.

"Get up, Eddie," the pastor said as he pushed the lever to elevate the head of his bed. "I ain't yer father, and only God has the power to forgive you."

"Sorry, pastor," the fallen disciple replied. "It's the way I was taught."

"Well, you got to unlearn it. You don't need no priest. In God's eyes, we're all priests."

"Not me," Eddie replied, shaking his head. "I can't believe God is even listening after what I done."

"You don't have to tell me," Freeman replied. "But you can if it'll make you feel any better."

"Not better, but at least lighter," Eddie said. "It's been weighin' me down and eatin' at my gut ever since, ever since I let you down."

"What happened?"

"Thursday night, the night you got hurt and nobody would tell me what was going to happen to you, I decided, all on my own, that whatever happened, somebody had to carry on. So I made a megaphone and went on down to the church steps and started to preach. I couldn't think of anything else to do, so that's what I did."

"So, what's so bad about that?" Freeman asked. "Did you get arrested, like me?"

"I only wish," Hazard replied. "'Cause then at least I'd still be able to face myself. Everything was going fine until this woman I used to know, Heidi she calls herself, came and sat down on the steps right next to me as if she was interested in what I was saying.

"Then, when some of my old friends walked by and saw her there with me, they stopped, too. For awhile, I even thought I was going to convert them all. But after maybe a half hour I realized that nobody was really paying attention. They were just waiting to see what was going to happen. Finally, I got so frustrated, I just put down the megaphone and stood there, mad at them, mad at myself, and even mad at God for not making them listen."

"God don't make nobody listen," Freeman replied. "He calls, but they don't have to come. Ain't his fault, or yours neither, if they decide not to." He paused and adjusted the bandage wrapped around his head. "That what's got you down—you preached and nobody listened? I been doin' that for months."

"I wish that was it, too," Hazard said, tears in his eyes. "But what's got me down is what happened after I shut up. You see—and I don't want to embarrass you, but I don't know how else to say it—the reason I knew Heidi was because she's a call girl. When I would come to Raptor, I'd call her just about every time.

"Anyway, when I'm finished, Heidi walks over, and

148

before I know what's happening, she's kissing me, right out there in public. 'Come on over, baby,' she whispers in my ear. 'And we'll have a good time tonight. No charge, just for old times' sake.'

"Well, after she left, I couldn't keep my mind on what I was trying to do. It seemed like the harder I tried to forget that she was waiting over at Alice's, the more I wanted to go there. As you probably figured out by now, I finally gave in. But when I woke up the next morning and realized what I'd done, I hated myself. It's taken me all this time to find the courage to face you. I'm sorry, pastor. I hope you don't hate me, too, but I already packed up my stuff to move out."

"Not necessary," Freeman said gently, reaching for the Bible next to his bed. "Ever hear of David, the king of Israel, who wrote a lot of the psalms? Well, he was not only a great king and a great poet, he was a great sinner. He sinned with a woman named Bathsheba, but here's what he wrote later. 'Create in me a clean heart, O God; and renew a right spirit within me. Cast me not away from thy presence; and take not thy holy spirit from me. Restore unto me the joy of thy salvation; and uphold me with thy free spirit. Then will I teach transgressors thy ways; and sinners shall be converted unto thee.'

"God gave me that the night I met you. And now I'm givin' it to you."

Eddie sat silently for a couple minutes before responding. "I don't have to *do* something to make up for it?"

"Ain't nothin' you could do, except maybe die for your own sins. But he already did that. So just confess it, turn away, and then be willing to do what he asks. We ain't lost the war, just one little skirmish. God uses broken vessels.

I got a broken heart, not to mention a broken head, and you got a broken spirit. I'd say we make a pretty good team."

Just as he said that, the phone rang.

"Nate?" Annie's voice said. "Are you okay? From the pictures in the paper, it looks like you should be dead."

"What pictures? What paper?"

"The *Pueblo Star-Ledger*. One of their reporters was there during the shoot-out, and got the whole sequence on video. They printed four segments—they're kind of fuzzy—in today's edition. It's right here in front of me. I nearly died of shock, myself, but the article said you were in Mountain View Hospital, so that's why I called. What happened?"

"Tell ya the truth," he replied, "it all happened so fast, I can't remember. Or maybe it's the concussion. The only thing I can't forget is Mocha's leg. Must've pushed her too hard."

"There's another possibility," Annie said. "I can send you the article, and I'll try to get a copy of the video. But Nate, won't you come down here, instead? They're out to get you, I'm sure of it now. And they won't stop until you leave or you're dead. Please . . . please . . ." Her voice melted into tears.

"Annie. Annie. Stop, please. I got a bump on the head, that's all. But what do you mean, another possibility? I got to know. I got to know what happened."

"Can you come down here? Now?"

"Doc says I can't drive for awhile. But . . . hold on a second," he said into the phone as he turned to Eddie. "How'd you get here?"

"Your pickup."

150

"Can you drive me to Pueblo?"

"I'll drive you to Boston, if you'll let me."

"Annie, I'll—we'll—be there for dinner. Me and Eddie, a former gambler God got ahold of. He's been stayin' with me, helpin' out. You'll like him."

"I'll like him if he'll drive you here . . . and then drive himself back to Raptor after dinner."

At the Hope Center, Bruce Davidson was walking around the grounds, talking with his new friend, Dr. Harold Williams.

"Since coming here," Davidson said, "I've had more dreams, at least dreams I remember, than I've had in years."

"It happens," Harold said. "Probably the subconscious coming back nearer the top."

"Well, last night's was pretty strange, but stranger than the dream was the fact that I woke up laughing," Bruce continued. "I've *never* had that happen before."

"Sounds pretty healthy to me. Care to tell me about it?"

"Okay," Bruce replied, "but it's just between you, me, and this grove of aspens. I was pulling a boat and trailer on an interstate, by hand—how, I never questioned, though I knew it was a dream. I was in it and watching it at the same time. It was a nice boat, a totally-equipped seventeen-footer, with two cushioned seats, a fish finder and two motors, a forty-horse Evinrude and an electric trolling motor with a foot-pedal control. I was headed for the lake, and starting to tire, when a van full of happy travelers pulled up alongside and asked if I'd like to hitch my load to the van and ride along.

"Relieved, I climbed aboard, suddenly realizing that I

knew everybody there. They were the members of our group, and Doris Oberly was driving. 'We'll get there, Bruce,' she said with a benevolent smile. 'We all want to go fishing.' Strange, huh?"

"Truth is stranger than fiction," Harold replied. "Any idea what it means?"

"Ah, there's the rub," Davidson chuckled. "Maybe I'll have to dream it again, just to find out."

"Perhaps your subconscious already knows, and you just need to listen. Freud might say you're expressing the need for sexual happiness, missing since your wife died and left you alone, far from the lake, without a way to get there. Just recently, you've met a woman you'd like to take fishing, and you've projected that same desire onto her."

"I always thought old Sigmund was obsessed with sex. Isn't it possible that I simply like to fish, and I'd like to do it with my new friends?"

"I didn't mean it as criticism. But your subconscious can't lie. It just finds creative ways to tell you the truth. It's only natural to be interested in a woman as . . . attractive as Doris. Some of us need a mother. Some of us need a lover. But all she wants is to be a friend, and facilitator of your recovery."

"Are you speaking from experience?"

"I needed a mother," the psychiatrist replied. "Somebody I could talk with about the things my own mother called unimportant. Somebody to give me permission to quit medicine, which was the only way I could really choose it freely. Somebody to let me unload all my resentment and bitterness about what I thought I'd been robbed of, so I could give myself permission to stop punishing the robber and use that energy, instead, to embrace living."

"Doris helped you with all that?"

Harold nodded, tears forming in his eyes. "The first week, I fought her. The second, I hated her. The third, I became dependent. And now, I guess I love her. I mean that in a healthy sense, not the way some people might take it."

"Care to make any predictions for me?"

"Well," Harold hesitated. "As long as you won't take offense. You're still in the fighting stage, and likely headed for infatuation, if you're not careful. But I hope that by the time you leave, you'll love her like a sister."

What would Clare Conroy think of that? Davidson wondered.

18

nnie!" Nate exclaimed as his wife ran toward the pickup.

He wanted to jump from the cab, pick her up in his arms, and whirl her around, but he was so sore from the effects of his tumble that he barely got the door open before she was standing there to help him step down.

"Nate," she said, hugging him and then stepping back to survey his injuries. "It's worse than you said. Your face is all bruised. Your forearms are scraped up real bad. And I'll bet you're black and blue everywhere else, too. Are you sure there's nothing broken?"

"Checked me head to toe," he said, limping toward the house. "Didn't find nothin' in the wrong place."

"Guardian angel," she said under her breath as she opened the door. "No doubt about it. I just watched the video. The reporter, Kevin White, brought it over, on the condition that he could stay and watch it with you. He's still here, waiting in the den."

"No interviews," he said. "I ain't up to it. But I do want to see that tape."

"You know," Doris Oberly said to Bruce Davidson. "Whenever you talk about Ellen, you mainly talk about the way she died. It's as if that moment is frozen in time."

"It is, like a permanent etching in my brain."

"But there was more to her than that . . . and to the two of you together, wasn't there?"

"Of course, but the end overwhelms everything else."

"When you think of her, what is your primary emotion?"

"Rage."

"Toward whom?"

"The bomb. The person who made it. Myself, for letting her take my car. God, for letting it happen. Take your pick."

"You forgot Ellen."

"Don't bait me," he responded.

"No, I mean it. If she hadn't gone out, she'd still be alive. At least, that's what you think. But she did go out, so she's at least as blameworthy as you are."

"I don't want to talk about this."

"Precisely why you need to. For years, you've suppressed your resentment that she died and left you here. Until you face that and forgive her, the true goodness of what you had together will always be hidden behind clouds of depression."

"What gives you the right to . . ."

"Intrude? Probe? Irritate? Nothing beyond my commitment to do whatever I can to help you get beyond it."

"What?"

"Your use of Ellen's death as an excuse for your drinking, your sadness, and everything that feeds that, including anger, guilt, hatred, and bitterness. And," she paused and looked him straight in the eye, "until you let it go and feed your soul with love instead of self-pity you will never really be free."

"So now I'm a slave."

"He who hates serves the one he hates."

"A pious platitude."

"Let's find out. Tell me who you hate, I mean who you absolutely, unequivocally *hate*."

"George Perelli, bomb expert and hit man for organized crime. He built the bomb that killed . . ." He stopped and stared at Oberly.

She nodded, because he was making her point. "Suppose this George Perelli were dead," she said.

"He's not. But if he were dead, I'd probably hate *myself* for not getting him first. Earlier this year I had the chance." He stopped himself. "But that really is confidential, so I can't say any more about it."

"Then let me conjecture, and you correct me if I'm wrong. You had the chance, but he escaped. But not long after that, by an interesting coincidence, you began to drink more heavily."

He nodded. "For years I wanted him, but when he practically fell into my hands, I couldn't put him away. Then I couldn't face myself. I had failed her all over again."

"Who?"

"Ellen."

"Is that what she would want?"

"For me to kill Perelli?"

"To kill *yourself*—your body with booze, your soul with

156

hatred, your mind with revenge. Do you really think that's what she would want?"

"I doubt it."

"You're not sure? What if Ellen could communicate with you, right now, right here, from wherever she is at this moment?"

"She's in heaven, if anybody is."

"Well, if that's where she is, let her tell you about that, first. Just close your eyes, breathe deeply, and try to relax. Now, count with me backwards from five, slowly. Five, four, three, two, one. Now, listen closely. You can hear her voice again, for the first time in years. She wants to talk to you. She wants to tell you about heaven. She wants you to know how she's doing. What is she saying?"

"'It's beautiful here, Ninj. Peaceful and happy. No more crying, pain, or sadness, only joy . . . just like I always dreamed.'"

Suddenly, Bruce Davidson jumped from the chair. "What's going on?" he yelled. "You're messing with my head. I almost thought I really heard her."

"Maybe you did, Bruce. Maybe you did, the part of her in you that never died. Sit down and listen and remember, no matter how deep it goes you can't fall through."

Nate Freeman grabbed the videotape player's remote control and punched the rewind button. "I seen it this time," he said through clenched teeth. "It was broke before she hit the ground. Watch." He hit slow motion, freezing the frame every split second until there on the screen, somewhat fuzzy but still clear enough to discern, was Mocha, just before her fall, her hoof still inches from the ground, skin and bone already dangling from her knee when only a split second earlier it had been totally intact.

"Shot," the cowboy shouted. "They shot my horse. They killed my horse!" Now he jumped up and began pacing around the room, as the reporter peeked inside his jacket pocket to see if his microcassette recorder was running.

"They stole my church, skinned my dog alive, and now they've killed my horse. Maybe they were tryin' to kill me! I'm going to make them pay, every last one of 'em."

"Nate, sit down. Let's think this through before you do something rash," Annie said, glancing nervously toward Kevin White. "Maybe we should pray about it," she suggested.

"Pray?" he yelled. "*That* would be rash. There is a time to pray and a time to kill. I've prayed long enough."

"Now you're talking nonsense, dear," she said, walking over to her husband and tenderly touching the bandage around his head. "It's his injury, Mr. White. Please, would you leave us now?"

"Certainly, Mrs. Freeman. I totally understand," the young man said. "And you can keep the tape, Reverend Freeman. It's a copy," he said over his shoulder, as Eddie Hazard escorted him to the door.

By the time White was gone, the minister had the tape cued and running again . . . just the last ten seconds before Mocha's injury. He sat on the floor, three feet from the TV screen, and watched it ten, twenty, thirty times, without moving a muscle except to control the remote in his right hand.

Then he switched it off, stood up, and faced the others, who had been standing behind him, watching helplessly as Nate withdrew from them as far into the electronic reality before him as he possibly could.

"I keep thinkin'," he said, "if I can only play it enough times, it'll change. But it don't because it can't. It'll always be the same. She's gone, and there's nothin' I can do to bring her back.

"I can't even tell who did it. They was all shootin'. So I can't get even. But," he paused, looking deeply into Annie's eyes, "I can make 'em pay. I *will* make 'em pay. If I die tryin', they can't get away with this!"

"Nate, please don't. Let it go. It's just a little God-forsaken, two-bit town. It's not worth dying for."

"Jesus would," Nate replied, resolutely. "Jesus did. And if I got to follow him that far, so be it. You can support me or not. You can wait for me, or not. But one thing I know, I got to go back and face 'em down, or I'll never be able to face myself again."

"Bruce," Doris Oberly said, as her client's inner vision of Ellen dimmed. "Let's try it one more way. Let me be Ellen for a few minutes and you just be yourself."

"Okay," he said, "as long as you don't push too hard."

"No problem," she said. "This is about you, not me."

She shifted slightly in her chair, then said, "Ninj, I left rather suddenly. We never got to say good-bye."

He stared at the doctor for a moment, then responded, "I'm sorry. If I'd only known, I never would have let you go."

"Nobody ever knows. But I'm the one who should apologize. I walked out and never came back. I'm sorry I left you so alone."

He choked up, but forced himself to continue. "I'm

159

sorry, too. I needed you. I still need you. It wasn't fair. I dared to love you, and then you were gone."

"I hope you weren't too angry. I really didn't mean to hurt you."

"Angry?" he replied. "I was sad, abandoned, disappointed. I was angry at everybody else, myself, God, Perelli—once I found out he did it. But it never occurred to me until today that I might be angry with you."

"Are you?"

He hesitated, looking down at the floor as he began to weep again. "I . . . I don't know. How can I . . ." he stammered. "Yes!" he finally blurted out.

"I understand," she said, softly. "Will you forgive me?"

Davidson looked at Doris Oberly and nodded. "Yes," he said. "I will. But the real question is can *you* forgive *me* for letting you die?"

"I already have, dear. A long, long time ago."

Stunned, Davidson looked at Oberly again. "I can't go any deeper today," he said.

"Fair enough," she replied. "We've made a lot of progress. But I just have one question. What is your primary emotion at this moment as you think about Ellen?"

He thought for quite a while, as the doctor watched him struggle to find just the right word.

"Gratitude," he said, finally. "I'm glad I knew her. Glad for the time we had."

"You see," Doris replied. "It *is* possible to change the past."

19

These are my life verses," Nathan Freeman explained, as he began his sermon. "That I may know him, and the power of his resurrection, and the fellowship of his sufferings, being made conformable to his death; If by any means I might attain unto the resurrection of the dead."

When he looked up from reading, the young minister was shocked to see that Dr. Martin Scerzy, bishop of the Rocky Mountain district of Living Faith churches, had slipped into the room and was now sitting in the back row. Freeman paused momentarily, wondering if he should recognize the senior pastor. But when Scerzy put his finger to his pursed lips, indicating he preferred anonymity for now, Freeman spoke for about ten minutes before reaching his conclusion.

"Anyone who wants to count for God," he said, "must be willin' to suffer, even die for the cause." He patted his bandage, unconsciously, as he spoke. "You probably heard, I had a little fall on Thursday. Well, I'm here to tell ya, it weren't no accident, just another attempt to run me outta town, which they been doin' ever since I started to picket.

"I been tryin' to stand for truth. And I'm askin' you to choose this day whom ye shall serve, yer fear or yer faith? It's time to stand up and be counted. If you're with me, stay after the service and we'll figure out the next step. If not . . ."

Suddenly, from the back of the room, an older, much deeper voice interrupted Freeman. "Pastor," Scerzy said, as he stood and walked down the very short aisle to the podium behind which the preacher had been standing. He stopped for a moment to shake hands with the only two elderly people left in the congregation, lifelong parish members Ellie and Sarah Smith.

"I'm reluctant to intrude in the affairs of any local church in my district, but it's clearly time to get involved here before your paranoia ruins our church's reputation."

"Paranoia?" Freeman replied.

"Please, son," the bishop said. "Don't make this any harder than it already is. Just let me read a little from the front page of this morning's *Star-Ledger*. 'They stole my church, skinned my dog alive, and now they've killed my horse. Maybe they were trying to kill me! I'm going to make them pay, every last one of them. There is a time to pray and a time to kill. I've prayed long enough!'"

"Let me see that," Freeman replied, snatching the paper from Scerzy. The front-page headline declared, "Minister Threatens Retaliation." The subhead explained further, "Clerical Crusader Claims Conspiracy."

"Reverend Freeman, did you in fact say these things?" the bishop asked.

162

Nate nodded, "In private, when I was so mad I could spit . . ."

"Or kill? Your crusade has become too personal. No one is exempt from adversity, but when bad things happen to you, it's a conspiracy."

"Ain't it possible?"

"Of course, but it's also possible you brought some of your recent difficulties on yourself."

"Such as?"

"Ending up in jail. You're the only minister in my district with a criminal record."

"Guess Peter and Paul shouldn't apply," Freeman tried to interject. But the bishop ignored him.

"Not only that," Scerzy added, "but that same weekend, you made a laughingstock of yourself with this—" he pointed toward Eddie Hazard as he fished for words, "—this well-known gambler, who has now taken up residence in the parsonage—"

"Ain't we still bringin' sinners to repentance?" Freeman interrupted.

"—where your own wife ought to be living. Beyond any question of your sexual preferences, just the fact that you couldn't manage your own marriage disqualifies you from leading this flock. My only regret is that I didn't confront you sooner."

Freeman fumed, "You callin' me gay? Annie left because she couldn't stand the idea of raisin' a family in this God-forsaken place. But if I had it to do over again, I'd still refuse to sell out."

"Your vote, your lone vote, cost this church, and our denomination, a *million* dollars!" the bishop continued, as if Nathan's input was totally irrelevant. "And why? To keep someone else from remodeling one pile of wood, mortar, and stone into a slightly different pile of wood, mortar, and stone. Apparently, you never stopped to consider what we could have done with that money. We could have built a new church, a school, and maybe even a new parsonage and still had funds left over to support the district."

"I can't believe my ears," Nate interrupted. "Whose side are you on?"

"When I was younger," the bishop said, "I thought every conflict had to be win-lose. But as I've matured, I've learned that nearly everything can be worked out. So now I try for solutions where everybody wins."

"What part has light with darkness? Truth with deception? Evil with good?"

"Since you asked the question, young man, I'll apply it to you. Whose side are *you* on? You call yourself good, but you've destroyed a century-old church. The next pastor will have to start from scratch."

"The *next* pastor?"

"I'm relieving you of your post. If you cooperate, with time you may receive another assignment. I suggest you leave immediately and become reconciled with your wife. An interim pastor will arrive Wednesday, by which time you will have vacated the parsonage. In the meantime, may the Lord restore your sanity."

Nate looked around the room, struggling for a moment to catch his breath, while at the same time looking for support. Yet, after four years of serving these people as faithfully as he knew how, the only one who would actually look him in the eye was Eddie Hazard, tears running down his face.

Freeman turned to face the bishop, and said, "Mr.

164

Scerzy, there's a war on here. You can take away the parsonage. You can take away the pulpit. But you can't take away the call. So I ain't leavin'. I'm stayin' till somebody wins and somebody loses."

"I'm sorry to hear that, son. Your ministerial credentials are hereby rescinded, along with their associated rights and privileges. From this moment on, any representation of yourself as an ordained clergyman, or pastor of Raptor Community Church, is unethical and illegal, and will result in punitive action."

"You do what you got to do. And I'll do what I got to do," Freeman said, as he picked up his guitar and headed for the door. "And the first thing I got to do is find a place to puke, you make me so sick."

"Last time we talked," Doris Oberly said, "you seemed to really break through."

"Glad *you* felt that way," Bruce Davidson replied. "I was one wrung-out dishrag when we finished."

"Not surprising, considering the energy invested. First of all, you had to overcome the resistance. Then you had to acknowledge Ellen's presence within yourself and listen to what she had to say. Then you had to deal with that, too."

"I've had my doubts," he said. "Was it fantasy, or was it real?"

"Real depends a lot on who's defining it. For instance, when I studied medicine, I thought the only reality was what could be verified empirically. That's okay when you're dealing with lab reports or CAT scans. But when intuition tells you the patient's pain is from internalized anger, it's pretty hard to prove, even if you know you're right. Some-body should invent a CAT scan for the soul."

"I'll leave that to you. For the moment, let's stick to facts."

"Fact is, it was real. But the crucial question is whether or not you'll accept its reality."

"I can't make something real if it's not."

"We used some creative approaches, but only as a means to make you aware of the family within Bruce Davidson. I'm sure, in your Ph.D. studies, you must have run across the concept of object formation."

"Obscurely."

"Too bad. It's the most concise way to explain the real you. The basic idea is that all of us have a family within us, a group of people, living and dead, to whom we relate in the present tense in one way or another. For you, this includes your father, your mother, your wife . . . and God."

"What does God have to do with it?"

"Everything, even if you want him out of your life. Ever fly a gas-powered model plane on a guy wire?"

"A few times."

"What happens to the plane if the wire breaks?"

"It flies off wildly and eventually crashes."

"Precisely what happens when people sever their relationship with God. To avoid crashing, most substitute another center—a cause, another person, or sheer will-power. But after flying for a while, they realize they're going to crash because their new center cannot hold. And many turn to booze or drugs to avoid facing the futility of life without God."

"Interesting analogy," he replied. "But there's another possibility. Perhaps God lets go of the handle, like some

166

demented cosmic joker who gets a charge out of filling his sky with little planes flying wildly about until they crash?"

"A cosmic joker certainly wouldn't deserve your trust."

"Of course not."

"But what if trusting is the only way to discover whether he is trustworthy?"

"It's a catch-22," he said. "God has me by the throat."

"Or by the guidance wire; maybe his reach is much longer than you can imagine. Either way, it's obvious that you do believe."

"I suppose so. But kicking and screaming all the way."

"Kicking and screaming is fine."

"What? I never heard that before."

"Remember the Bible story of Jacob, the one who wrestled all night with the angel of God, and wouldn't let go until he had received the blessing?"

"Vaguely."

"Let me refresh your memory, since it's the story of your life. Jacob wrestled with God, just like you've been doing for thirty-two years."

"But I never got the blessing."

"Because you're still wrestling. But I need to remind you that even though Jacob got the blessing, he emerged from the experience lame. There's a price to be paid for confronting God."

"I thought you said kicking and screaming are okay?"

"They are, because they imply that you believe in a person and you live in a relationship, even if it seems adversarial at the moment. It's still better than the atheist shouting his protests even if he's convinced no one's listening."

"Ventilation is good for the soul."

167

"Unless you believe nobody's listening and nobody cares."

"Maybe *you* think God cares. But if so, why did he let my father die in my arms? Why did he let my wife burn to death before my eyes? Why did he let me become an alcoholic? And why did he stick me in a place like this?"

"Where you have to contend with a person like me?" she added. When he nodded, she continued, "A person, I might add, who is committed to your best interests, just as *he* has always been."

"And who keeps answering questions nobody's asking, instead of actually dealing with what's really important to me."

"The why questions?"

He nodded.

"You've mentioned three. How many are there?"

"Hundreds, maybe thousands," he replied. "I never counted, and it doesn't matter anyway, since I can't even get an answer to the first one."

"Perhaps before our next meeting you should write them all down."

"So you can answer them?"

"No, not me. That's impossible. They're between you and him."

"You don't even want to referee?"

"I only want you to recover. I urge you, though—be ruthlessly honest with yourself, and him. Do you want his help, or not?"

"The Lord helps those who help themselves."

"An ancient proverb from the school of self-sufficiency, whose God is too small to remake you from the inside out."

"Give me a better one, then."

"A better proverb, or a better God?"

"Either will do."

"I can't give you a better God. But here's a better proverb: Blessed are the poor in spirit—that is, those who know their need of God—for theirs is the kingdom of heaven."

20

No wonder they call this Mule Skinner's Pass, Clare Conroy mused as she struggled to catch her breath. *Takes a mule to make it to the top.* For thirty minutes she had been climbing the summit path up Fool's Gold Gorge by moonlight, after leaving her vehicle in the parking area maintained by the state. Three hundred feet up the path, in the darkness, she had transformed herself from Juanita Rodriguez into an FBI undercover agent, dressed in a black knit cotton pullover and hiking boots. Her destination was a midnight rendezvous with Fred Billings at a remote ridge-top turnaround roughly ten miles east of Raptor, and accessible only from the north.

Billings's Blazer appeared right on schedule. As soon as he had turned off the headlights, Conroy stepped out of the brush where she had been waiting, trying to catch her breath.

"Evening, Ms. Conroy. You seem a little winded. I guess you've learned that the steeplechase is a strenuous race." He laughed at his little play on words.

170

"It's also dangerous," she replied, "based on what happened to Freeman the other day."

"I read about it, but I wanted an eyewitness report."

"News photos told it better than I could," she replied. "It happened so fast, to the naked eye it just looked like the horse broke her leg. But now that I've seen the video, I can see the padre's point." She handed Billings a videocassette, delivered to her three hours earlier by Nathan Freeman.

"It would be nearly impossible to prove, though, without exhuming the horse and checking for fragments. Even then we'd never know who fired the shot."

"Our crusader sure complicated the op, threatening the others," he said.

"Complicated his own life, too," she replied. "His bishop defrocked him today, right in front of his congregation. And he has to vacate the parsonage by Wednesday so a replacement minister can move in."

"May be a blessing in disguise," Billings said. "Charges of conspiracy should come from us, *after* the key players have been ID'ed. Tip our hand too early, and they'll skip town before we can nail them."

He reached behind the seat, pulled out a soft leather fanny pack, and began to empty it item by item.

"PVS-7 night goggles. A PRN-34 surveillance microphone with lightweight headset and microcassette recorder. Field of sound is six feet at three hundred yards, from which distance you can hear a whisper. Nightscope and camera, with infrared illumination for absolute darkness.

"With the goggles, you should be able to see what the witches are brewing pretty clearly. But . . ."

"You still wonder if it's worth it?"

"I was going to say, don't look directly at any light source, or you'll get ballooning glare. But since you brought up the other issue, I chased some supposed satanists for a while once, Bruce's orders, and came back empty-handed. In this country, people are free to worship Satan or God, or anything in between. Personally speaking, I don't think there *is* anything in between, and sometimes I wonder whether there's anything at either extreme. But my main point is that, unless the people you're observing actually break a law, you cannot intervene. I hope I'm making myself clear enough."

"I believe there's a connection between this group and Stephanie's murder."

"We have no body, no motive, no means, no suspects, and no witnesses. You might as well be looking for a ghost."

"At least you believe in ghosts. But if I'm 'ghostbusting,' I hope you've included a PKE meter like in the movie *Ghostbusters*."

"Too bulky," he laughed. "But here's a dainty little unit you'll enjoy." He handed her what looked like a silver eagle pin, perhaps an inch-and-a-half wide. "Look at the eyes," he said.

"Exquisite, though it's hard to see in this light what they are."

"Actually, they're a lot like yours. High-resolution auto-focus lenses. Left is wide angle. Right is telephoto. You activate by twisting the talon on whichever side you want to use. Pull both feet together and push down on the head, and the wings become a flash unit with built-in rechargeable battery. Twelve flashes and you'll need to plug it in overnight. Here's the cord; it attaches inside the beak."

"Where's the film?" she asked, turning the wafer-thin unit over several times without locating a seam.

"Nowhere," he said. "It writes a super-VGA encrypted binary file to its built-in chip. Capacity is twelve shots. Then you have to download, which is accomplished in a variety of ways. For example, you could fire it into our Boulder computer via the modem built into your Micro-Tac Ultra Lite. Or, in an emergency you could dump it onto CompuServe, since nobody—I mean nobody—would be able to read it.

"Intermediate solution," he continued, "is to temporarily store it on this."

He handed her a belt, comprised of twelve silver medallions, each with an eagle etched into its face, linked by a silver chain; the eagle pattern was duplicated in a slightly larger belt buckle.

As she tried it on for size, he continued, "There's a one-meg chip embedded in each medallion, with wires in the chain connecting them all in sequence. The belt buckle contains the battery, and the eagle's eyes are microphones. It's voice-activated, but sixty minutes is all you get before it shuts down.

"If anybody tries to take these apart, an automatic self-destruct will melt everything down. You can activate it yourself by holding your fingers over the eagle's eyes for a count of ten. Infrared sensors do the rest."

"Neat stuff. Anything else?"

"One other item. To fill out your jewelry ensemble, here's a new watch, fully loaded. Notice the twin controls at two and four o'clock—sizeable for a lady's timepiece, I realize, but the .22-caliber hollow points have to have some way to get out!"

"How does it fire?"

"Twist the dial right one click, left two, and back to twelve o'clock. But be careful. Point blank, they'll explode a medium-sized gourd, so imagine what they'll do to a human face, including your own, if you forget what kind of jewelry you're wearing."

An hour later, Clare Conroy sat in her darkened hotel room, using the night goggles to watch activities on dimly-lit Second Avenue, right through her lace curtains. The lane ran east from Main Street, starting almost directly below the gable of her room in the Regis Hotel, affording a clear view of the entire street.

"If Main Street is Casino Boulevard," she muttered, "Second Avenue is Tavern Alley."

The only saloon still open was "Alice's." At 2 A.M., when its lights finally went off and the street became almost totally dark, Conroy noticed a vehicle moving slowly westward, without headlights. *Police car. Late-night security check?* Against the street's reflected moonlight she recognized the profile of Leonard Price.

The vehicle pulled up in front of Alice's and stopped. Almost immediately, a figure stepped from the darkness and slipped in next to the driver as the car pulled away from the curb.

In the illumination of the dome light, Conroy had seen that the rider was a woman. The agent scrambled to activate the PRN-34 surveillance microphone. She slipped on the earphones, barely in time to hear Price say, "I'd like to kill the jerk, Kelly. He really gets under my skin."

"Freeman? You almost did, three days ago," the woman said.

"No, I mean Hawkins. Thinks just because he pays my salary I got to kiss his boots all the time. Even when I succeed, I fail."

"You put the minister in the hospital. Did he want you to blast him on Main Street in broad daylight?"

"Nope. He was bugged about the newspaper story. And now the reporter's back in town, snooping around. Hawkins wants him outta here, and he's willing to pay big bucks for it."

"How big?"

"Five thousand."

"Blackmail becomes me," she laughed. "Consider it done."

The vehicle turned the corner and headed north, out of Conroy's sight and range. Before it disappeared, Conroy saw through the goggles that the woman was leaning against the chief's shoulder, evidently convinced that it was safe to do so on Raptor's dark and deserted streets.

You can get anything you want, at Alice's, Conroy hummed as the car drove out of sight. *No wonder the boys badgered Eddie Hazard the other day. There's more to Second Avenue than meets the naked eye. Now if I can blackmail the blackmailer, maybe I'll get something substantial on Price . . . and Hawkins, whoever that is.*

21

Bruce Davidson arrived at Doris Oberly's office with a sheaf of legal pad pages in his hand. He dropped them perfunctorily on her desk.

"There," he said, throwing himself into the leather chair in the corner. "All the why questions I've ever had or ever hope to have."

She picked up the sheets and slowly read through them, stopping every so often to glance at Davidson, who was watching with a little smirk on his face. When she finished, she spread the pages side by side on the desktop between them, the bottom edges toward him.

"You've always been a questioner," she said.

"Good background for a G-man, don't you think?"

"Evaluate your case."

"Incriminating. Indisputable. A guilty verdict is virtually assured."

"So, God is responsible for all the bad things that have happened to Bruce Davidson."

"There's no way around it."

"Nobody else shares the blame?"

"Not in the ultimate sense."

"Just for argument's sake, let's take your first question, why God let your father die in your arms. You've already admitted that your father drowned because you weren't strong enough to hold his head above water until he regained consciousness. Nobody blamed you, of course. And you couldn't blame your father. So, you blamed God, and still do."

"Tell me something I don't know."

"Why bad things happen to good people."

"What?"

"A few years back, Rabbi Harold Kushner addressed that question after his only son, Aaron, died in his teens from a rare disease that caused him to age prematurely." She grabbed a slim book off the credenza behind her and opened to a page marked by a Post-it note.

"Here's his famous conclusion. 'I believe in God. But . . . I recognize His limitations. He is limited in what He can do by the laws of nature and by the evolution of human nature and human moral freedom. I no longer hold God responsible for illnesses, accidents, and natural disasters, because I realize I gain little and lose so much when I blame God for those things. I can worship a God who hates suffering but cannot eliminate it, more easily than I can worship a God who chooses to make children suffer and die, for whatever exalted reason. . . .'"

"So the rabbi declares God not guilty, because he can't do anything about it?" Davidson asked. "I always figured either God was in control or he wasn't. If not, he wasn't God. If so, he can make things happen or keep things from happening. Therefore, since he didn't keep Daddy from dying, he was responsible."

"I agree."

"Then why'd you read me that?"

"To make you define the God you believe in. If you embrace Kushner's God, you'll never get to step two, for if he has no power over evil, he has no real power to do good. In which case, believing he can restore you to sanity is an exercise in futility. On the other hand, if he has the power to intervene, it's valid to question why he failed to do so."

"Like I said, God is guilty as charged."

"Yes, Judge Davidson, because he created a world where the possibility of suffering existed. But, tell me, exactly what is he guilty of?"

"I don't know, never took it this far. How about divine malpractice?"

"Okay. And the sentence?"

Davidson thought for a moment, then said, "To hurt as I have hurt. To feel the loneliness, fear, confusion, and guilt. To agonize and suffer. Maybe even to die; yes, to die in Daddy's place. To die in Ellen's place . . ."

He stopped mid-sentence, and stared at Oberly.

"To die in Bruce's place?" she added. "So he can be released from his own death sentence?"

"I get the point," he said quietly, tears forming in his eyes. "But it's so hard to comprehend."

"That's not necessary, as long as you accept it. Like I said, the only way around it is through it, and the only way through it is by embracing his way with you."

"Everything?"

"You don't have to understand it. You don't have to like it. You just have to do it. That's what faith is all about."

***

"There." Nate Freeman pointed upward toward the cliff overlooking the secluded valley he and Eddie Hazard had been traversing on horseback for about an hour. "A Ute Indian cave, just like I said. See how it's dug out?"

Eddie, who was totally absorbed with staying on one of the formerly-wild stallions Freeman had broken, nodded and then asked, "We riding up *there?*"

"Not straight up, naturally. There's a trail loops up behind it and then back down. Don't worry. It's safe."

"From what?"

"Coyotes, cougars, bears. Even bad guys if they decide to get any more unfriendly than they already been."

"They'd have to find us first. We must be five miles from the nearest road."

"You ain't lost, are ya?" Freeman laughed.

"Not as long as I'm with you. But I'd sure hate to try to find my way here by myself, especially in the dark."

"Easier than you think. All you got to do is find where the west branch of Remington Creek crosses the road, and follow it right to here."

"Sounds easy, except sometimes it goes underground and sometimes there's beaver ponds and sometimes there's not enough water to brush your teeth."

"Then how we gonna catch our supper?" Freeman asked, as he dismounted.

Eddie did likewise, eyeing the small trickle of water. "You'll have to be a fish magician to catch anything here. Besides, we didn't bring any fishing poles."

"Don't need none," Freeman said. He knelt at the edge of the stream and reached under the embankment with his right hand. "Spring runoff cuts these banks back every

179

year, so . . . every time I check . . . there's more and more fish hiding back there in the dark!"

Triumphantly, the mountain minister pulled his hand from the water, grasping a struggling eight-inch native brook trout just behind the gills.

"I can't believe it," his companion laughed. "You are a fish magician!"

"Nothin' to it," Freeman said, tossing the flapping trout at Eddie, who caught it, dropped it, and caught it again before the fish could fall to the ground.

"The farther you reach under," Freeman said, narrating his progress as he felt for another trout, "the more they try to scrunch up against the bank." He grunted as he stretched. "'Cause that's where they think they're safe. All you got . . . to . . . do . . . is come up under their bellies real . . . slow . . . get your thumb on one side and your forefinger on the other . . . and . . . grab right behind the gills and flip 'em up on the bank," he added rapid-fire as another trout of about the same size flapped its way through the air toward Eddie Hazard.

"Your turn," the preacher laughed. "I got my supper, now you got to catch your own."

"But you're having such a good time," Hazard laughed back as he hung the second fish on a forked stick from a nearby alder.

"What you mean is, you don't think you can do it. Okay, I'll let you do it like the Ute's did," Freeman said, cutting a second alder branch. "Give the man a fish, and you'll feed him for a day," he said as he whittled the limb into a barbed fishing stick while Hazard watched. "Teach him how to fish and he'll feed hisself."

He grabbed a couple medium-sized rocks from the bank

180

to block the exit of the little pool. Then as the water level began to rise slowly, he handed the trident to Eddie. "We got about ten minutes before the water runs again. I'll flush 'em out, and you can harpoon 'em. But you gotta be quick, 'cause once they get out in the open, they don't stand around waitin' to be stuck! And you got to get out into the water or you'll never get close enough."

Hazard yanked off his boots, grabbed the fishing stick, and stepped into the ankle-deep water, surprised to find it ice cold. He hopped around on the gravelly bottom until his feet got used to the chill.

"Well, now they know you're here," Freeman chuckled. "So they got no excuse. Get ready, here comes a herd of brookies," he announced, as he reached in under the bank again. This time he made a sweeping motion and almost immediately five fish flashed from the darkness into the pool, where Eddie jabbed, jabbed, and jabbed again, twenty times, as he chased them. Finally, just before the trout darted back under the bank, he connected.

The piscatorial neophyte proudly displayed his six-inch trophy to his instructor, who fell back on the bank, howling with delight. "Ain't seen nothin' so funny since . . ." Freeman tried to say, but couldn't continue, he was laughing so hard. "As a matter of fact, I ain't *never* seen anything so funny!"

"Glad to entertain you," Hazard replied, smiling, "but are we gonna gab or are we gonna jab?" He tossed the tiny trout into Freeman's lap, and reached in under the bank himself, scaring the fish back out where he could see them. A moment later, he splashed his way to his friend's side with an impaled ten-incher to add to their wilderness larder.

***

"Sometimes you're like a broken record," Bruce Davidson said to Doris Oberly. "No matter what issue I bring up, you make it into a discussion about faith. But I fail to see what difference faith can possibly make in relation to my . . . illness."

"Explaining it to someone who hasn't experienced it is like trying to describe the taste of real Vermont Grade A maple syrup to someone who's only had that artificially-flavored and sweetened pancake topping before. I could talk all day about the delicate sweetness and exquisite aftertaste, but the only way you could really understand would be to actually go to a sugarhouse in March and sample a teaspoonful direct from the evaporator."

"I've done that," he said, "and I know exactly what you mean—about maple syrup. But you're asking me to trust God so I can discover the value of trusting God—" he picked the papers off the desk "—despite the evidence that he's not trustworthy."

"Those questions will lead you to better questions, if you let them," she replied.

"No answers? Aren't there any answers?"

"Suppose God sent someone, a great prophet, who could answer every one of the questions on your sheet."

"I'd be impressed."

"But would you trust God then?"

"I might trust the prophet. But God, I don't know."

"That's because the real issues aren't cognitive, but volitional. Heartbreak hides that, which is why you have to keep asking until you get to the questions behind the questions."

"Such as, why do bad things happen to good people?"

"Precisely. When you answer that one, you will have answered everything on those pages, plus all the questions you've asked in the past but forgotten, and the ones you'll ask in the future, but haven't thought of yet."

"What's the answer?"

"That wouldn't be fair. It would be like handing my spiritual eyeglasses to you. You might see better, but you wouldn't see clearly until you got your own prescription."

"I have to discover the answers myself?"

"Not *by* yourself, but *for* yourself. There's a huge difference. In other words, God wants you to search for, and find, answers for your best questions. But he doesn't make you search without guidance."

"Are you talking about yourself?"

"No, about him. For only he knows the way you take. But when he is finished, your faith will be like refined gold."

"Shakespeare?"

"Job, who also had more questions than answers, but refused to stop searching until he was satisfied."

She rose from the desk as she spoke, walked to the closet, and emerged a few seconds later with a fly rod case, a fishing vest, and a trout net; she handed these to Davidson, along with a thin-line Bible from her desktop. "I never gave this assignment to anyone before, but let's call it personalized therapy. I want you to take the whole day tomorrow by yourself, down at the river, equipped with four items: your list of questions, a Bible—so you can read Job's story for yourself—a sack lunch, and this fishing stuff."

"*You* fly fish?" he said, unwrapping the rod to find a Sage eight-foot, six-inch rod, with matching reel and #5 weight-forward floating line.

"I understand you're an Orvis man," she replied.

"Billings again? You certainly did your homework."

"After you use that rod, you'll eschew bamboo forever. There's always a couple good rainbows in the big pool at the bend. Since it's on our property, I'm the only one who fishes there, though I don't get out as often as I'd like.

"Here's some flies I tied, number twenty-two Tricos, BWOs, and a few RS-2s. If you run out, or if there's a hatch on that nothing here matches, there's a field tying kit in the vest. The tippet's only 6x, because anything bigger puts 'em down. But tie into anything over eight pounds and you'll be there all day just trying to land it."

"If that happens, I'll think I've died and gone to heaven."

"I'm hoping. Not that you'll die and go to heaven, but that you'll live and let heaven come to you."

22

Eddie Hazard's scream catapulted Nate Freeman from a deep sleep into wide-eyed consciousness in a split second.

"What it is, Eddie?" the pastor said, rubbing the sleep from his eyes as he searched his pack in the dark for his glasses.

"A cat, biggest one I've ever seen, just started to come in here. But when I yelled, it ran off. I think it dropped something."

"How big was it?" Nate Freeman asked, as he crawled toward the cave's opening.

"About this long," Hazard indicated, holding his hands three feet apart. "Not counting the tail."

"Jehovah-jireh," Freeman muttered as he picked up the blue grouse the cougar had left behind.

"Funny name for an animal."

"Cat's a cougar—mountain lion. Jehovah-jireh's a name for God, from Genesis, from the time Abraham was about to sacrifice Isaac and God provided a ram instead. Abraham named the place Jehovah-jireh, which means 'the

Lord will provide.' So now we got a name for this place, Camp Jehovah-jireh, 'cause he delivered breakfast right to our door."

"I . . . thought *I* was going to be *its* breakfast!" Hazard replied, his voice quavering.

"Not a chance. Though this may be the critter's breakfast nook. Cougar's ain't man-killers, unless you get one cornered and it has to kill you just to get away. Must've had its nose full of that bird's scent so it didn't smell us until it was too late.

"But do me a favor. Next time you order breakfast in bed, let's sleep in till daylight."

"Wouldn't matter. I didn't sleep a wink all night," Hazard replied.

"Sorry. I keep you up with my snoring?"

"No. It was the other night noises. Soon as the moon rose, the screeching and howling was nonstop. And, you won't believe this, somebody's been playing a flute all night a few hundred yards up the valley."

Just as he said that, an eerie but delicate flute-like trill echoed down the canyon on the frosty air.

"See what I mean? Guy must be crazy to be out here."

"Crazy for romance, that's what," Freeman said with a laugh. "Elk romance. Ain't you never heard an elk bugle?"

"You're kidding. How can an animal that big make such a delicate sound?"

"Don't know for sure. It just can. Trust me," Freeman replied, still holding the bird by its feet. "We could sneak up on him, if you want to see for yourself."

"What about the cougar?"

"Probably headin' for the next county." He looked down

at the bird, saying, "Unless she thinks it'd be easier to come back and retrieve this grouse than try to catch another!"

He laughed, but when he saw the panic in his new friend's eyes, he added, "Just foolin'. She ain't gonna bother us. You build a fire and brew the coffee, and I'll take the bird down to the creek and clean 'er up real good. Then we'll have a breakfast fit for a king."

In the pre-dawn darkness, Bruce Davidson sat motionless, his back against a large cottonwood on the east bank of the South Platte River. The river gurgled quietly along as a four-point buck meandered to the water's edge on the west bank, directly in front of him. The animal took a drink and then headed for the timber to Davidson's left without detecting the agent's presence.

Suddenly, Bruce remembered one of Ellen's favorite posters of a deer taking a drink, captioned, "As the hart pants for streams of water, so my soul pants for you, O God."

He shifted a bit and pulled the list of questions from his pocket. He spread them on the bank and then lay back and looked up at the star-studded sky. "Okay," he said. "I'm listening. You can answer them one by one, or one at a time. We have all day."

"Never had a better breakfast in my life," Eddie Hazard said as he licked the grease from the bacon-wrapped grouse off his fingertips.

"That breakfast was the Lord's doin', that's for sure."

"Quite a contrast to what he's been doing the past few days," Hazard retorted.

"Depends on what yer thinkin' of."

"I was thinking that you almost died, and Mocha did die. I was thinking of the newspaper article, the bishop, and the parsonage. Enough adversity to fill anybody's week."

"You forgot your one-night stand, and my flying off the handle when that reporter was still sittin' there."

"You blaming God for those things, too?"

"I'm pointin' out that askin' why good things happen to bad people is just as good a question as why bad things happen to good people."

"Sounds like a riddle. But are you saying *we're* bad people, after what they've done to you?"

"Maybe we're not as bad as really bad people, but that only makes us relatively good, not really good."

"Is anybody really good?"

"Only one man ever was—Jesus. And they crucified him. So, if you're gonna figure out the riddle for yerself, you got to figure out why God let his own Son die, when he never did nothin' to deserve it."

"Is there an answer?"

"Same answer as to both questions. Love. God loved us enough to give us what we needed, instead of makin' us earn it, because Jesus loved us enough to pay the cost hisself."

"So bad things happen because God *lets* them . . . and good things happen because God *makes* them?"

"Not exactly," Freeman replied. "But God can make the bad things he lets happen into good things, like he did with Jesus, if we'll trust him enough."

"Forgive my doubt, pastor," Hazard replied. "But Mocha's dead, and your dog, too, right? Nothing can change that."

Freeman nodded, tears filling his eyes.

"And your ministerial career, and your place to live, and maybe even your fight to get the church back. Maybe they're all dead issues, and you should just walk away from here and start over, like Annie said, before something worse happens."

"What more can they do to me?" Freeman replied. "There's nothin' left to lose."

"What about your life?"

"He who keeps his life shall lose it; but he who loses his life for my sake, shall gain it."

"Another riddle?"

"A promise. Which reminds me, I promised someone I'd be on the church steps at noon today. You can come, or you can stay here and wait till I get back. It's up to you."

"I'm not staying here alone," Hazard replied, "until you teach me how to shoot that revolver. Too many wild beasts around, looking to have somebody like me for lunch."

As the sun's first rays hit the snow-topped Rockies to the west, Bruce Davidson began reading the story of Job, finding in the very first chapter support for his own complaints, still laid out by his side.

"One day the angels came to present themselves before the Lord, and Satan also came with them. The Lord said to Satan, 'Where have you come from?'

"Satan answered the Lord, 'From roaming through the earth and going back and forth in it.'

"Then the Lord said to Satan, 'Have you considered my servant Job? There is no one on earth like him; he is blameless and upright, a man who fears God and shuns evil.'

"'Does Job fear God for nothing?' Satan replied. 'Have

you not put a hedge around him and his household and everything he has? You have blessed the work of his hands, so that his flocks and herds are spread throughout the land. But stretch out your hand and strike everything he has, and he will surely curse you to your face.'

"The Lord said to Satan, 'Very well, then, everything he has is in your hands, but on the man himself do not lay a finger.'"

In one day, the man lost everything he had, Davidson thought, as he scanned the rest of the chapter. *All his possessions and all his children. And then, to add injury to insult, he lost his health.*

The FBI agent held the Bible in his left hand and picked up his list with his right. "Just as I thought," he said out loud, holding the two documents heavenward. "You *are* responsible. You not only let it happen, you *selected* Job. Why couldn't you let him live in peace? Why couldn't you let *me* live in peace? Did our happiness make you unhappy, and our sadness give you joy? If so, you've been happy all my life, and right now you're up there mocking my futile attempt to find some meaning and purpose in it all, when there really isn't any. It's just a colossal, capricious, cosmic joke."

He paused, folded up his list, stuck it inside the Bible, and stared blankly upriver to the north, where a mule deer doe and its two fawns were slowly grazing their way to the river. As Davidson drank in the scene, its serenity a total contrast to the turmoil in his soul at that moment, a movement along the embankment caught his eye. A lone coyote was waiting, downwind of the deer, totally concealed in the longer grasses.

190

Stop! he wanted to shout to the deer. *Go back! Get out of here while you still can.*

He considered shouting out loud, but decided to observe a little longer, to see if the doe would somehow sense the danger in time and get her little ones out of there. After all, if he intervened this morning, and she didn't learn from it, tomorrow the predator would come again, its breakfast only delayed by twenty-four hours.

The deer were thirty yards away from the water when a little swirl of breeze carried the scent their way. In a flash the doe was dashing west, away from the danger as fast as she could go. On the open range, the coyote would never catch her.

For her youngsters, however, the outcome was still in doubt as the hidden hunter charged. Momentarily frozen in place, partly from fear and partly from confusion, their first good fortune occurred just as the coyote pounced and they separated instinctively, heading in opposite directions, one west toward its mother, and the other east, toward Davidson.

The coyote hesitated just long enough for the westward-bound fawn to escape, then turned to pursue the other, which had thrown itself into the river and was now desperately trying to swim across. But the pool was deep, and the adversary was strong.

Leaping from the bank, the predator nearly caught up to the wide-eyed, frantic fawn before Davidson, unwilling to witness the slaughter, launched himself into the river.

"Sorry, pal," he said, as the would-be killer nearly turned itself inside-out to escape. Then the deer, sensing danger from too many fronts simultaneously, gave up and started to sink beneath the surface.

"Bambi, you're too young to die," his savior said as he gently lifted the animal in his arms, draped it across his shoulders, and walked out of the water on the west bank. In the distance, the doe and other fawn watched Davidson set the trembling animal down and help it stand up. For a moment, the fawn seemed confused and a little unsteady. But when it heard the sound of its mother's bleating from across the meadow, it ambled slowly in her direction, looking back twice toward Davidson as if still wondering what had just happened.

Davidson, meanwhile, began to shiver, not just from the adrenalin surge, but also from the fact that he was now totally wet and the sun had yet to warm the valley air much above freezing. He waded back to the other side, seriously considering if he ought to return to the Hope Center and call it a day.

Can't, he thought. *I've got to complete the assignment, regardless of the distractions.* He searched the fishing vest until he found a capsule filled with waterproof matches and kindled a fire on the riverbank, using the top sheet of his questions to get it started.

Then again, maybe it wasn't a distraction. Maybe it was part of the plan. Whose plan? The coyote's? Mine? Doris's? God's?

He unfolded a paper-thin foil-coated survival blanket he'd also found in the vest, and hitched it to a couple of tree branches to create a life-sized reflector oven. Then, when the fire grew hot enough, he stripped to his underwear, hung his shirt and jeans on sticks by the fire, and waited for everything to dry. "If Clare could only see me now!" he chuckled.

Toasty hot on one side and freezing cold on the other,

he picked up the Bible again and continued his journey with Job.

"But ask the animals, and they will teach you, or the birds of the air, and they will tell you; or speak to the earth, and it will teach you, or let the fish of the sea inform you. Which of all these does not know that the hand of the Lord has done this? In his hand is the life of every creature and the breath of all mankind."

23

Wally Courier, you weasel," Nate Freeman said to the new minister, who was standing on the front porch of the parsonage when Freeman and Hazard arrived on horseback. "Never thought you'd stab me in the back."

"Nothin' personal, Nate," his former Bible school comrade replied. "Scerzy speaks, we jump. What other option is there if we want to advance in the district? Besides, he said it would only be until the dust settled."

"That case, you could be here forever."

"I don't need any trouble, Nate."

"Trouble? Eddie and me thought somebody should officially welcome you to Raptor. But I see you already been welcomed, by the *Chronicle*," Freeman said, pulling a tightly rolled-up newspaper from his saddlebags. "Nice photo, but ain't it a bit deceivin' to use your graduation picture when you've lost most of yer hair since then, and put on about thirty pounds?"

Freeman laughed, but he didn't dismount. Courier

194

chuckled, too, but he shifted his weight nervously from one foot to another. "They interviewed me by phone. Scerzy sent the photo."

"He tell you what to say, too?"

"Nobody tells me what to say, Nate. I'm just trying to spread some oil on the waters."

Freeman unrolled the newspaper and read from the interview:

"Chronicle: Do you plan to continue the anti-gambling campaign launched by your predecessor?

"Reverend Courier: Gambling is as old as humankind. It was even used by the disciples to select a replacement for Judas. Shall we say that something useful to Peter, James, and John is evil, in and of itself? The main issue isn't whether or not a man wagers from time to time, but whether he loves wagering more than he loves God.

"Chronicle: Then will your church officially give up its crusade to repossess the Community Church property?

"Reverend Courier: That crusade was solely the former pastor's. We have no claim on the Cathedral Casino.

"Chronicle: What about Freeman's charges of conspiracy?

"Reverend Courier: Nate was devastated to lose the facility. But our work has to do with saving souls, not saving face. The real conspirators today are fundamentalists who try to impose their values on the public at large."

Freeman stopped reading and threw the paper at Courier. As it fluttered to the ground, he said, "Oil on the waters? I'd call it salt in the wounds."

"Yours, maybe," Courier replied. "But the church people seemed to appreciate it."

"Which?"

"The Millers, Bishops, Thorpes, and Arnolds, for starters. I make that a one-hundred-percent gain in one day."

"Deserters, after the vote. Every one of 'em work at casinos."

"What other work is there? How they make a living is not my business, as long as they attend church and pay their tithes."

"Puttin' dirty money through an offerin' plate don't make it clean."

"Maybe not. But it'll pay the bills, which is more than you've been doing, judging from the treasurer's report." He paused, looked his former classmate straight in the eye, and said, "Look, Nate. I didn't come here to duke it out with you. In fact, I've always liked you, because you were so . . . unique—riding, roping, shooting, and all the rest. But I also wondered if you really had a pastor's heart. I mean, you challenged everyone from Calvin to our professors. You took every issue as another opportunity to throw down the gauntlet. Church people need encouragement, not fire and brimstone week after week."

"You want fire and brimstone, I can show 'em to ya. But I got a sneakin' suspicion you don't really want to know what's going on behind the scenes."

"I have quite enough work to keep me occupied, thank you, especially if you plan to interfere."

"You want me outta yer face? Then come along with me and Eddie tomorrow night. If you ain't convinced this town needs defendin', I'll leave and never come back."

Courier hesitated, then said, "Intriguing offer, Nate. But I can't risk my reputation by showing up somewhere with you."

"In this case, nobody will even know you're there. Promise."

The sun was almost directly overhead when Bruce Davidson awoke from his nap in front of the fire that had dried his clothes. When he opened his eyes, he was lying on his back, staring straight up into a clear blue sky, framed by golden aspen leaves quaking in the gentle midday breeze.

As Davidson's eyes focused beyond the foliage, he saw an eagle soaring five-hundred feet up, effortlessly riding the thermals, looking for its lunch.

The agent put his hands behind his head and watched the magnificent bird glide. For the first time in years, he felt relaxed. No place to go. Nothing to do, when for as long as he could remember he'd been hurried and worried, always rushing, but never getting anywhere, ever since his father had drowned.

Lying there, mesmerized by the raptor's heavenly gyres, he was nine years old again, lying in front of a campfire down near Misty River, with his dad, listening to the hoot owls and trying to get them to answer. Little Brucie's voice was too high, his call too shrill, to merit a response from any self-respecting owl. But T. Bob was good at it. He got an answer every time.

What did they say? What did they say? I knew then, but I can't remember, he thought. *Something about life being good, safe, peaceful, and happy because there was a natural order of things and we were part of it and glad to be . . . just glad to be alive.*

Suddenly, the eagle plummeted, a talon-tipped harpoon into the heart of the quiet pool directly in front of Davidson. A second later, the bird emerged with an eighteen-inch fish and carried it away to its nest atop a nearby crag.

"Perfect size for lunch," the observer muttered, realizing that he, too, was hungry, but the sandwich he'd packed had turned to mush when he rescued the fawn.

Okay, Doris. Let's see if your flies work well enough to keep me from starving.

He picked up the rod, amazed at its light weight, wondering how it could possibly handle a fish as large as the one he'd just seen snatched from the pool's waters. Blue-winged olives were hatching, but not one fish was feeding on the surface, probably because the water had been disturbed so often since dawn.

But maybe there's a lunch-sized rainbow in that riffle at the tail of the pool, he thought, opening the small case of nymphs and streamers tucked into the fishing vest's back pocket. *RS-2s, scuds, hare's ears, brassies, midge larvae, San Juan worms, and woolly buggers. Nice selection. Better than mine! Wonder if she tied these, too?*

He selected a pink San Juan worm, tied it on with a turle knot, and crept along the bank until he was sure the broken surface of the short run between the pool he'd been watching and the longer, shallower pool just below it would prevent any fish from seeing him.

He knelt behind a fallen log, laid the fly out at the head of the rapids, and watched the line bump its way through the rocky sluice until it hesitated momentarily. He lifted the rod tip slightly and a moment later a twelve-inch rainbow trout catapulted skyward, trying to shake the hook. The light rod and the stream's current made the brief battle much more enjoyable for the angler, but from the outset the outcome was virtually assured. He slid the still-struggling silver-scaled beauty into Doris's collapsible net and carried it triumphantly to the shore.

"Is your twin still in there?" he asked, leaving the fish behind the log. He cast again to the same spot, with the same result. Fifteen minutes later, he had rekindled the fire, using another of his pages of complaints, and stoked it with mesquite. The dressed fish were split and laid open between latticed layers of wet alder branches. *Three minutes, each side, should be perfect,* he mused, as the pink flesh sizzled and the smoky aroma heightened his anticipation of the forthcoming feast.

When the meal was ready, he sat cross-legged on the ground, set the fish on a flat rock, and laid the Bible open on an aspen stump before him. He ate, holding the fish like corn on the cob, as he continued reading Job's lament.

"Man born of woman is of few days and full of trouble. He springs up like a flower and withers away; like a fleeting shadow, he does not endure. . . . At least there is hope for a tree: If it is cut down, it will sprout again, and its new shoots will not fail. Its roots may grow old in the ground and its stump die in the soil, yet at the scent of water it will bud and put forth shoots like a plant. But man dies and is laid low; he breathes his last and is no more . . . till the heavens are no more, men will not awake or be roused from their sleep. If only you would hide me in the grave and conceal me till your anger has passed!"

Bruce Davidson nodded in agreement. *You got that right,* he thought. Then he stopped mid-bite and stared at the stump, where a small shoot tipped with two yellow leaves bravely proclaimed that, despite appearances, it wasn't dead yet.

The tree lives, as the wise one says. And Daddy lives, too, and Ellen, not only in heaven, but in my memory . . . and even in my thoughts and actions. They're inside me, as Doris said.

And even you live, Job, through your words. Maybe even your pain wasn't as wasted as it seemed. Maybe my *pain wasn't as wasted as it seemed.*

He turned away from the Book and stared west toward the Rockies, pondering the question as with each new bite he gained energy from the flesh of the fish.

After a moment, he continued his perusal of Job, whose "comforters" just made his agony worse. "Then know that God has wronged me and drawn his net around me. Though I cry, 'I've been wronged!' I get no response; though I call for help, there is no justice. He has blocked my way so I cannot pass; he has shrouded my paths in darkness. . . . He tears me down on every side till I am gone; he uproots my hope like a tree. . . . Oh, that my words were recorded, that they were written on a scroll, that they were inscribed with an iron tool on lead, or engraved in rock forever!"

Davidson again nodded in agreement, glancing toward his remaining pages of questions, themselves but reproductions of the permanent etchings in his personal memory bank. *But what is* this, *Job?* he asked, as he read on. "I know that my Redeemer lives, and that in the end he will stand upon the earth. And after my skin has been destroyed, yet in my flesh I will see God; I myself will see him with my own eyes—I, and not another. How my heart yearns within me!"

You went psycho from the pressure, Davidson mused. *One minute you're wishing you could die, and the next you're rejoicing. Laughing and crying at the same time. What kind of a response is that?*

The mid-afternoon sun reflected off the steeple of the former Community Church, shimmering on its steps where Nathan Freeman stood, holding his open Bible in one hand as he preached the sermon of his life.

"Turn back, oh men, forswear yer foolish ways," he shouted. "It ain't too late. It's never too late to repent, go home, return to your families. Don't cast your substance before the god of chance. Don't cast your souls before the altar of fortune, mammon, greed. But cast your souls before the throne of grace, where there is forgiveness and mercy and power to live the way you should."

Unknown to Freeman, a group of hecklers had been hired by the Casino Owners Association to harass him. With every sentence they mocked, jeered, and shouted obscenities, pushing ever closer to the speaker, who retreated up the stairs until he was standing with his back against the front door.

Freeman was wondering if a riot might be developing, when suddenly from the street below, someone announced on a bullhorn, "This meeting is against the law. You have two minutes to disperse. Anyone trespassing on the property of the Cathedral Casino after that time will be subject to arrest."

When only Freeman and Hazard remained, Chief Price handed the preacher a folded piece of paper. "Mr. Freeman," the policeman said. "You are hereby served a restraining order issued this morning by Circuit Judge Bernard Luce. The next time you obstruct the entrance of this, or any other casino in Raptor, you will be confined in the county jail and be subject to a fine of five thousand dollars or thirty days in jail, or both. I trust this makes things clear enough, and I surely hope you're smart enough to take your trouble elsewhere."

"I'm a free man, and it's a free country," the preacher replied. "I'll preach in the middle of Main Street if I have to."

With that, he ripped up the court order and handed it back to Price.

"There ain't no way, short of killin' me, to shut me up," Freeman declared as he turned on his heel and walked away.

As he passed the door of the Regis Casino, from which Juanita Rodriguez had observed the entire exchange, she suddenly stepped out, directly in his path, and bumped him hard enough to knock the Bible from his left hand.

"I sorry," she said, slipping a ticket to the 4 P.M. performance within the Book's pages as she handed it back to him. "Be there," she whispered.

Eddie Hazard, walking right behind Freeman, saw the exchange and heard her words; he glanced around to make sure no one else noticed. *Have to ask Nate about this sometime,* he thought. *Maybe he's not as pure as the driven snow!*

Looking out his office window toward the street below, Stanley Hawkins had witnessed the same event, though he couldn't quite see what the actress had done.

But he was sure he had seen the woman somewhere other than on the *Dracula's Mistress* posters plastered all over town. Try as he might, however, the mafioso couldn't recall any Spanish woman with the combination of agility, figure, and gait he saw in this one as she walked back inside the Regis Casino.

Have to see the play, he said to himself, as he turned from the window, rubbing his scar. *See the lady in action. Maybe that'll jog the memory.*

24

Bruce Davidson caught the just-emerged fly in his hand, and compared it to Doris Oberly's selection of drys. *Trico, black-and-white, number twenty-two. And there's only one in this box.*

As he studied the fly, one of many hatching at that moment all around him, he noticed for the first time a small ring, a minuscule circle, in the backwater behind a fallen log directly across the pool from his position. His experience with trout hunting over the past twenty years told him this was a large fish, since smaller trout often splashed when feeding. But the monsters had a habit of lying just below the surface, slurping emerging flies without leaving much evidence they were there.

Easy to see why she's a big one, he whispered to himself as he picked out the only fly in the box matching the current hatch. *She's feeding right under that overhanging branch, facing downstream in the eddy. Probably been doing that for five years.*

Davidson's heart began to beat faster as he captured another trico in his hand and compared it to the imitation

203

he had just tied on the end of his line. All the while, the fish kept feeding, breaking the surface slightly every thirty seconds or so.

In any other situation, the approach would have been straightforward enough: Creep to a position thirty degrees downstream, then cast up and across, leaving a small loop at the end to eliminate drag as long as possible. A fish this experienced would never take a fly acting peculiar in any way. The look-alike must drift through the fish's feeding field as naturally as the scores of others it had already passed up, or it would not be fooled. Worse, if it sensed something amiss, it might spook to another location, or quit feeding altogether.

Davidson finally settled on a strategy, one he'd never used himself, and only seen used once before—by his father. When the granddaddy bass refused to come out from behind a log in Misty River, T. Bob Davidson caught him anyhow by looping his cast over the log, showing the fish six seconds worth of dragless drift before the line would pull it back, toward the river's main flow.

As far as Bruce could see, the same approach might work here, but there was no room for error. The cast had to be perfect the very first time, or the line would snag on the log and the fly would be lost. Even if the fish took, if it headed upstream, the fragile leader would snap immediately. But if the hooked fish ran downstream, away from its hiding place, it might pull the line and leader free and leave fisherman and fish with a fair fight.

Davidson waded out gingerly into the river, a half step at a time, slowly working his way into position. When he finally reached the middle, still out of range, he tried a few casts, to get used to the high-tech equipment, since the earlier fish hadn't really tested it.

The Sage's range was amazing. At twenty feet, the fly traveled effortlessly. Even at thirty feet, there was hardly any drag on the back cast. At forty feet, he still hadn't reached the rod's maximum effective distance. But it was enough, since that was about as far as he could cast with the degree of accuracy needed for this particular fish.

His adrenalin surged as Bruce laid the line out once, twice, three times. On the fourth forward roll he dropped the tip and watched the tiny fly float toward its target. But at the very last second, a small gust from the south blew the nearly weightless fly back upriver just enough so it landed on the log. He tried, gently, to nudge it off the obstacle so he could cast again, but as soon as he raised the rod, the miniature barb hooked and held. When he tried to pull the hook free, the leader parted.

No! he protested. *She won't take anything else.*

He retreated to the bank, discouraged, while his quarry kept right on feeding.

What would Job say to this? he muttered, leafing through the document still open on the bank. "But if I go to the east, he is not there; if I go to the west, I do not find him. When he is at work in the north, I do not see him; when he turns to the south, I catch no glimpse of him."

That's the way it's been all day. What did Doris think I'd find out here, some kind of special revelation? The big fish eats the little fish—that's what I see, unless the little fish is lucky. And the wind blows where it will. There's no way God can take a personal interest in every tiny detail.

But the next verse hooked him, partly because Doris

Oberly had prepared the way. "But he knows the way that I take; when he has tested me, I will come forth as gold."

I know the way that trout takes, and I'd like to test her and find out what she's made of. But I can't do it. I don't have the right fly. Then again, maybe I do.

Davidson fumbled in the vest's back pocket and found the field fly-tying kit. He jabbed the vise into the stump, laid another freshly-captured *Tricorythidae* fly next to it, and began to tie a pattern to match it, starting at the tiny hook's bend. First the tail, then the body, wings, hackle, and finally the head, cemented in place with one small droplet of fingernail polish.

This time, as he false-casted, Davidson waited for a break in the wind before he dropped the tip. The fly landed perfectly, hardly denting the surface. It drifted for about three seconds, then disappeared. *Submerged, or sucked in?* he asked himself. He raised the tip and was suddenly connected with solid piscine power. Instantly, the calm surface boiled as the fish turned and ran downstream, stripping twenty feet off the reel before the fisherman had time to react.

At the south end of the pool, the giant rainbow launched herself heavenward in a spectacular, twisting, turning leap, spray flying from her back, tail, and fins in all directions, haloed by the sun.

It seemed to Davidson that the fish was tail-walking its way south in order to get a good look at its adversary. He stood stock still, transfixed by the acrobatics. Never in his life had he even hooked such a rainbow, much less landed one.

Upon reentry, the trout tore downstream through the riffle into the next pool. She was already into the reel's backing before Davidson had stumbled his way to the lower pool. But he tripped as he arrived, and fell headfirst into the icy water.

Got to keep the line from tangling, he thought as he struggled to right himself, *or this fish is history.*

When he finally regained his feet in the waist-deep water, his line lay limply on the surface, stretching nearly to the other end of the pool. Disappointed, he sucked in a long breath, not knowing if he should laugh that he'd had the opportunity of a lifetime or cry because he'd blown it. He began to slowly retrieve the line.

Twenty cranks later, the pole was nearly torn from his semi-numb fingers as the trout, which had been sulking in the shadows of the pool's far reaches, realized it was still hooked. Leaping once again, its head wagging fiercely to dislodge the hook, the fish rocketed skyward. Again and again she leaped, falling heavily back into the water, trying desperately to deal with something she didn't understand. Each time she jumped, Davidson dropped the tip, then recovered a few more inches when she landed.

Frustrated by her foiled attempts to escape, the fish did the only thing that made sense to her. She streaked back upstream as fast as she had charged down, at one point passing within three feet of Davidson as he helplessly watched the monster tow the limp line the other way. *One rock, even a small twig, is all it'll take to snap the line*, he reminded himself as the leader dragged along the bottom.

But the river was kind, and when at last he felt the fish again, Davidson had regained all the backing. Only ninety feet separated him from his prize.

Again she leaped, but not as high. Again she turned and ran, but not as far. This time he kept her in the pool.

207

Slowly, inch by inch, he gained, letting the rod tire the fish, constantly alert not to overstress the slender, possibly frayed, tippet.

Now she was just fifteen feet out, still trying to escape. But with each gentle tug from Davidson, the fish fought less and showed her side more—nearly three feet of speckled rainbow—green on top, fiery stripe down her side, and silver below.

Finally, she turned on her side in the current, her yellow-and-black eye staring up at the victor as he gently guided her head—that's all that would fit—into the net. Then, grasping his prize firmly by the lip, the exultant fisherman pulled her into shallower water, where, exhausted, he sat down, the fish between his knees in the water, and began to laugh out loud.

"All my life," he said to her, "I've been trying to catch you. And all my life, you've gotten away. You tested me, and won, until today, this very moment. Now."

He scrutinized the exhausted fish, still barely able to keep itself horizontal.

"Any other day, we'd have a date with the taxidermist. But, my friend, we've learned too much from each other today to waste half of it by hanging you on any wall. No, I want to remember you as queen of this pool, maybe monarch of this river. But I am king of you, and if you forget what you learned and we meet again, I may not be so merciful."

When the trout was strong enough, Davidson unhooked the barb that had nearly killed her, laid her up against the rod one last time to mark how large she really was, and then released her. For a moment, she hung suspended in the water. But when she realized there was nothing holding her back, she burst away, her powerful tail splashing Davidson. Then she disappeared from sight.

As if frozen in place, the fisherman, drenched to the skin for the second time that day, lifted his eyes to the hills. "Am I also free?" he asked out loud. "No hook, no net, nothing holding me back? It's almost too good to believe."

Shivering, he turned toward the shore where the rest of his pages of questions were spread out next to the stump in which the vise was still imbedded. *Don't need another fire,* he realized. *It's time to go back. But there's still one thing left to do.*

Slowly, deliberately, he selected twelve stones from the riverbank and stacked them into the shape of a small altar. Then he laid the papers on top and set them afire. And as the flames devoured his unanswered questions, he followed their sparks aloft. Through his tears, he asked a question he had never asked before. "What do you want from me?" he asked. "You'll have to show me, because I have no idea where to start."

haven't seen you much this week," Juanita Rodriguez said to Nate Freeman. They sat in the balcony after her afternoon performance.

"Eddie and I been settin' up camp in a cave in the national forest. Rent's reasonable, and nobody can throw us outta *there.*"

"Am I on my own tomorrow night, then?" she asked.

"Nope. I'll be there, and Eddie's comin'. Wally Courier, too. That'll make it a group snoop!" He laughed at his own joke.

"Do they know what's going on?" she demanded. "Do they know about me?"

"No," he answered, confidently. "But Eddie goes everywhere I go. And I made a deal with Wally. I'm sick of bein' called paranoid."

"In this business, you can't let your feelings get in the way of good judgment," Conroy replied. "Or you end up dead . . . like your friend, Stephanie," the agent added, for emphasis.

"I got to do it," he insisted. "If I back out now, Wally

will tell the bishop, and I'll never live it down. Now I have to go, even if you don't."

"Well, then. You're on your own," she said. "I can't risk anyone else knowing my mission. But if you won't listen to reason, maybe you can at least get some photos, and then we'll have some ID's."

She handed him a Nikon N90, attached to the night-vision scope. "It amplifies available light six thousand times. And with the infrared illuminator, you can see when it's dark as pitch. Just remember, infrared is invisible from the side, but you can see its source if you look directly at it.

"The camera's loaded with high-speed film, thirty-six exposures, so be selective. Don't bother to unload it, just bring the whole thing back here after the late show Saturday night, and I'll take it from there."

She gave him another ticket. "Good luck," she said.

Doris Oberly was standing at the stained-glass bay window of her apartment in the Hope Center complex, watching a thunderstorm roar eastward from the mountains, when she noticed Bruce Davidson walking slowly up the path from the river. Even from a distance, it was clear he was totally soaked already, so another deluge would make no difference. But another fact was also clear, even at a distance. His gait told her something extremely significant had happened that day.

Since arriving, the FBI man had alternated between rushing here and there, and ambling aimlessly toward whatever was next. But as he approached the center after his day in the field, there was a bounce in his step she'd not seen before, which to her trained eye could only signify one thing—life!

211

Tears flooded her eyes as she grabbed some of her personal bath towels and rushed to meet him in the garden. *Professional distance, Doctor,* she reminded herself as sternly as she could manage. *Stay detached, or everybody just gets hurt.*

As she opened the back door, however, the addictionist glimpsed herself reflected in the glass and, by instinct, fixed her disheveled hair. *Whoa!* she thought as she settled herself down. *Does the doctor like the patient a little too much?* Nonetheless, when Davidson saw her coming, his response nearly unglued her.

He smiled.

With the fly rod over his shoulder, he looked like an ordinary fisherman returning from an enjoyable outing. It was hard to remember that this particular angler had made this particular trek because she had prescribed it.

"I lost one of your flies," he said, "and used up some of your tying supplies." He shivered from the cold as she wrapped the dry towels around him. "But I had the most amazing day. I wish I could show you, because I certainly can't put it into words."

"I can see it in your eyes," she said. "But I want to hear about it, too. Everything. Don't leave anything out."

"That would take hours," he replied. "And I'll freeze to death if I don't get into a hot shower in the next five minutes."

"No problem," she said. "We can talk tomorrow. But, tell me, how did you get so wet?"

Now his smile became a laugh. "She pulled me in!"

"She? Who?"

"The queen of the deep, to be precise," he replied. "The biggest river rainbow I've ever seen, or imagined. Took a

212

number twenty-two Trico, black-and-white. Fought her up and down that stretch until we were both so exhausted I ended up sitting in the water with the fish lying in my lap, gasping for dear life."

Doris had never seen him this animated, or even imagined that he *could* become this enthusiastic. *Is he manic? Has he been down there doing crazy things all day? Did I push him so hard, he decompensated?*

"How big?"

"Only her head would fit into the net."

"Bruce! You're exaggerating."

"I measured her. Nose to the vee in her tail, she stretched from the butt of your rod to the first guide."

He held the Sage out, for emphasis, and watched Doris's reaction; a big grin stretched across his face.

"That would make her over thirty inches!" she exclaimed, trying to envision a rainbow that large lurking in the pool she fished so often. Then, for the first time, she noticed the extraordinarily large scales still clinging to his jeans where the fish had rested. "Leviathan," she said.

"She has a name?" he asked. "You've seen her?"

"Only in my dreams," Oberly said, taking the Bible from his hand. "'Can you pull in the leviathan with a fishhook or tie down his tongue with a rope?'" she read. "'Can you put a cord through his nose or pierce his jaw with a hook? Will he keep begging you for mercy?'" She searched his face for a flash of recognition. "Evidently you didn't finish Job's whole story."

"I didn't have to," he said. "I experienced it."

"Nate, help."

Eddie's weak voice barely carried from the cave to the

213

stream below, where Nate Freeman was watering the horses. The distress cry was so soft, it didn't really register for a moment. When it did, the minister jumped enough to startle the horses whose reins he was holding.

"What?" he yelled up the cliff. When he got no response, he yelled again. Then, when the only sound he heard was the echo of his own voice, Freeman looped the reins haphazardly over two alders and scrambled straight up the incline, slipping and sliding in the gravel.

His friend was lying on his back, unconscious, at the mouth of the cave, his right hand clutching a rock.

"Eddie!" Nate hollered, feeling for a carotid pulse as he tried to elicit a response. *Slow pulse. Cool and clammy skin. Respiration, rapid and shallow. Why? What happened?*

Freeman rolled Hazard onto his side, placed his left arm under his face to keep him from choking, and his left leg over the right to keep him from rolling over. As he moved Eddie's left foot, he noticed a puncture in the heel support of the lightweight canvas climbing boots he was wearing.

Rattler! Freeman exclaimed, internally. *Explains the rock. But is it still alive? Is it still in here?*

He flicked the flint on the lighter he always carried, and immediately saw a semi-coiled three-foot-long pygmy rattlesnake, its head smashed and its body evidently dragged toward the entryway by its victim's attempt to escape.

Must've fainted, Freeman assured himself. *Venom don't work that fast. Have to get to that bite, though, right now.*

As the minister removed his friend's shoe and sock, the injured man started to stir. "Snake," he whispered. "In my sleeping bag. Never saw it until it was too late. Didn't know what the buzzing sound was."

"Rattles. End of the tail. But don't talk now. You fainted.

Most likely, venom never got past the canvas. But we can't take any chances. I got to cut you."

The preacher retrieved a small, razor-sharp knife from his pack, and held it over the flame from the lighter until the blade glowed red hot. "Sorry. But faithful are the wounds of a friend," he said, handing him the still-ignited lighter. "Hold this so I can see. But don't move. And don't wimp out on me, either."

He firmly grasped Eddie's left ankle in his left hand and made a single half-inch incision an eighth-inch deep along the axis of his leg, just inside the wound from the fang. He applied suction with his mouth, once, twice, and then again, at twenty-second intervals for two minutes. When he was finished, he dropped two drops of antibiotic into the wound and covered it with a bandage. Finally, he wrapped Eddie's lower calf with gauze strips, taking care to impede, but not eliminate, the flow of blood below the constrictor.

"You've done this before," Eddie said, when Nate was finished.

"Nope, but I seen it on video when I trained to be an emergency medical technician."

"Am I going to die?"

"Not from the snake, but maybe if you faint again and fall down the cliff."

"What's going to happen?"

"If it don't swell up terrible, or turn purple or green, the only thing you got to worry about is keeping the cut clean."

"If it does swell up?"

"Then we get back on our horses and find some antivenin for that pygmy rattlesnake that got one fang into your heel. Luckily, you got its head before it really nailed you."

He stabbed the snake with the trident they'd made for spearing trout, then stuck the handle in the ground just outside the entrance to the cave. "That'll be the new symbol; Eddie the serpent killer lurks in these rocks!"

Hazard chuckled nervously. "Nate," he said. "Would you build a fire? I'm kind of cold."

"'Course. Anything else?"

"Please check the rest of the cave for more snakes."

"Every square inch. But this one's rare enough. Don't worry. Just try to relax. Everything's going to be all right." Freeman used the lighter to ignite the dry sticks already stacked in place.

"I hope so. But every time I relax, something else happens."

"That's the way the enemy works. We let down our guard, he strikes. When he leaves us alone, that's when it's time to worry."

"Why's that?"

"'Cause it means we ain't no threat to his program."

The cowboy poet picked up his guitar and strummed gently. The chords filled the cave, then the valley, and drifted toward the starlit sky as Eddie Hazard relaxed and then slowly drifted off to sleep.

Every fifteen minutes, Nate Freeman checked his friend's vital signs, as well as the tightness of the lymph restrictor. At midnight, he checked the wound itself, and found it unchanged. *Thank you, Lord,* he muttered. *'Cause I don't know how we would've made it to the hospital in time.*

***

"Looking for some action?" Kelly Mitchell asked the blue-eyed, blonde, well-conditioned young woman who had taken the stool next to her at Alice's, just before the bar's closing.

"Depends," Clare Conroy replied.

"Ditto to that, honey," the auburn-haired prostitute said. "You want to work this town, you need a license."

"Says who?"

"Charlotte. You want to sign on, I can arrange it. Split's sixty-forty. Otherwise, if you want to stay pretty, stay off this street."

Conroy sipped the Perrier and lemon she'd ordered, taking in the other woman's striking beauty and wondering how she could possibly tolerate selling it night after night.

"Already got a license," Conroy replied, checking the bar area one more time to be sure it was vacant. "I'll show you, if we can talk more privately."

"Get out of my face," the younger woman said. "I got work to do."

"Such as blackmailing Kevin White?"

"What?"

"Because blackmailing becomes you . . . but mostly because it's worth as much as five thousand dollars."

Kelly stared at Conroy, speechless.

"Now, shall we continue this conversation in private?"

"I have a room upstairs. Actually, I have a room upstairs in every hotel in town. Take your pick."

"Over there in the corner is fine. What I have to say won't take long."

They walked to the booth and sat down.

"I'm listening," Kelly said.

217

"Okay, see if this sounds familiar," Conroy said, handing the prostitute her mini-recorder and an earphone.

"I'd like to kill the jerk, Kelly . . ." the tape began.

"Freeman? You almost did, three days ago."

"No, I mean Hawkins. Thinks just because he pays my salary I got to kiss his boots all the time. Even when I succeed, I fail."

"You put the minister in the hospital. Did he want you to blast him on Main Street in broad daylight?"

"That's enough," Kelly said. "You working for Hawkins, too? He'll kill Leonard."

"I don't know Hawkins."

"Then what's your angle?"

"Let's say I'm simply interested in what's going on behind the scenes in the sleepy town of Raptor, Colorado, and I think you could help me."

"You haven't given me one good reason why I should."

"To save your own skin."

"From what?"

"Spending a few years behind bars. By the time you get out, you won't be too pretty yourself."

Conroy reached into her pocket and produced an FBI photo ID, which listed her name as C. W. Montclair. Kelly was obviously convinced.

"Cooperate," Conroy said, "and we never met. Refuse, and I've already got enough to nail you—prostitution, collusion, blackmail, and I haven't even begun to dig."

"What do I have to do?"

"For starters, I want everything Leonard Price knows about the recent trials and tribulations of Nathan Freeman, including what happened the other day in the shoot-

218

out and how this Hawkins fellow was connected to it. Who is he, anyway?"

"Runs the bank behind the scenes. Wants to run the town."

"Is that all?"

"No. He's set up a big-time week-long poker game, starting Saturday night, in the Cathedral Casino. At least one high roller coming in from New York, and Skip Sanders is coming from Acapulco."

"How do you know Sanders?"

"Used to be a regular client. Nice guy. Big tipper. He's staying for the whole month of October."

"How do you know that?"

"He's reserved my services the whole time. Thousand bucks a night. Not bad for a high school dropout, eh? Better than the FBI."

"True, but at least I don't have to worry about getting HIV from any Tom, Dick, or Harry who walks in the room."

"They might catch it from me," Kelly replied, staring evenly at Conroy, who could hardly believe what the younger woman had just said. "Goes with the territory," the prostitute continued. "Half my friends have it already, and the other half are just waiting their turn."

"I can help you get out of here once I have the information I need," Conroy offered.

"I'm not interested in leaving. Hookers get hooked, too, and I don't mean on the sex. The real issue is how much can I make working nights? A hundred thousand, two hundred thousand a year? What am I supposed to do, settle down in Podunk, U.S.A., and read the *Ladies' Home Journal* while I wait to die?"

"Sorry," Conroy said. "I find your lifestyle hard to fathom."

"Ditto," Kelly replied. "But I suppose there must be some kind of rush when you take down a big-time crook."

"Wouldn't know," Conroy lied. "I just get assigned to places like Raptor, to figure out which, if any, laws are being broken by various small-time villains. Then I file my report and go on to the next case."

"Well, then, let's get it over with, so you can move on to something bigger, and I can get the FBI out of my face. How long do I have to cooperate?"

"Three days. I'll meet you here Friday night, midnight, and give you a mike. Don't worry, it'll be very creative, totally camouflaged. In fact, I'm wearing one right now and you never even suspected."

"Show me," Kelly said, nervously, eyeing Conroy's body-suit incredulously.

"Trade secret. You'll have one for yourself in forty-eight hours."

"Who you after?"

"Hawkins, sounds like. And maybe you can get Sanders to talk about the bank deal. Otherwise, I don't know."

"Not Price?"

"You like him?"

"He's my insurance policy. I keep him happy, he lets me operate."

"I can't promise anything. I think your best bet is to try to save your own skin."

26

will lift up mine eyes unto the hills, from whence cometh my help," Nate Freeman read to Eddie Hazard, as the sun began to dry the valley's morning dew. "My help cometh from the LORD, which made heaven and earth. He will not suffer thy foot to be moved. . . . The sun shall not smite thee by day, nor the moon by night. The LORD shall preserve thee from all evil: he shall preserve thy soul. The LORD shall preserve thy going out and thy coming in from this time forth, and even for evermore."

"Sometimes it doesn't make sense to me," Eddie said, lying on his side atop his sleeping bag. "Why do we keep getting smitten, to use one of the words you just read?"

"Smitten, but preserved. That's the whole point. You could be lying in a hospital, venom eatin' its way through your leg. Instead, you're eatin' your way through that oatmeal."

"I'm not complaining," Hazard replied. "Just trying to understand how it all works."

***

"I guess you died and went to heaven," Doris Oberly said to Bruce Davidson, who was sitting in the leather chair in her office.

"True," he answered, "but it was more than that. Heaven came to me, like you hoped."

"You found the answers you were looking for?"

"No, but I found some better questions."

"Such as?"

"Do you hunt like a lion? Do you see the doe give birth? Do you make the eagle fly or build his nest on high? But the real kicker was, 'Will the one who contends with the Almighty correct him? Let him who accuses God answer him!'"

Bruce paused, and looked deeply into his therapist's eyes. "When I got to the root of it, I discovered that his questions were better than mine."

"Every question led to a better one?"

"More than that. All my questions led to the same choice—either I would recognize him as God, or I would have to create my own universe."

"And?"

"Not being very creative, the former seemed more rational to me than the latter."

"What happened to all your 'whys'?"

"They evaporated into thin air. Actually, I burned them on a little altar I made, down by the river."

"So they're gone?"

"I've started over, with a clean slate. So far, there's only one thing written on it: What do you want me to do?"

"That's good, but it's just another way of asking why," she said. "Some people shake their fist at God and demand a reason for everything that happens. Others gaze in his direction and seek to understand."

"I've moved into the second group."

"You've made a decision to turn your will and your life over to the care of God as you understand him."

"Step three? That's all?"

"Have you made a searching and fearless moral inventory of yourself?"

"Isn't that what you've forced me to do?"

"Yesterday was just the beginning. One day before the face of God cannot heal all the wounds."

"Why not? I thought he was the great physician."

"I'm thinking about the wounds you've given others, all the people you've forced to meet your needs without regard to theirs."

"What kind of needs?"

"It's easier to show you than to describe it," she replied, walking to the closet, and returning with a short piece of pine two-by-four, a nail, and a hammer. "Here," she said. "Drive in the nail."

After he had done that, she said, "Now, pull it out."

When he had accomplished that, she said, "Now, pull out the hole."

"Get serious. The molecules are rearranged. The wood will never be the same again," he replied.

"So it is with your friends," she said. "You had a series of losses, driving spikes into your psyche, some of which you managed to pull out. But the holes were still there, and you needed your friends to fill them."

"It's wrong to have needs?"

"We all have needs, but it's wrong to require others to meet them."

"You've never done that?"

"I have. I did it constantly before I realized what was happening. For example, I came to understand that my cousin's sexual advances were a response to the messages I was leaving all over the place: Won't somebody please love me?"

"Are you exonerating him?"

"No, but I've forgiven him and tried to fill the hole with more positive, healthy, constructive, mutually-fulfilling relationships." She stopped and looked directly at him. "Bruce, the issues aren't just between you and God. Your character defects have hurt others, perhaps many others. But are you willing to admit these wrongs and let him take them away, the same way he took away all your questions?"

"You're tearing down the progress I made yesterday."

"I want you to build on it. You have to see yesterday as a new beginning. But there's still a long way to go before the power you've tapped is internalized enough to use it to help someone else."

"Use both hands if you have to," Nate Freeman instructed Eddie Hazard, who had been trying to learn how to shoot the minister's .357 Magnum Ruger Black-hawk. But every time Hazard pulled the trigger, he closed his eyes and flinched so badly he never touched the McIntosh apple serving as their target, even from fifteen feet away.

"You got to keep your wrist firm and your eyes open, or you might as well be shootin' blanks," Freeman said, pulling Black Bart from his holster. "Watch."

He raised the .45-caliber six-gun, pulled the hammer

back, and aimed carefully, holding the firearm with both hands. At the shot, the apple exploded. "See, it's easy," he said. "Just takes a little practice."

"Power is power," Cynthia Stamford said to Stanley Hawkins. "You use guns and bombs. Hitler used words. With this group, I use spiritual power. It's all the same in the end."

"I disagree," Hawkins replied. "The real power is money. After we buy out every casino in Raptor, twenty million a month will have to pass through our hands. It's a real gold mine!"

"So what's the problem?"

"Costellini wants another video. The Lockwood tape is selling great, but suicide doesn't satisfy snuff buyers for long, even if she did it on a satanic altar. The next one needs more violence . . . brutality."

"Any candidates?" she asked.

"Only the preacher. But now that he's not living in the parsonage, he just appears and disappears like a timber ghost."

"Too bad we don't have him now. We could do it tonight on the grave of Elyse Morais. These people really believe in the curse, and every time we feed it another victim, their faith is strengthened that much more."

"How can you do all the hocus-pocus if you don't believe it?"

"The only real issue is whether or not it works. The end justifies the means."

"Harold," Bruce Davidson said to his new friend, as they walked through the compound's rose garden after supper. "You're leaving Sunday, so I need to pick your brain about step four."

"Tough one, like I said in group. Self-inflicted dissection, that's what it felt like. You think you're ready?"

"I thought so until I met with Doris this morning. Yesterday, I finally broke through and it felt so good. But now she says it's just the foundation for the rest. It nearly killed me to get to step three. If she's right, I can't imagine how I will ever finish the program."

"The program isn't finishable, until your higher power is finished with you. But your ego will desperately cling to every shred of self-respect. For me, that was the biggest hindrance. I didn't want to believe I'd hurt all those people."

"Can you give me an example?"

"My mother, my wife, my kids, and all my patients. I wallowed in self-pity because I believed my mother had forced me to become a doctor. But I expected my wife to bow and scrape once I became a doctor. I neglected my kids because I let my patients take all my time. I projected all these conflicts onto my clients, and then charged them a hundred bucks an hour to address my issues instead of their own."

"I can't believe it was intentional."

"I didn't even realize I was doing it until I stopped blaming everybody and everything but myself for my unhappiness. When I did the inventory and saw myself for the first time, I felt the pain I had inflicted on others, because every character defect had a person's name attached to it, to whom I must now make amends, if possible."

"Haven't you just exchanged one load for another?"

"Seems that way, but it's not the way it works out,

because you carry the first load by yourself. But when you start making amends, some former adversaries become allies and the loneliness that used to be filled with whiskey is filled with love."

"Wally," Nate Freeman said. "You'll freeze to death in that suit and tie."

"Where are we going, Nate?" Courier replied, grabbing a sweater and wool overcoat from the hooks by the door.

"Behind the scenes, like I promised. That's why we're goin' on horseback, just in case they have sentries on the road."

"Sentries? I can't be involved with anything questionable."

"Okay. I'll give it to you straight, if you swear to keep it confidential."

When Courier nodded, Freeman continued. "Sixty-one years ago, a Haitian witch named Elyse Morais put a curse on Raptor, just before she was hanged from the steeple of Community Church. Every full moon since, the local coven has renewed that curse by holdin' a ceremony on her grave at midnight. Usually, there's a sacrifice. It is possible that last month, the sacrifice was human."

When Freeman said that, Courier stepped backward and his mouth dropped open. For a moment, the interim minister stared at his predecessor; then he fixed his eyes on Eddie Hazard, who was standing behind Freeman, holding the reins of three horses. Hazard nodded emphatically.

"When I use the word conspiracy," Freeman said, "this is part of it. But no newspaper's gonna print that. Don't worry, we'll stay back in the timber. Nobody will even know we're there."

"You're sure they aren't just a bunch of kooks?"

227

"They're absolutely serious."

"And if I'm not convinced, you'll give this up?"

"Count on it."

"Okay," Courier said, climbing aboard the third horse. "But I'll hold you to it."

27

What are they doing, Nate?" Wally Courier asked. Two men dressed in black robes were circling a small cluster of people. Courier, Freeman, and Eddie Hazard had watched the group gather at the grave of Elyse Morais in the last half hour before midnight.

"They're closing the circle," Freeman said. "So they can commune with the devil without danger from any forces their worship might release."

The three men crouched in the deep pines, a hundred yards east of the group. As they watched, the same two men lit a fire; a woman, obviously the leader, carried a lamb to the monument. She laid the animal on the slab and held it there, as the others began to move slowly around it, counter-clockwise, chanting, swaying, moaning. Above the low murmur of the human voices a football field away, the forlorn bleating of the lamb could be heard plainly, echoing off the cliff behind the cemetery.

Freeman, who had begun snapping photos moments

earlier, noticed his colleague's level of interest. "Here," he said. "With this you can see like it's daylight!"

The new minister took the camera-mounted night-vision scope from Freeman and looked through it for a few seconds. "Where'd you get this?" he said. "It's amazing!"

"Mail order," Freeman lied. "Russian military surplus. With the cold war as good as dead, Boris must be tryin' to turn hardware into greenbacks. Keep watchin'," he continued, waving off Courier's attempt to hand the unit back. "You're the one needs convincin'."

Three hundred yards southwest of the ritual, Clare Conroy crouched in the underbrush, using her night-vision glasses to watch and earphones to listen as the boom mike recorded the event.

The leader faced away from Conroy. "Behold the sacrificial lamb," she said, lifting the whimpering animal toward the sky. "A lamb without blemish or spot, to honor the memory of Elyse Morais. We renew her curse," she proclaimed, as she slit the animal's throat, "and release her spirit to roam this village another month."

The blood filled a small channel and ran into a silver chalice held by a young woman kneeling at the altar's corner.

I know that voice, Conroy thought, straining to see more clearly through the glasses.

"From Therion, the great oracle," the woman said. "These words of truth we dedicate to her memory: 'Imminent over me thy hatred hangs; / Thy slow blood trickles on my swollen sides, / The curdling purple where those poison fangs struck, slays desire; and only death abides. / Imminent over me thy hatred hangs!'"

The group joined arms and moved rhythmically around the circle, their volume growing with each passing minute. "Baphomet," they repeated. "Baphomet, come." Again and again they said it as if actually expecting the goat-headed god from ancient days to appear.

Bored by the repetition, Conroy switched off the recorder but continued watching through the night goggles. In case something really did happen, she didn't want to miss it. *On the other hand,* she thought, *if this Baphomet character really does make an appearance, he might not show up on this scope anyway.*

By mistake, Wally Courier pressed the trigger of the infrared illuminator. Immediately, the scene in his viewfinder brightened, bathing the dancers in macabre green as their movements became more brisk and their incantation more urgent.

In Conroy's glasses, magnified fifteen thousand times, the small red dot in the dark forest behind the coven seemed like a torch, though with the naked eye she could hardly make it out.

Nate! she begged. *Don't use that part. You don't need it. They might see you if . . .*

Yet even as she silently exhorted the minister to turn the signal off, she saw the woman point, and heard her shout, "Randy, Peter. An intruder. Find him, and bring him to me!"

"Nate," Wally Courier whispered. "Something's happening. The woman is pointing in this direction, and two guys are walking right toward me, almost like they can see me."

"Ain't possible," Nate replied. "It's pitch black in here, and they been looking at a fire. There's no way, unless . . ."

Freeman grabbed the camera. "Unless you been pushing this trigger here."

"I have," Courier admitted, sheepishly. "You didn't say not to. But how could they see it? It's black."

"All except for this," he said, activating the device for a moment right into Courier's eyes. "Infrared," he said.

Quickly Freeman analyzed their options, then he told the others. "We run, they'll hear us and sound the alarm. We'll never get away. But these guys will follow the red dot wherever it goes. Stay low, as low as you can get. Don't move; don't hardly breathe. But you better pray, 'cause they get their hands on us, they ain't likely to treat us kindly."

With that, Freeman crawled away into the underbrush. Thirty yards to the south, he activated the illuminator again long enough to snap a picture of his pursuers.

"There!" Randy said. "I just saw it again. Let's go."

For about ten minutes, Nate Freeman managed to elude the human hounds, leading them away from his friends. But when it became obvious they were safe and he wasn't going to get away, he stood up and said, "Howdy, boys. I'm just out lookin' for an eye of toad and tongue of newt. How 'bout you?"

"Shut up, scum," Stebbins said, grabbing the camera from the minister's hands. "You should've got out while the gettin' was good."

They tied his hands behind his back and triumphantly led him to the group. When they saw who it was, they roared their approval with diabolical glee. "Well, well," Aradia said, taking the camera and throwing it into the fire. "The great one has provided a better sacrifice . . . our enemy."

"Your enemy is the one true God," Freeman said. "I am only his servant."

"Silence!" she screamed, slapping him across the face. "Or I will cut out your tongue."

Stunned, Freeman shook his head, quickly surveying the faces of the group, all crowding around him. But the shock of the blow was nothing compared to the shock of seeing in the circle two of Community Church's most faithful members, Ellie and Sarah Smith.

"What are you doing here?" he started to say, but was interrupted by another slap. This time as he tried to shake off the sting, he realized that the Smith sisters and all the others in the group were wearing the choir robes from Community Church.

Does their blasphemy have no bounds?

The woman spoke again. "What shall we do with our victim?"

"Kill him," one said.

"Slowly," a second chimed in.

Other suggestions came fast and furious.

"Slit his throat."

"Cut out his heart."

"Burn him at the stake."

"Hang him from a tree!"

"Hang him from *a cross!*" Ellie Smith said, grinning.

"Yes," Aradia grinned. "The perfect execution!"

She turned to the men who had captured Nate, and commanded them, "Cut a stipes and patibulum."

She said to the woman still holding the chalice, "Get the video camera, battery, and lights. We'll give Perelli his new video all right, and watch him lose his lunch."

***

233

For Clare Conroy, suddenly everything became clear. *That witch is Dr. Florence Bradley! She must be using this group to continue her eugenics work. And Perelli's in this, too. Hawkins must be his alias! That explains why Nate's been having such a tough time. Get in Perelli's way and he'd sooner step on you than step around.*

As Conroy watched, wondering how to help Nate out of his predicament without putting the investigation at risk, the men returned, dragging a crudely-hewn pine cross roughly six feet long. They leaned it against the tombstone of Elyse Morais, and made the victim stand before it.

The woman returned with four lightweight battery-operated floodlights which members of the group quickly mounted on tripods, two in front of Freeman, one behind him, and the fourth on top of the cross.

The witch, meanwhile, had fashioned a wreath of wild rose vines. When all was ready, she nodded for the camera to begin taping, and then walked to Freeman and jammed the crown down upon his forehead hard enough for its thorns to penetrate his skin. Blood began to trickle from the wounds as the woman said, "Cursed is every man who hangs on a tree."

"My Lord broke every curse at Calvary," Freeman replied.

"Then let him save you from the teeth of this one," she growled. "There is no lord but Lucifer, to whom your life is forfeit."

In the woman's eyes, as they reflected the dancing fire behind him, Nate Freeman saw something he'd never seen before. Beyond malevolence, anger, hatred, and spite—or any motive he'd ever recognized in himself or anyone else—he saw cold, dispassionate evil.

"Father, forgive them," he prayed. "They don't know what they're doing."

"We know exactly what we're doing," she screamed. "Prepare the victim!"

Immediately, twelve pairs of hands ripped at Freeman's clothing until only his underwear remained. As the tormentors tore away piece after piece, he said to each, "Fear not those who slay the body, but those who slay both body and soul in hell."

As a result, the group was worked into an emotional frenzy by the time Aradia picked up a horsewhip. "Turn him around," she ordered. When this was done, she cracked the whip off his upper back, first one side then the other, until the wounds were oozing blood. But the minister did not flinch, nor did his knees buckle.

"Bind him to it," she commanded, and immediately his hands were tied to the crosspiece and his waist to the stake. She walked to her victim, grinning. "Where is your Lord?" she asked. "He cannot save you now, because"—she grabbed his hair and jerked his head back—"because he is dead. But Lucifer will save you, if you will worship him."

"Jesus is Lord," he said. "I worship only him."

She grabbed the knife and raised it. But her mouth said, in a voice not her own, "Defile him."

Bradley turned to see who had spoken. Then, obviously shaken, she heard it add, "He must drink his last communion."

Obediently, she laid down the knife and picked up the chalice filled with lamb's blood. Again she grabbed Freeman by the hair, and, forcing his head backward hard against the stake, poured the liquid into his mouth.

Before she could move, however, Nate Freeman spat the blood back in her face.

"Blasphemer!" she cried, grabbing the knife again. "Die!"

But just as the dagger started downward, Clare Conroy leaped from the hiding place to which she had crept while the group had become totally absorbed with the rite.

"Freeze," she yelled. "FBI. You are all under arrest."

As if on cue, the coven scattered into the darkness. Only the leader was left to face the new intruder when Conroy stepped into the glare of the lights. The witch's mouth dropped open. "Clare Conroy. What are you doing here?" she said.

"You took the words right out of my mouth, Dr. Bradley. Now, don't make me use this," Conroy replied, brandishing her Beretta.

"You underestimate the power of darkness!" Bradley laughed. "You have broken our circle," she shrieked, "and violated our sacred space! Now you, too, will die!"

Suddenly, both of Conroy's arms were seized from behind. She struggled to free herself from the powerful grip, but when she twisted to see who it was, there was no one there. What is this? Some kind of trick? Conroy tried harder to pull away, falling to her knees as she did so. Yet, as soon as she hit the ground, strong hands made her stand again. She turned a second time to see two men holding her by the forearms. *Must have been the black robes,* she thought, as one of them tried to grab her gun.

At that moment, the agent heard Nate Freeman say, "In the name of Jesus, I command you to free her." Conroy pulled the trigger with all her might. As the gun spoke, the man holding her right arm yelled, grabbed his left leg, fell to the ground, and started to crawl away.

236

The witch raised her dagger and rushed at Conroy, who pulled free from her second assailant, rolled on the ground, and fired a quick shot toward Bradley. The doctor dropped the knife and staggered backward into the dark, holding her right hand. Conroy turned, expecting an assault from the second fellow, only to find he had vanished into the darkness.

Got to get Bradley, Conroy urged herself as she darted past the fire into the graveyard. But as the agent paused to allow her eyes to adjust, she heard Nate Freeman say, "They're already gone."

Clare stared into the night for a moment longer, her handgun ready, searching for a target. Then she realized that the minister's plight had to take precedence for the moment.

Embarrassed for the first time by Freeman's near-nakedness, Conroy tried to focus only on his bonds as she cut him loose, from behind. Two things hindered her work: working in the shadows with a fairly dull pocketknife, and the fact that both the rope and her hands were becoming increasingly slippery as blood dripped on them from the minister's back.

"I'm sorry," she said, fighting her increasing nausea. "I shouldn't have given you the equipment. You shouldn't even be here. If anybody should be hanging here, it should be me."

Freeman's knees buckled when the last rope broke, and he started to fall toward the fire. Conroy sprung to his side and caught him, just as he steadied himself. As a result, for a moment they ended up in a rather awkward embrace.

Freeman stepped back and looked at Clare's blood-stained, fleece-lined lambskin coat. "Sorry," he said. "It's ruined."

"Here," she replied, removing the coat and wrapping it around him. "It's the least I can do. Now, if you huddle by the fire you should be able to keep warm enough while I go after the others. Maybe I can still catch up to the one I wounded."

"Ain't no use," Freeman replied. "They're all gone. The second fella picked up the one you shot and carried him off like he was a sack of potatoes. There are powers beyond what we can imagine."

In the distance, a vehicle started, roared its engine, and tore off down the gravel road.

"I believe you," she said. She reached out and gently removed his thorny crown.

"So do I," a voice said, as Wally Courier and Eddie Hazard stepped into the circle of firelight. Instinctively, Conroy whirled and leveled her gun at the men, who froze in place.

"Don't shoot," Eddie said. "We're on your side." He stared at Clare, then added, "Miss Rodriguez. I thought something funny was up when I saw you pass that note to Nate yesterday."

"Hopefully, you were the only one who noticed," she replied, lowering the weapon. "You've stumbled into the middle of an FBI investigation, but you're the only people in Raptor who know my cover. Either you keep it secret, or we call this off. Somebody could get seriously hurt."

She paused, glanced toward Freeman, and then at the other two. "Somebody already has been seriously hurt. Why didn't you two intervene?"

"We were going to, right when you showed up," Hazard replied. He handed Nate a sweatshirt, his hat, and a second pair of jeans, which he'd left in his saddlebags. "But there were so many of them, we were afraid they might overpower us. Maybe a gun makes courage a little easier."

"I'm sorry, Nate," Courier interrupted. "I doubted you, but you still nearly gave your life to save me. Come spend the night in the parsonage. Tomorrow I'll move out."

"Not a good idea," Conroy commented. "If we're going to keep this investigation alive, it should be business as usual, especially since the bad guys think you're on their side. Nate," she continued, "you really should see a doctor tonight."

"I just saw one," he laughed. "But she didn't do me much good! What happens to all our work if I walk into a hospital and try to explain these wounds? I'm an EMT. I can take care of myself."

"Until Sunday?" Conroy asked. "I think by then we can set a trap."

"Forever," Freeman replied, "if it'll mean saving my church. Besides, there's nothing like a good cave when you've just been crucified."

28

"ello, Fred?" Clare said into her MicroTac Ultra Lite. "When we finish, I need to download some files."

"Good hunting at the cemetery?"

"Pretty good. About an hour's worth of audio, and twelve pictures with my telephoto eagle."

"You didn't use the Nikon?"

"Loaned it to Freeman and it ended up fried."

"What about him?"

"He almost ended up dead . . . crucified, to be exact."

"Crucified? Pretty poor joke, Clare."

"You'll see for yourself. Maybe then you'll finally be convinced. You'll see something else, too. Actually some*one*; specifically, Dr. Florence Bradley, who just happens to be the priestess of the satanic group in question."

"What?"

"Not only that, Bradley said she was videotaping Nate's execution for none other than George Perelli. He's called Stanley Hawkins around here. Maybe he's still connected with Costellini, but I'll bet he's embezzling big time."

"We'll check it out. Anything else?"

"Skip Sanders is coming to town tomorrow."

"How do you know that?"

"From a local hooker, whose services he's booked. I had her nailed—prostitution, blackmail, collusion. So I traded immunity if she would wear a mike for three days."

"Listen, Clare. It sounds like things are getting pretty hot up there. I'm coming up. Somebody has to receive what our new undercover agent transmits. When do you need the mike?"

"Midnight tonight."

"I'll drive down Main Street in a twenty-foot Winnebago camper at 10 P.M."

"But Perelli and Bradley know you, Fred." She added thoughtfully, "You can bet Bradley's already told him I was there last night."

"Yeah, you better operate from now on as Juanita Rodriguez. I'll come as a retiree with gray hair, beard, spectacles, and cane—.44-magnum cane to be exact. If I don't see you on the street, I'll meet you in the Regis Casino at 11 P.M."

"George," Florence Bradley said. "We've got a problem."

"It better be big, to interrupt me here."

They were standing in the Cathedral Casino's Upper Room poker parlor, where Perelli was supervising final preparations for the upcoming game.

"You need to see this," she said, pulling out a videotape. "As soon as possible."

"Don't have time today. Tell me about it," he replied, taking the cassette from her.

"You have time," she said pointedly. "Last night, when we were meeting at the cemetery, Freeman showed up. He

241

had a high-tech camera, which I trashed when we caught him. And then I decided to get rid of him, too, and film it, so you'd have some raw material for Costellini. Seemed to be the perfect solution."

"Maybe I *will* watch this," Perelli grinned, walking over to a small integrated video player and monitor. "Take a break, boys," he said to the men who were laying carpet. "Take a half-hour break, on me."

When the others had left, Perelli ran the tape, with Bradley watching over his shoulder. "Great stuff, Doc. Didn't know you did impressions."

"The voice came . . . from somewhere else," she said. "Actually, from someone else, but I don't care to go into it."

"And what about *that* voice?" Perelli asked, as Conroy's yell could be heard off-camera, followed by the screen going blank. "It sounded like she said—"

"FBI," Bradley nodded. "That's why I brought this in. Just when I was going to kill Freeman, Clare Conroy jumped out of the bushes with a gun in her hand. She shot me in the hand." The doctor showed Perelli her bandaged hand.

"Conroy!" Perelli roared. "How did she find us?"

"I have no idea. But maybe she only found *me*. How could she know about you? I was lucky to get away last night, but I can't take any chances with the project. The girls and I stayed up all night packing. They're waiting outside in the van. I'm out of here. If you're smart, you'll get out, too."

"Are you kidding?" he laughed. "Run from a woman I could break in half with my bare hands? I have a score to settle with that broad," he continued, rubbing his scar and

242

suddenly realizing the identity of the Spanish woman he had seen bump into Freeman on Wednesday morning. "And I think I know where to find her. Make a nice surprise for Costellini. He wasn't too happy when the little lady shut down his best laundry and cut off his supply of girls from Jamaica. Maybe Vincent and I will take in a matinee tomorrow, then pay our respects to the star of the show."

"You want to fool with her, that's your business," Bradley said. "Here's the keys to the mansion. The master tapes are in the safe. By nightfall, I'll be as far from here as I can get."

"Nate, the horses are gone!" Eddie Hazard said, as he clambered back inside the cave where Nate Freeman was still lying in his sleeping bag.

The minister groaned as he turned to face his friend.

"Didn't you hobble 'em last night?"

"I thought so, but it was awful dark, and I kept wondering if that lion was hanging around. Maybe I didn't tie them tight enough. Now what are we going to do? You're in no condition to chase 'em, and I wouldn't know where to start."

"I should let you hunt 'em all day, just to learn yer lesson," Freeman chuckled. "But there's a better way. Bring the oat bucket. Let's just hope they're still in range."

The men made their way to the edge of the small meadow just below their campsite. "Now," Freeman said, "beat on that bucket with a stick."

Within thirty seconds the first horse came into view, with the other hot on its heels. They trotted directly to

Hazard, who gave them each a handful of oats, as he grabbed their reins.

"I never would've thought of that," Eddie said.

"Me neither. Learned it from my daddy. Works most every time, unless they've wandered too far away. Then you might never see 'em again, especially the ones that was wild to begin with."

This time, Freeman supervised as Eddie hobbled the horses. Then the minister said, "Kind of like us and God. We want to wander. He wants to keep us close, so when it's time to give us a treat we ain't off somewhere runnin' wild."

"Is that what we've been doing?"

"Maybe a little. Last night, when I thought I was going to die, all I could think of was Annie. How she tried to warn me. How she would feel puttin' me in the ground. What she would do afterward. If she would marry somebody else. Crazy things like that. And I promised myself if I lived through the night, I'd go and ask her to forgive me for treatin' her the way I have."

"Funny," Eddie replied. "When I got bit by that snake, all I could think of was Karen. Here I was maybe dying in a remote mountain cave, instead of being home with her. I wonder if it's too late."

"Only way to find out," Nate said, "is to go see her. Last night we promised we wouldn't show our faces in Raptor till it's time to work the plan Sunday afternoon. You can stay here, or you can ride out with me, but I know what I got to do. I'm headin' for Pueblo."

"Don't want to stay here alone and get eaten," Eddie replied. "But I'm not too anxious to let Karen have me for lunch, either. I don't know."

"All you can do is try to make amends. If she don't want to forgive you, that's her business. All God asks is that you risk it and leave the results to him."

"I talked it over with Harold," Bruce said to Doris Oberly. "And what he said was pretty scary. Is it really necessary to start another list, one that might be even longer than the first?"

"Scary is the operative word. It's necessary for the same reason it's so scary. Tell me who you are."

"Forty-one-year-old FBI bureau chief, instructor of psychology, gourmet cook, fly fisherman, and, I thought, a recovering alcoholic."

"How about orphan, widower, and contender with the Almighty?"

"Those, too. What's your point?"

"You've just made it for me. The real Bruce Davidson is obscured by his personas. A searching moral inventory is the only way to recover your real identity. But the personas you evict will leave the premises kicking and screaming that you will never survive without them."

"What are you talking about? Personas? I thought I needed to make a list of all the *persons* I have wronged, find them, and make amends."

"That comes later. If you just chop the tree down, it'll grow up again from the same roots. But if you eradicate the root, you can keep the tree from growing back. In step four, you need to identify root causes without worrying about the implications. After that, we can talk about the wrongs that have resulted, and what to do about them."

"Your diagnosis, Doctor?"

"I can only guide you away from the pitfalls. You'll have

to guide yourself toward the truth," she replied. "But you could start with the seven deadly sins: pride, greed, lust, anger, gluttony, envy, and sloth. Or, if you prefer a psychological model, I believe you'll find that root causes are usually misdirected natural drives—for survival, security, significance, or sex.

"For me," she continued, "the root was my struggle for significance. After Mom and Dad died, I was suddenly a nobody, no longer the daughter of two successful parents, but an adolescent set adrift in a world that didn't seem to notice or care. I vowed to make them notice even if I couldn't make them care. So, gradually, everything I did—from graduating valedictorian, to becoming a doctor, to marrying David, to building the nicest house in the subdivision, to becoming a party animal—was designed, at least subconsciously, to feed my ego's desperate need for significance.

"With each new achievement, my awareness of the need increased, because as my list of 'if onlys' got shorter, the emptiness got deeper, along with the pain, which I tried to dull with alcohol and drugs."

"So, how did you finally overcome it?"

"I haven't. Recovery is a continual searching and fearless moral inventory, or we'll substitute new lies for old ones."

"I don't think I have the energy," Davidson replied. "I've been just barely surviving."

She nodded, knowingly, and walked to her closet, returning in a moment with an exercise unit. "Here," she said, handing him the spring-loaded tube. "Put one end on the floor next to the chair, push down on the other end lightly, and keep it compressed."

Bruce did as she directed. Doris walked back to her desk and sat on its corner, watching. After about a minute, when his arm began to tremble slightly, she said, "Playing the persona game is a lot like what you're doing. At first, it doesn't seem very difficult to maintain all the fronts in order to prevent others from knowing who you really are."

Now Bruce's arm was quaking as he continued pressing down on the exerciser.

"But eventually," she continued, "you become so exhausted that all you can manage is survival."

"Arghh," he yelled, letting the exerciser go. He began to massage his upper arm, as he stared at her.

"Let me see if I have this right," he said. "You want me to risk exhausting myself in this process so I'll have more energy to invest in being who I really am?"

She nodded.

"Any guarantees?" he asked.

"Only the one hanging around your neck," she replied. "Hope, personalized and actualized. You asked God what he wanted you to do. Maybe this is your answer."

29

Nate," Annie Freeman cried, when she answered her doorbell. "What a nice . . ." She stopped mid-sentence, shocked by her husband's appearance. She reached out to touch the ugly gashes on his forehead.

"That ain't the worst of it," he said, following her through the door. "Look at this." He peeled off his shirt, revealing numerous severe welts on his back, along with several deeper wounds, still oozing blood.

For a moment, her medical training took over; she led him into the bathroom where there was more light. "These are dirty, Nate. We should go to the emergency room."

"No," Nate replied.

"My insurance might cover it."

"That ain't it. What if the newspaper hears about it? You know what happened last time. Just do what you can, please."

She laid him down across her bed, then fetched a clip-on reading light, a large bottle of antibiotic, clean wash-cloths, and as many bandages as she could find. As she started to work she said, "So they finally came after you, personally."

"Not exactly," he replied. "I was after them, but they caught me, instead. The coven . . . in the cemetery."

"I thought that was just legend."

"Me, too, until Stephanie Lockwood got murdered—by them, I believe. Said she was part of the group."

"From the looks of it, you're lucky to be alive."

"You can say that again," he murmured between winces. "They had me tied to a cross when the FBI rescued me."

"So it's over? You're out of there for good?"

"I promised to be there Sunday. But I won't go unless it's okay with you."

She stood up and walked around the bed to look him in the eyes. "Since when does that matter?"

"Since I was hangin' on that cross thinkin' about this whole deal, but mostly how I've treated you. I came here today to say I'm sorry. I ain't lookin' for sympathy, just forgiveness."

She sat down next to him and stroked his hair, still caked with blood. "But . . . do you want to be there? Do you need to be there?"

"Since when does that matter?"

"Since I know you're willing to put me ahead of your own agenda."

"Look at my back," he said. "Put your finger into the thorn prints from the crown they made me wear. Remember Mocha, and Rowdy, and answer your own question."

She sat down again, next to his head, and touched his forehead wounds.

"I'll go with you," she said.

He pushed himself up on his elbow. "Never thought I'd

hear you say that," he admitted. "But you should stay here. It could get pretty ugly."

"Uglier than this?" she asked, touching his back.

"Maybe. We're dealin' with some underworld types that don't much like the idea of goin' to jail."

"One more day, promise?"

He nodded.

"Then what?" she asked.

"How about Liberty Riding Center? Maybe tomorrow you and me can sit down with Jim and Jenny and see if a trick-shootin', bronc-bustin', cowboy preacher might fit into their plans. Whaddya think?"

"I think . . . if something happens to you and you don't come back, I'll never forgive myself for letting you go."

Over a hundred miles north, Eddie Hazard received a different reception.

"What are you doing here?" Karen demanded.

"I . . . I came to apologize," he said.

"A little late," she replied. "By about ten years."

"But I really have changed," he said, still standing outside the screen door.

"You've changed a million times," she said. "And you expect me to pretend nothing's happened, when I'm the one who fights off the bill collectors." She paused and looked at him. "Do you have a job?"

"No, but—"

"Don't give me any buts. Get a job, go to confession, and tell the priest all your sins, I mean all of them. And then ask him what he thinks about you becoming a Baptist!"

"I'm not a Baptist just because I got baptized. I'm a Christian."

"You were a Christian before, but it didn't make any difference. Why should it now?"

"Because now he's inside me."

"Who?"

"The Lord."

"That's what David Koresh said. That's what they all say. You've just gone wacko, that's all. I don't care if I ever see you again."

Saddened, Eddie Hazard turned away and started walking aimlessly down the street. *Now what?* he wondered, fingering the twenty-dollar bill in his pocket, the only cash he had left. *Nothing to do and nowhere to go.* He stopped in front of West Side Tavern, where he had downed more than a few "brewskies" through the years. *Twenty won't go far in here*, he thought, as he opened the door and walked in. *But I have to dull the pain somehow. Nate would understand. Nate would forgive me.*

But when Nate came to mind, along with the memory of the previous night's horror, Eddie Hazard suddenly realized the bottle wasn't the answer. He turned on his heel and walked out, down the steps, and down the street to the bus station. *Our stuff's still in the cave. I'll be okay there for two nights.*

Bruce Davidson sat in his room at the Hope Center, perusing the A.A. book, *Twelve Steps and Twelve Traditions,* trying to make some sense of what Doris had told him that afternoon. The word that kept jumping out at him was "security."

When I played war with the other kids in the woods behind our house, he recalled, *I always pretended to be*

251

wounded. I would lie there crying for somebody to help me, somebody to hold me.

Does big boy Brucie communicate the same thing to his grown-up playmates? At least Clare was honest.

He stood up to stretch, walked to the window, and gazed out at the nearly-full moon. *And what about Fred? We had some intimate talks, but I was always drunk, and he was always sober.*

"There's a clue," he said. "It was always one-way. I've always been afraid to let anybody know me, really know me, because I thought that once they discovered who I really am, they wouldn't like me anymore. Even with Ellen there was always a little wall, but it certainly wasn't built by her!"

Staring at the moon, he started to weep silently, mostly for himself, for what his character defects had kept him from experiencing—authentic, unobstructed, transparent, two-way love—but also for what this weakness had done to others.

"I'm sorry," he said, to everybody. "I didn't know what I was doing to you, or to myself. I only hope there's a way to recover."

"Nice necklace," Kelly said, taking the string of dark blue sapphires set in solid silver from Clare Conroy. "Where's the mike?"

"Look carefully at the setting of the largest stone."

"It's surrounded by pinholes."

"And backed up by a strong condenser," Conroy said. "It'll pick up any sounds within six feet and transmit them to a vehicle parked outside. So," she couldn't help a little

252

grin, "if there's something you don't want us to hear, you better remember to turn it off."

"Maybe I'll give you such an earful you'll beg me to turn it off!" Kelly winked. "Where's the switch?"

"No switch. Just twist the stone to the right of the one with the mike. Forward for on. Backward for off. Here, let me show you."

"It's working perfectly," Fred Billings said as Conroy climbed into the camper parked behind the North Star Tavern.

"And she's not wasting any time, either. Almost as soon as you left Alice's, Leonard Price called. As we speak, they're on their way out of town in his squad car. Listen . . ."

He switched on the overhead speaker.

"Glad you were available, babe," Price said. "I didn't want to spend the night alone in the old Kingsford place."

"Why would you go there?"

"Occupants moved out today, and Hawkins insisted I keep an eye on it."

"Do you have to? I mean, do *we* have to?"

"What difference does it make where we go?"

"It's haunted," she said. "Ever since the Kingsford baby was sacrificed to Satan and buried in the mine. Everybody knows that."

"It's been over sixty years. What self-respecting ghost is going to hang around for that long with nothing to do?"

"Time means nothing to a ghost," she said.

"How would you know that?"

"*Ghostbusters.*"

"Fiction, my dear. Pure fiction. But don't worry, if they

253

come after you, they'll have to get past my trusty .357 Magnum."

"Guns mean nothing to ghosts, either."

"Well, then, I guess we'll just have to find out what they do respect," he laughed. "Because that's where we're going."

"No, please," she said, starting to cry. "Keep the money, just take me back."

The transmission became garbled as the distance increased between the miniature transmitter and the FBI listening post.

"Let's follow them," Clare said. "I have an idea."

"Where are we going?" Billings asked.

"To the Kingsford mansion, of course."

"But it's haunted," he chuckled.

"By us," she replied. "I'll bet the occupant who moved out today was Florence Bradley, and Perelli wants the place guarded because she left some evidence behind. Can you monitor this transmission with a mobile unit?"

"Piece of cake," he said.

"Then if she leaves the mike on, we should be able to keep our distance. What do you say?"

"We *do* need some hard evidence. I'm game."

A half hour later, Conroy and Billings, dressed totally in black with their hands gloved, stood at the back door of the Kingsford mansion. Clare also wore a fanny pack stocked with plastic sample bags. When only one light was left still burning in the upstairs bedroom, Billings whispered, "Time to go." He tapped the mobile unit. "They'll be occupied for a while."

He pulled the earphone out, disgusted, reached for his

254

pouch of lock picks, and was just about to step up to the door when Conroy whispered, "Wait. There's a sensor."

She knelt down and breathed on the invisible beam, her breath fogging the frosty air just enough so Billings could see it.

"Let me climb on your back," she said.

"What?"

"If you were nine feet tall you could reach over and pick that lock, right? Well, on your shoulders, I am nine feet tall. Once the door's open, I'll swing myself through and disarm the controls. Then you can waltz on in."

A moment later, as the door swung open with a loud creak, Conroy reached for the crosspiece, swung herself through, and landed harder than she had intended.

She looked back through the open door to see her partner crouched on the landing, the earphone back in place.

Upstairs, Kelly Mitchell said, "Leonard. Did you hear that? I told you, the place is haunted."

"I didn't hear anything. But if it'll make you feel better, I'll go look."

"Please," she said.

"Okay."

Billings snapped his fingers to get Clare's attention, then pointed upstairs. "He's coming," Billings whispered. "Close the door."

Clare grabbed the inside knob with her left hand and lifted the door as she closed it. This time its quieter squeak was overwhelmed by the sound of creaking wooden steps as Price came down the spiral staircase in his stocking feet. Conroy dove for the closet to her left, just as the lawman came into view, gun in hand. He tested the knob and discovered the door was unlocked. "Thought I locked

255

this," he muttered. "Must've had my mind on other things."

He walked around the corner, paused briefly to check the alarm control box, then went back upstairs.

"Just the wind in the door," Billings heard him say. "Alarm's still on. Nothing gets past that."

Clare peeked through the door's window, wondering what she should do next. "Get what you can," he told her, using a combination of mouthed words and hand signals, "and I'll stand sentry out here."

30

lare stole silently through the downstairs of the Kingsford mansion, looking for Bradley's office. Having worked with her before, she knew how it would be organized. *Lots of records, and a wall safe to keep them in.*

Finally, she found what she was looking for, a small room, three walls of which were waist-to-ceiling bookshelves. Using her penlight for illumination, Conroy checked the titles. The west wall was mostly medical textbooks, including manuals of anatomy and physiology, surgery, obstetrics and gynecology, embryology and cytology. But the largest section had to do with reproductive technology and genetics. She examined the titles carefully: *Genetic Prophecy, Population Genetics and Evolution, Molecular Genetics, The People Shapers, Brave New World,* and *Jurassic Park.* Prominently displayed at eye level was a leather-bound, gold-embossed copy of *The Master Plan of the Ages.*

On top of a tall filing cabinet in the corner was a stethoscope, a pharmaceutical mixing bowl, and a few vials of drugs in a variety of forms.

Turning to her left, Conroy found the shelves full of books by or about Adolf Hitler, including *Mein Kampf, The Final Solution, Secret Diaries of Hitler's Doctor, Spear of Destiny, Horns of the Moon,* and *The Seventh Secret.* Centered in a collection of Nazi memorabilia was what appeared to be a personally-signed photograph of the führer.

Most surprising, however, was the massive collection of books about the occult, witchcraft, paganism, and satanic worship that totally covered the north wall of the room.

She's coming back, or she never would have left these, Conroy thought. *Maybe the tapes are still here.*

On the corner of the doctor's mahogany desk sat a small videotape player and monitor. On the wall behind it hung a large picture labeled "Gregor Mendel," slightly awry. Conroy peered behind it and found the safe.

If this stethoscope works, she said, grabbing the instrument from the doctor's display of medical memorabilia, *it'll save me a lot of work!*

It did, and in less than a minute, the agent was staring into a much smaller space than she'd expected, roughly sixteen inches wide by twelve inches deep by eight inches high. *Not built for files, but just right for these.* She reached in and drew out a master videotape, one of ten in the safe, and read the embossed title: "The Ultimate Sacrifice." On the second tape, the title was scrawled in indelible magic marker, "The Crucifiction." *Couldn't even spell it right! Or maybe didn't want to.*

Conroy inserted the first tape into the video player. She punched play and fast forward simultaneously just to get a quick overview of the action. *Snuff, just as I thought.* But suddenly, as she watched, the surreal became real as the face of Stephanie Lockwood filled the screen. Sickened, the agent continued watching for another minute or so and then ejected the tape. *Bradley made her commit suicide somehow. I'll see her hang.*

She slipped the tape into her fanny pack and then cued the second tape in the machine. Within seconds her suspicion was confirmed. It was the original of the tape made in the cemetery Thursday night. She took this one, too, but that was all the room she had in the pack. She laid the others out on the desk, so that their titles were all clearly visible, then pointed her eagle pin at them, pulled both its feet together while pushing down on its head, and twisted the left talon. Immediately the eagle's wings flashed, filling the room with light.

Nice unit, Clare thought, stuffing the tapes back into the safe. *Can't believe how bright it is!* She turned and snapped photos of each wall of the doctor's office. *Need to remember your favorite reading material,* Conroy chuckled.

Upstairs, Kelly Mitchell whispered, "What was that?"

"Lightning," Leonard Price replied.

"On a cloudless night?" she answered.

"There it is again, but it's not coming from the sky."

"You're dreaming."

"More like a nightmare. A couple ghosts are duking it out downstairs."

"Chill out. I'll take another walk. But if I don't find anything this time, it's your turn. I need to get some sleep. Tomorrow's a big day."

"There won't be any tomorrow if they get us tonight!"

Billings, who was listening, crawled through the shrubbery bordering the north side of the house. As Conroy took the second and third pictures, he honed in on the right window. When she snapped the fourth, he tossed a pebble against the glass to get her attention.

She peered through the pane and saw him gesturing wildly. "Cut, cut. Get out of there. Price is coming down again!"

She reached to shut the safe, but as she started to do so, she noticed a small button just inside its door, on the right side. She pushed it, and immediately a panel of witchcraft books pivoted silently, revealing a small tunnel behind them.

She snapped the safe shut, twisted the dial, slid the picture back in place, and dove for the tunnel. The solid four-inch-thick oak door swung shut automatically, five seconds after it opened. A moment later, Leonard Price stepped into the room, flicked on the light, and said, "Don't move and you won't get hurt."

Clare Conroy was now immersed in total darkness. In the small circle of illumination from her penlight, she saw that the tunnel she had entered took a sharp bend about twelve feet in front of her. She followed the four-foot-wide shaft, hands extended to left and right and the penlight in her mouth, for another hundred feet. Then, just as her little light gave out, she stumbled and fell forward down a small flight of stairs to the floor of a much larger cavern.

Pretty poor engineering, Kingsford! she commented angrily, standing to her feet and checking for broken bones. Her left wrist was protesting, and her back was a little sore. Her mouth was bleeding because the pen had been torn from her lips. *Thank God it wasn't higher, or I*

260

might be in here forever! But then again, where am I exactly?

She knelt in the darkness, feeling for the flashlight. It was useless. But she did find something else, railroad ties nearly covered with dust, from which the rails had been removed. *The mine! Cecil Kingsford's private entrance. The guy was a real mole!*

She crawled on the floor, trying to estimate the distance to the far wall. *Twenty feet, maybe, and I can't touch the ceiling. The main shaft, no doubt. But what's that awful smell? Rotting meat? Would someone use a gold mine for a garbage dump?*

She followed the gradual incline toward the mine's entrance for about two hundred feet; then suddenly she bumped into a very solid waist-high obstruction, right in the middle of the cavern.

Startled, she tried to determine the structure's identity. *Metal draped with soft cloth. Candles. A cup. A dagger and a skull!* By now she was on the other side of the object, facing down the incline, though it made little difference in terms of what she could see. Then she had an idea. *Snap a picture. Fred may never believe it, otherwise.*

Feeling her way, she aimed her eagle camera toward the altar. When it flashed, for a millisecond she could clearly see the whole setup. *This is where they did it. This is where they made Stephanie Lockwood kill herself.*

But as the light turned again to darkness, Clare Conroy was first startled, then terrified by what she saw. In the blackness, a goat's face grinned, phosphorescent, its eyes blazing red. And she seemed to hear a voice, the same voice she'd recorded the night before, saying, "She has violated our sacred space! She, too, must die!"

Clare Conroy turned and ran uphill, toward the mine's

261

entrance, as fast as she could possibly manage in the dark. She stumbled, fell, then regained her footing several times before she finally saw a thin sliver of moonlight shining through the heavy wooden doors blocking the entrance to the Kingsford mine.

She pushed against them, but they didn't budge. *Locked! Lord Jesus, help me find a way out of here!*

Lift the beam, she urged herself, though at that point she didn't even know there was a beam blocking her exit. She searched and found it, then lifted the three-by-six piece from its place. The doors practically flung themselves open, and she dashed out into the moonlight.

"Hello, Fred," Conroy said, when she had crept to within ten feet of where Billings stood waiting by the office window. "I'm sorry I took so long to—"

Billings, turned, his mouth open and his face as white as a sheet, even in the moonlight. "Clare," he stammered. "I thought you were gone."

"I was," she laughed. "Come with me and I'll show you where."

As they snuck around the rock outcropping that hid the mine's entrance from view, she asked, "Do you have a lighter?"

He nodded. "But why do we need it?"

"There are candles."

"Candles? In a mineshaft?"

"On the altar. There's a human skull, too, and a goat's head, and I don't know what else."

"I don't know about this," he said, stopping in his tracks.

"Well, Fred," she said, pulling the mine door wide enough for them to slip through. "I don't either, because there's something in there that spooks me to my bones.

But if we're going to solve this case, we can't walk away from it now."

"Fair enough," he replied. He turned on his penlight, and led the way down the slope. After descending a hundred paces, they came to the altar. Without comment, Billings lit one candle after the other until he came to the one embedded in the human skull.

He started to light the candle in the wax-coated cranium. Then he pulled the lighter back, extinguished it, and stepped back next to Clare. "Table is gold," he said. "Could be worth a million bucks."

"Cecil Kingsford did this," she said. "He was the only one who could have. Elyse Morais was telling the truth. Kingsford killed his own daughter on this altar, just as Stephanie Lockwood killed herself on it."

"You don't know that."

"It's on this tape," she said, patting the videocassette for emphasis. "The whole grisly ritual. I wonder how many others have died here."

"Just because they found the Kingsford girl in here doesn't mean she died here, or that Kingsford did it. It could have been anybody with access to the shaft—"

He stopped, because she had turned toward him with a look of horrified comprehension, a combination he'd never seen before on her face, or anywhere else.

"I think we can find out," she said, quietly.

"What?"

"How many have died on this altar, because they're all buried deeper in the shaft. I smelled the stench of death when I was down there. I just didn't recognize it. This altar is the gateway to Hades. I think we better leave."

"Fine, I'll go by myself."

"I can't let you do that."

"Decomposing bodies bother you?"

"There's more to it in this case, Fred. Trust me."

"What do you suggest, praying? You pray, and I'll dig," he said, starting down the dark tunnel.

She followed him, carrying the lighter and praying, *Our Father, which art in heaven. Hallowed be thy name. Thy Kingdom come. Thy will be done in earth, as it is in heaven. . . . And lead us not into temptation, but deliver us from evil: For thine is the kingdom, and the power, and the glory, for ever. Amen.* She prayed it silently over and over as they descended.

When they passed the opening to Kingsford's secret passage, Clare pointed it out. "This is how I got in," she said. "It connects to the mansion."

Fred nodded, then turned without a word and kept walking. Fifty feet further, he stopped and stared at the lower edge of the mine shaft's wall, where someone had created a three-foot-high gravel wedge. Its surface appeared undisturbed.

"The worst stench is right here," he said.

He stuffed tissue in his nose, put the penlight into his mouth, knelt down, and started to dig away the loose stone by hand.

"It's a body, all right," he announced a few moments later. "A woman, judging by the clothes."

"Let me see," Clare said, leaning closer. "It's Stephanie. The pattern matches the video. Rip off a piece."

She held out a small, clear plastic bag from her fanny pack.

"What's in her hand?" she asked, staring at the partially decomposed flesh.

"Jewelry of some kind," he replied, trying to fish the metal away from the putrid mass surrounding it. "It's a cross," he announced after a moment, lifting it up and dropping it into the still-outstretched plastic bag.

She snapped pictures as he continued to dig around the girl's upper body and face.

Through her tears, Conroy said, "Maybe Nate got to her more than he thought. And maybe they got to her less than she thought."

"Unfortunately," he said, dropping some hair into the bag, along with the end bone of her little finger, "they got the final word."

"Only *he* gets the final word," she replied, but the words were only half out when a gust of wind blew out the lighter she was holding.

"What?" he said, standing up. "We closed the door and bolted it behind us."

"Maybe that was a mistake," she replied. "Because it's definitely time to go, and it'll be just that much harder to find our way out."

"Okay, let's go," he said. "We have what we need. But forensics needs to come in here with more than a sample bag, that's for sure."

They ascended toward the door, their path illuminated by Fred's penlight. Clare held the little bag with the cross in it out in front of her in the dark, counting steps as they went. When she reached seventy, she said, "Fred. The altar. It's around here somewhere. Haven't you seen it yet?"

"Not yet," he replied, "but this light is getting very dim. I can hardly see the ground now. The wind must have blown the candles out."

"Then let me see if the lighter will help," she said, reaching for the gadget, when suddenly less than twenty feet in front of them, a candle ignited itself, then another, and another, until all the candles Billings had lit the first time were blazing again.

"Fred," she said, taking his hand. "Go around it. Don't stop. It's a trick to keep us here."

"But how?" he asked. He stepped past the table, then turned to face it. "They must have been smoldering but not quite out."

As if to answer him, the candle in the skull ignited next, its blood-red wax running down across the forehead and into the eye sockets and out the mouth. "How did that happen?" he asked. "Sparks?"

"Run, Fred! Run!" She pulled at him, but he stood stock still, whether intrigued by the mystery or mesmerized by the flames she couldn't tell, nor did it matter. For one long, interminable minute, he stared into the grinning face of Baphomet, engraved in gold on the altar's black satin drapery. He turned to her. "Did you hear something?" he said. "Is someone else here?"

"Yes," she shouted. "But greater is he who is within me, for he is the Christ, the Son of the living God, whom even the gates of hell cannot hold captive!"

At that moment, the mine doors flew open in the distance, the cross beam exploding from the pressure of the wind roaring through the canyon outside. An instant later, the candles were torn off the altar, along with everything else on it, and sucked out the door into the night.

"Now, Fred!" she screamed above the howl. This time, she didn't have to say it twice.

31

ddie Hazard awoke with a start. All night long, he had sat facing the fire, his back against the cavern wall, Nate's .357 Magnum in one hand, and a Bible in the other. Whatever happened, he wanted to be ready.

A crackling fire had kept him from hearing the nightlong feral serenade, but occasionally an owl would fly by and screech at the blaze. And several times he did hear coyotes yipping, right down by the stream.

Now that it was daylight, and he was still alive, the city boy's first impression was to feel rather proud of himself. A split second later, that sliver of self-esteem vanished as he suddenly realized what had beckoned him from dreamland.

In the mouth of the cave, not six feet from his face, a cougar crouched, its tail twitching as it studied its intended victim, watching for any indication of weakness.

Hazard froze. He returned the cat's gaze, unflinching, as his hand gradually tightened on the firearm. *One false move and one of us is dead,* he thought, as his other hand tightened on the Bible.

"Help!" he prayed.

The cat crouched lower, the muscles in her shoulders and loins bulging with the tension. Then she leaped.

Hazard fired and rolled, all in the same motion, barely evading the animal, which landed next to him, twisting and clawing at the grazing wound the gunman had just inflicted. Infuriated, she snarled and lunged for his leg as he tried to crawl to safety. Her teeth sank into the solid leather heel of his new cowboy boot, which she tore off his foot and attacked.

The diversion gave Hazard just enough time to aim and fire again. This time the bullet struck the boot first, passed through it, and drove the cat backwards against the wall. Its body hit the ground with a thud.

Shaking, Eddie peered into the darkness, training the gun on the animal until he couldn't hold his hands up any longer. Then, step by step, he approached its furry form, watching for even the slightest twitch. His shoe, still in its mouth, was his first objective.

When he was sure the cat was dead, he pried his boot from its mouth, amazed by the gaping hole the bullet had made. He pulled the boot on, grabbed the animal by the tail, and dragged it out into the sunlight.

Eddie the serpent killer has slain the lion, too. But what should I do with it?

He glanced to his right, where the snake still hung on the stake, and then he had an idea. *This is my castle,* he chuckled. *And just like in the days of old, I will have these beasts guard my gate!*

He laid the animal out on its belly and propped its head off the ground with a short forked stick he'd pulled from the fire. The small, flat boulder under its chin hardly showed. In fact, from almost any direction, the cougar seemed to be lounging in the sun, daring anything to try to invade its space.

Then Hazard picked up the Bible, and opened it to the passage he'd been reading before he fell asleep: "My strength and my hope is perished from the LORD: Remembering mine affliction and my misery, the wormwood and the gall. My soul hath them still in remembrance, and is humbled in me. This I recall to my mind, therefore I have hope. It is of the LORD's mercies that we are not consumed, because his compassions fail not. They are new every morning: great is thy faithfulness."

He looked toward the sky. "Forgive me, God. I'm not used to talking directly to you," he said, "so I hope you don't zap me if I say something wrong. But this guy, Jeremiah, I don't know what to make of him. One minute he's crying and the next he's full of hope. I wish I could be full of hope. In fact, I wish I had any hope at all. But sometimes it seems like getting born again messed up more than it fixed. I tell Karen I've changed my ways, and she laughs. I tell her why, and she throws me out. And then I go back and try to make amends, and she won't even let me in the front door. I've done everything I can to make things right, so I guess the rest is up to you. Or was it always up to you, and I just didn't know it?"

"I thought about it all night," Bruce Davidson said to Doris Oberly. "I reviewed my whole life, looking for clues. I'm exhausted, but I think I'm starting to solve the mystery. Funny, the solution is more like a story than a bunch of indisputable facts."

"Tell me your story," she said.

"Once upon a time," he replied, "there was a little boy named Brucie, who was desperately lonely but afraid that if he let people know that, they would laugh and walk away and he would be even lonelier than before. So Brucie learned to pretend. The first thing he pretended was that it didn't hurt to be lonely, which made it that much easier to pretend nothing really hurt.

"After a while, nothing hurt, but nothing felt good, either. However, he had to pretend about that, too, if he wanted to relate to anybody, since all they wanted to talk about was what made them happy or sad.

"When he was in college, he pretended to love one girl-friend after another, because when they loved him back that made him feel good, at least until they figured out that the love was all flowing one way. So after getting ditched by a dozen girls, Brucie made a choice—subconsciously. He forgot girls and tried to find something else to make him feel good, something that didn't expect the same in return.

"Espionage was the perfect answer. He could grow long hair and a beard and pretend he liked it so he could spy on his fellow classmates in the anti-war movement. Later, he pretended to be a pacifist so he could spy on the Mennonites, and filed disparaging reports even though they were the most consistently moral people he'd ever known.

"Bruce built a career on his ability to lie and make others believe him, until he came up against a lady named Ellen, who forced him to tell the truth because lying to her would have been like mugging Mother Teresa. For the first time since he started pretending, he actually began to let somebody see who he really was.

"It wasn't easy, because he was always afraid if he took

off all the masks, and let her see how empty he was inside, she would walk away like all the others."

"But she didn't."

"No. But here's the crucial point. I never really took off *all* the masks, even with her. I was still holding back when she died. You'd think by then I would have wised up. The most devastating thing I realized, at maybe three o'clock this morning, was that, even with Ellen, I never had real intimacy—I'm not talking about sex, but something deeper."

"Letting somebody really know you . . . and knowing them, too. But how did you realize this?"

"I was thinking about Fred, how over the past few years he's told me just about everything a guy would care to hear—maybe more—about his hopes and dreams, his marriage, his kids, his finances, and even his doubts and fears. Fool that I was, I never recognized those things as a gift entrusted to me. And I never gave him anything back. I talked about the Broncos, the cases we were working on, hunting and fishing, the news, the weather. But I *never* talked about anything intimate, *unless I was drunk.*"

"So then you were stuck," she said. "The bottle helped you be yourself, but when you were drunk you weren't really yourself, and Fred knew that. But he pretended to be satisfied with the friendship, so you thought everything was okay."

"But inside somewhere I realized that even this relationship wasn't real, so I drank more to hide from that loneliness and to avoid facing the alternative."

"Which was?"

"Telling him I didn't want to pretend anymore, because his friendship was more important than my fears. Letting

271

him decide how close he wanted to be, instead of trying to control him through my drinking and my masks."

"Could you tell him that, now?"

"As in this minute?"

"This weekend, sometime?"

"I . . . I . . . think so," he replied. "But it's easier telling you."

"That's because you believe I won't reject you, no matter what you say. But you're afraid he might."

He nodded.

"You pointed a loaded gun at him, and he didn't reject you."

"But I lied to him. I made him relate to a false person."

"Which he freely chose to do . . . but that isn't the worst thing you did to Fred, or anyone else. By hiding the way you have, you've robbed everyone you've ever known of *yourself*—the beautiful, deep, sensitive, and creative person who is Bruce Davidson."

Bruce blushed.

"Setting that person free is what this whole process is about, and confession is a major part of it, though if I explain why it would be like reading your story from the back of the book. But I'd like you to contact Fred this weekend and tell him whatever you need to. I'm taking the day off tomorrow, but we can talk about it Monday."

"Okay," he said, as he stood up to leave.

"And another thing I'd like to talk about then," she said, also standing, "is why, when you surveyed all your relationships, you focused on Ellen and Fred, but not Clare Conroy?"

"I don't know," he replied. "Maybe because I haven't known her as long, so I haven't lied to her as often?"

"Or perhaps because even when you tried to lie to her, she still told you the truth?"

"I do like her," he admitted. "I've asked her to marry me, twice. But she turned me down both times. She said she needed more time."

"Maybe what she really meant was that *you* needed more time, because she could see past the personas of Bruce Davidson into his soul; maybe she liked what she saw, and was willing to wait until he found a way to release it."

He looked directly into Doris's eyes, and said, "I hope that's true, with all my heart. But are you speaking for Clare Conroy, or for yourself?"

Now it was her turn to blush, but she managed to return his gaze. "Therapists risk emotional involvement with their clients," she replied, "if they're really going to help them."

"Now who's pretending?" he laughed over his shoulder, as he turned and walked out of the room.

She watched him go, then stared at herself in the mirror. "He's right, you know," she scolded her reflection. "But I can't use him to fill my own loneliness. I must find a way to use the attraction to pry open his heart, without filling the void with myself."

"You were right," Fred Billings said to Clare Conroy as they finished breakfast in the parking area at Fool's Gold State Recreation Area, where they had both grabbed a nap after leaving the Kingsford Minc.

"About Stephanie Lockwood? I saw it on tape."

"About the supernatural factor."

"You mean what happened at the altar?"

He nodded, thoughtfully. "The candles, the skull. Especially the face of the goat. I would have sworn it talked to

273

me, telling me to bow down and worship, and everything I've ever wanted would be mine. That's what it said, directly to my mind."

"Did you believe it?"

"I was tempted. But when the gate burst open, another thought obliterated the first, though the only voice I heard was yours. When you said the phrase 'the Son of the living God,' my mind was filled with light—I can't explain it any other way. In that instant I realized two things. The goat's-head god is death personified. But more importantly, the living God was waiting to provide all my needs if I would only bow and worship him, instead."

She looked at him and smiled. "And is that something you think you could do?"

"I have been, since that moment," he said. "And my intention is to never stop." He returned her smile. "When I walked out of that tomb, it was as if everything that had kept me from believing, especially my bitterness, melted away; I was a new man."

"Mr. Hawkins," Leonard Price said over the phone. "Something strange happened out here last night. About two o'clock, a fierce wind roared through the canyon behind the house and tore the doors of the mine almost off their hinges."

"Well, go out and close it back up."

"I did, already. I put on a new latch and a chain," Price replied. "But before I locked it, I walked down in there and took a look around. And you won't believe what I found."

"Try me."

"A gold table. I'm not talking gold paint, either. Must weigh three hundred pounds. I tried to lift it."

274

"Three hundred pounds of gold?" Hawkins said. "I need to see that. I'll be there in a half hour. Whatever you do, don't tell anyone about this."

"It's our little secret," Price said. "I'll give you the key when you come."

He hung up the phone, then turned to Kelly Mitchell, reclining next to him on the sofa in the mansion's living room. "Figured that one right," he said. "Hawkins wants the gold for himself. But he'll pay me a finder's fee, or face a very unhappy Vincent Costellini."

32

N ate Freeman watched Annie gently lead the handicapped child's horse around the ring. Two volunteers walked alongside, in case the boy might lose his balance, or the horse might act up.

"Look, no hands!" the rider cried.

"Good job, Christopher. Great job!" Annie cheered.

"Annie's the best I've ever seen," Big Jim commented, his boot resting on the lowest rail of the corral as he chewed on a piece of grass. "Hope she can come with us, full-time, once the center is built."

"Tell me about that," Nate replied.

"It's a dream," Jim said. "But it's going to happen, I know it. The need's too big for it not to happen."

"You mean there are a lot of kids like this in Pueblo?"

"Hundreds, most of them a lot worse off than Chris. Actually, when he first started riding two years ago, he was pretty bad off, too. But look at his confidence now. He could probably ride that horse without any help, and when he came to us, he could hardly walk."

"Take a pretty big place to house a hundred kids. And what about their families?"

"They wouldn't all live with us. Most of them don't need to live with us. They're doing okay by themselves. It's the families who've just had a child become disabled that need the most help. And they need it for at least a year."

Jim turned toward Nathan. "You're a pastor," he said. "So you've probably thought a lot about why bad things happen to good people."

Nate nodded.

"But I'll bet, in all your classes, you didn't talk too much about what happens to good people who end up caring for other people to whom bad things have happened. More than eighty percent of marriages break up within two years after the disabling illness of a child."

"I didn't know that. Why is it?"

"Before the child becomes ill, there are often little problems in the parents' relationship that both partners overlook. But after the crisis, one of the parents—usually the mother—becomes totally absorbed in trying to help the little one recover. And the other partner—usually the husband—goes out and finds happiness elsewhere, most often in another woman's arms. And in the end, they simply decide to go their separate ways, with the result that everybody suffers, especially the child, who, if he or she is able to understand what's going on, feels responsible for the parents' unhappiness in some way."

"I'd expect a tragedy like that to glue people together."

"It does, at first, but over the long term it's more of a wedge than a glue, unless there's somebody to help them survive that first year and get adjusted to their new 'normal.'"

Nate followed Big Jim to the stable; on the wall was pinned an architect's rendering of Liberty Wellness Center, a constellation of six living units in the shape of a star, all connected to a central facility by short hallways.

"This is where the families would live," Jim said, pointing to the individual units on the periphery. "Four families per quad, all coming into the program at the same time, with the intention of staying a year. Every second month, once the whole facility is finished, four families would come in and four others would leave. The central unit would be for meetings, including worship, recreation, physical therapy, and counseling."

"Good plan," Nate said, impressed. "But what's the bottom line?"

"Eight hundred thousand dollars," Jim said. "A hundred for each quad, and two hundred for the central core. Know anybody looking for a worthy project to support?"

"Not really," Nate laughed, "but I do know somebody who owns the cattle on a thousand hills. Maybe he'll auction off a couple. What would it take to get started?"

"A hundred thousand. Plans are already passed, septic's in, and we own the land. In fact, Jenny and I will match the first fifty thousand from anybody else."

"I would if I could, but I ain't got a cent," Nate replied. "I ain't even got a job, so all I can do is pray for you." He looked at Jim's tattered blue jeans and his nearly worn-out boots. "But if you don't mind me askin', how'd you come up with that kind of money?"

"Same way we got acquainted with the need," Jim replied, motioning for Nate to follow him to the house. "Ten years ago our son, Jesse, was a perfectly normal and healthy five-year-old, always getting into things and giving his mother fits. When he was two, the first time he had an ear infection, we discovered he was allergic to penicillin. Fortunately, that doctor was right on top of it and no real harm was done. But when he was five we moved to Illinois, and about a year later, he got tonsillitis. Jenny told the new doctor about Jesse's allergy, but for some reason it didn't register. He prescribed ampicillin, and Jenny went ahead and gave it to Jesse, figuring the doctor knew what he was doing.

"To make a long story short, our happy, bouncy boy was reduced to a vegetable overnight from the brain damage. He never talked again, and can barely navigate. The doctor's insurance company settled for five hundred thousand, which we used to buy this land and establish a trust fund for Jesse. And we tithed fifty thousand as a matching grant to build the Jesse Rogers Wing in the new center."

When Jim opened the top portion of the door to the specially constructed playroom, a stocky, sandy-haired adolescent looked up from the Playskool bench where he'd been stuffing stars and moons through their matching holes. "Daddy's home," Jim said; the boy simply smiled and returned happily to his work.

"I think I'd like to work with you," Nate Freeman said a few minutes later, as the two men sipped coffee in an adjoining room. "But now that I see the need, I don't know . . ."

"Love to have you, Nate, but all I can offer is a dream."

"And all I can offer is myself, which ain't much, considerin' the pain people like you must have."

"Pain is pain, as far as I can see," Jim replied. "And from what Annie's told us, you've had your share. You just need

279

to help other people handle theirs the way you've handled yours."

"Or *not* to handle it the way I've handled mine," Nate said, "'cause I ain't been no model of virtue."

"But have you been faithful and truthful and persistent?"

"I tried."

"What else is there? Handicapped families don't need some sanctimonious spiritual speculator fooling with their fragile souls. They need someone who understands what it means to live with ambiguity, to struggle with God, to question, and yet still trust, even if it doesn't seem to make sense."

The big man paused, and looked at Nate. "I need someone like that myself, because sometimes when I look at Jesse, I hurt so bad I can hardly stand it."

"Maybe we can help each other," Freeman replied. "We have more in common than I thought."

"That her?" Vincent Costellini asked George Perelli, as *Dracula's Mistress* got under way. The partners in crime were seated in the VIP balcony box with the secret passage leading to Clare Conroy's dressing room.

"Hard to believe," Costellini continued, "how much she cost me last spring. Our Jamaica connection dried up, and we had to find another laundry without any warning. And all that cocaine, a million bucks up in smoke, not to mention the hassle of getting our Swiss assets unfroze. Me and this lady got to have a heart-to-heart talk."

"I'd like dibs, if you don't mind," Perelli said, rubbing his scar. "We were leaving for a fantasy getaway when she gave me this. I won't kill her, promise. We just need a little time alone, and then you can turn her into fish bait."

"She's an actress. Maybe we can create a role for her in one of our full-length feature flicks. How about *Dracula's Mistress II*, only with a real Dracula?"

"Sounds like a nice twist. Maybe get your million back."

Costellini pursed his lips, and leaned forward to get a better look at Clare, about thirty feet away on the stage. Perelli followed suit; for about ten seconds the overhead lights illuminated their faces against the dark background.

Conroy nearly choked in the middle of her line. "But dear," she was supposed to say, "I understand you, even if nobody else does. I love you, even if nobody else does." But suddenly, as she spied Perelli and Costellini, her mouth went dry and nothing came out. So she grabbed Dracula and kissed him passionately, peeking over his shoulder to see if her eyes had deceived her. But her adversaries had sat back in their seats again, waiting for the final curtain.

My cover's blown, she thought, *and he knows about the passage to my dressing room. Or are they just here to be entertained, and sitting in that box by chance?*

What am I going to do? she wondered, still clinging to Miguel Ortiz, who returned her kisses wholeheartedly.

If those two get their hands on me, I'm history.

"She likes to kiss, I see," Costellini said. "We should have a nice time tonight."

"She's mine," Perelli protested, respectfully.

"Since you found her, we'll make her part of the game."

"The *poker* game?"

"Gentlemen's agreement. You put her up for collateral, and I'll give you a million-dollar line of credit."

"Deal. But you'll never beat me."

"We'll see about that."

Suddenly, a loud explosion blanketed the stage with

smoke as Count Dracula disappeared through the trap-door; a bat was seen flying toward a full moon projected on the back of the set. But this time, as he slid to a stop in a large tub of sponge balls, Miguel Ortiz was surprised to find his co-star right behind him.

"So, you really meant it," he said, happily, reaching to embrace her. "Finally came around after all this time!"

"Sorry to surprise you, Miguel," Conroy replied, removing her wig and colored contacts. "But I followed you down here because upstairs, as we speak, two mafia men are trying to find me, and not because they want my autograph."

"What are you talking about?" he asked, leaning back to look at her. "I should say, *who* are you, and what's going on?"

"I'm going to trust you because I desperately need your help. I'm an FBI agent working undercover on a case involving the men in question. They may have figured out my cover."

"You're serious," he said, sitting up straight. "What a rush. I've been making out with an FBI agent! Wait till the boys back home hear about this."

"Breathe a word of this to anybody, and I might end up dead. Is that clear enough?" she replied.

He nodded solemnly. "What do you want me to do?"

"Take off your clothes," she said.

"Make up your mind."

"I don't mean all your clothes, just your shirt, pants, and cape. I have to get out of here before they tear the place apart to find me."

"On one condition," he said. "That you let me bite your neck."

"I don't have time for jokes, Miguel."

"It wasn't a joke," he answered with an appreciative glance at the agent. Then he responded to her stern look by unclasping his cape.

Upstairs, in Conroy's dressing room, Costellini and Perelli waited in the dark, one on each side of the door.

"She's taking her own sweet time," Costellini said.

"It'll be worth it," Perelli replied, as the sound of foot-steps could be heard in the hall.

The doorknob turned and in walked the star of the show, skirts rustling as they brushed against the doorposts. But as soon as the door closed, each man seized an arm. Perelli, holding a gun behind the captive's ear, said, "So, Agent Conroy, we meet again. But this time you won't escape, I promise."

"I don't know what you're talking about," a man's voice answered. "Please let go."

The two gangsters, totally surprised, let go and stepped back a half-step. "What is the meaning of this?" Perelli demanded, still pointing the gun at the actor, who very cautiously flipped on the lights.

"My question, exactly," Ortiz said, as calmly as he could manage. "Me and Juanita, we like to play after a hard day's work. This is the only way I can get in here without every-body talking. But who's Conroy, and who are you?"

"None of your business, punk. And if you know what's good for you, you'll forget you ever saw us," Perelli said, aiming the gun right between the actor's eyes and pre-tending to pull the trigger. "Now get out of here."

33

y the time Perelli and Costellini reached Clare Conroy's hotel room, she was sitting in the dark on the other side of the two-way mirror.

If he knows about this passage, it's the end of the line, she thought as she watched the men tear her room apart. Her heart raced, and her index finger twitched involuntarily against the trigger guard of her Beretta. *Not much firepower,* she mused, *but it'll have to do if they come through the looking glass.*

"She must have seen us," Costellini said, obviously miffed at his henchman.

"How? Had to be dumb luck. She's downstairs playing the slots, or blackjack, or somewhere else in town. We'll find her eventually. She has two shows a day, and you'll be here all week. Don't worry, we'll get our hands on her soon enough."

"Around her neck, mostly," Costellini replied, "though we wouldn't want to mess up her snuff career."

Perelli glanced at his watch. "Sanders is probably waiting in the Upper Room," he said. "We wouldn't want to delay him from giving back some of that hard-earned pay-off, would we?"

"To me, or to you?"

"Don't much matter to me."

"Well, don't try to take it all tonight, okay? Play it smart and we might even separate him from what we still owe him."

"Two million? It'll take some pretty big pots."

"Getting cold feet? Don't forget your collateral. That should keep you in the game for a while. But I'm a little worried. If Sanders doesn't keep coming back to the table, I won't have anything to do in this hole-in-the-wall town."

"You could play the slots."

"Do you have hundred-dollar slots here? I wouldn't invest the energy for less than that."

"There is an escort service."

"In that case, let's have a football party tomorrow afternoon. I have ten g's on every game, but I hate to laugh or cry alone. So invite the ladies—no dogs please—and get it catered."

"Have to truck it in, but no problem," Perelli said. "Prime rib, lobster, caviar, champagne, the works?"

"Pizza, too, with anchovies, and some beer. Spare no expense."

"Consider it done," Perelli said, as he closed the door behind himself on the way out of Conroy's room.

Perfect, Conroy said to herself. *When the others show, these guys will be half sauced.*

"Nate," Annie said, as she changed the dressing on his back. "Do you really have to go back? Let the FBI handle it. That's their job, after all."

"For the plan to work, we all have to be in the right place

at the right time. My spot's the middle of Main Street. What can possibly happen to me there?"

"Almost anything, if the past couple of weeks is any indication."

"You've changed your mind. You want me to stay."

"I always wanted you to stay, but I also knew you needed to be there."

"I like to finish what I start."

"I know, but you're in no condition to drive, with your back like this. I'll take you there."

Nate turned on his side and stared at Annie. "I thought wild horses couldn't drag you back to Raptor."

"Actually, I loved that beautiful little town before the casinos ruined it . . . and almost ruined our marriage. So, I have some unfinished business with the bad guys, too. More importantly, though, from now on I want to be wherever you are."

She reached out and took his hand, tears in her eyes.

He paused, thinking it over.

"You're right about my back," he said, finally. "The trip down here nearly killed me. Every bump felt like somebody was whippin' me again. I suppose you could drop me off in the middle of town, if you promise to stay out of the way. Ain't no sense takin' any chances."

"So you will be in danger."

"Not if everything goes accordin' to plan," he replied. "But Black Bart will be loaded with real bullets, just in case."

"Evening, Mr. Sanders. Welcome back to the old stomping grounds," Perelli said.

"Nice to be home, Stanley. But a few months away, and

286

a guy can forget how little oxygen there is at ninety-six hundred feet."

"Let me introduce the other players, Skip. This is Vincent Costellini, from New York. His organization is behind the Cathedral project, and he wanted to meet the man who helped us acquire the property." Sanders and Costellini shook hands.

"And this is Leonard Price, our police chief. Don't worry, he's off duty, or we're all in big trouble, hey!"

But I'm on duty, Clare Conroy mused, from behind the confessional screen. *So I hope you'll all feel free to discuss business.*

"Tonight we'll play draw poker, anything opens. Tomorrow, seven-card stud. Monday, Texas hold-'em, and Wednesday, California draw. Black chips are five hundred; red, a thousand; white, five thousand; silver, ten; and gold, a hundred. Five-hundred-buck minimum. Your buy-in is on the table. Gentlemen, choose your seats and let's get started."

Sanders sat down facing Clare's position, with Perelli on his left and Price on his right. Costellini sat with his back to the booth, about ten feet away. Costellini's bodyguard stood silently in the corner, to Clare's right.

"Ante up," Perelli announced, and each man threw five hundred in the pot. He handed the deck to Price, who dealt the first hand. As he did so, Conroy calculated the buy-in at a hundred thousand apiece. *Where did Price get that kind of money? Bankrolled, no doubt, to make a fourth player. He'll last an hour at most.*

"Let's start with five hundred dollars," Sanders announced, pushing another black chip into the pot.

"I'll see that, and raise it five," Perelli responded.

"Call," Costellini replied, tossing in a red chip.

"Me too, and raise it a thousand," Price said, pushing two red chips into the center of the table.

Conroy studied Costellini's hand, wondering how high he'd go with a pair of twos.

"Call," Sanders said, adding two thousand to the pot.

"Ditto," Perelli said, following suit.

"I'll see your two and double it," Costellini said, flicking four more chips into the pot.

Price smirked a little, "You're on. Call your four and raise you five."

"Call," Sanders said, a play matched by the others; when Price's three sixes beat Perelli's two pair, the policeman was thirty-eight thousand dollars richer than he had been three minutes earlier.

Nice work, dude, Conroy thought, unable to believe that Costellini had thrown away fourteen thousand dollars rather than fold. *Must be setting up Sanders.*

Outside in the parking lot, Fred Billings eavesdropped on a conversation between Kelly Mitchell and Charlotte, madam of Raptor's only escort service.

"Here's your eighteen thousand," Charlotte said. "Sanders paid in advance. Must like you. And, by the way, your presence is required at a party tomorrow afternoon upstairs at the Cathedral Casino, as his escort, of course. Connie, Heidi, and Ruthie will be there to entertain the others. A football party, I was told, and the rest I'll leave to your creative minds. Just keep the boys happy, and there's an extra five hundred in it for each of you."

"Double-dipping," Kelly laughed. "I like it."

"Keep it to yourself," Charlotte warned her, "or I'll run into trouble with the others."

By 10 P.M., when the bets started to escalate, Price checked out, his original table stake doubled, and a satisfied look on his face. He put his chips in the rack, noted his standing at that point in the week-long game, excused himself, and left the room.

Sanders and Costellini had each won a few hands, with Sanders roughly fifty thousand ahead. But so far, Perelli was the big loser, much to Conroy's satisfaction. By the time Price quit, Perelli had squandered his original stake and was well into his second hundred thousand, which he had laid on the table in cash. Clearly, he was determined to beat Costellini before the night was out.

"This'll be my last hand tonight, boys," Sanders said with a sly smile. "Got a date, and I wouldn't want to keep the little lady waiting. You know what I mean."

"Sorry you can't stay," Costellini said. "With your line of credit, you could play forever."

"Two million doesn't go as far as it used to," Sanders chuckled, as he dealt the cards. "I have to make it last all week."

Costellini picked up his cards slowly, as Conroy watched from the confessional. *Jacks high full house. It's a lock. Go for the jugular.*

"Ten thousand," Costellini said, tossing a silver chip on the table.

"Twenty," Perelli responded, throwing out two chips.

"Call," Sanders said, adding two more silvers to the pile.

Without even looking at the others, Costellini doubled the bet again. "Forty."

Perelli paused for a moment, examining his diminishing supply of chips. "Sixty," he said, nearly depleting it.

"Sixty?" Sanders said, eyeing Perelli for a moment.

"Call," he said, adding another sixty to the pot.

Two hundred ten thousand and counting. This one's going big time!

"A hundred," Costellini said, quietly, and with a little grin at Perelli, who only had five silver chips left in front of him. He added one gold chip to the pile.

"I'm out," Sanders replied. "But I have a feeling this one's not over yet."

"Two," Perelli replied, coolly.

"Excuse me," Costellini replied. "Have you been hiding some chips?"

Without a word, Perelli produced a piece of paper, upon which he wrote something, folded the paper, and then pushed it over to Costellini. He unfolded it carefully as Clare read, over his shoulder, in large block letters, a single word: CONROY.

Shocked, she wondered for a moment whether Perelli had seen her through the booth's screen and was tipping off his boss to her presence behind him.

Then she realized they were playing for her. *Scum bags! First they have to find me, and then they have to deal with my little side arm.*

As she watched, Costellini nodded, slashed a line through her name, and wrote a one followed by six zeros. Then he refolded the paper, placed it in the bank, and handed Perelli ten gold chips.

On the other hand, she thought, *nobody ever told me I was worth a million bucks! Not bad.*

Perelli threw two of the chips back onto the table and stared at his boss.

"Three," Costellini said, adding three more one-hundred-thousand-dollar chips to the pile.

Holy cow, Conroy thought. *They're over eight hundred thousand dollars and neither one is even counting!*

Sanders was sitting back, smoking a cigar, a look of disbelief on his face as he watched the others duke it out.

"Three-fifty," Perelli said, without hesitation, pushing the chips forward.

"Four," Costellini replied.

"Call," Perelli said, tossing all but one of his remaining chips into the pot.

It was impossible to tell from behind, but Clare was sure Costellini was grinning as he slowly turned over one card after the other, first the two fives, and then, one by one, three jacks.

"Full house," he said, glancing for a moment toward Sanders, who nearly inhaled his cigar when he saw the hand. He started to cough loudly. Perelli rose, moved to his left, and clapped Sanders on the back. As he did so, however, he dropped his cards on the floor.

"Clumsy," Costellini commented. "Just put them on the table, and quit stalling."

Perelli knelt next to Sanders and picked up his cards. But in the fleeting moment when he was out of Costellini's view, Perelli slipped two cards into his shoe and substituted two others in their place. Then he took his seat again.

Conroy couldn't believe her eyes, considering the consequences for Perelli had he been caught.

Mimicking his boss's revelation of his hand, Perelli laid down two sixes followed by a three. Next he turned over a third six, and then, after pausing again, a fourth six. "Four of a kind," he grinned, reaching out to clear the more than two million dollars from the table.

"Just a minute," Costellini said, leaning back from the table.

Count the cards, Vincent. Count the cards! Conroy wanted to yell.

291

Perelli stopped dead, his elbow cradling the small pile of large denomination chips. From Clare's hiding place, Perelli's face seemed to turn a little pale as he waited for Costellini to continue. After about five seconds, Costellini said, "You redeem the loan, or I will."

Perelli, visibly relieved, stuffed his cards into the deck and stacked his chips into three five-hundred-thousand-dollar piles, and a fourth that was slightly higher. He pushed the middle two piles toward the bank.

"Easy come, easy go," he said.

"She'll be mine by this time tomorrow," Costellini said, smirking.

Over my dead body, Conroy protested silently.

"And," he continued, with no inflection in his voice, "Skip and I will separate you from the rest of your little plastic discs before the week is out."

"Is that a threat or a promise?" Perelli responded.

"Neither," Costellini said, standing up to stretch. "A fact. Now why don't you show our guest to the door; you and I need to talk a little more business."

Perelli nodded and escorted Sanders down the spiral staircase. When they were out of earshot, Costellini's bodyguard stepped up next to him and said, "He cheated, boss. I'm sure of it."

"I noticed," Costellini replied. "You think I'm blind? But he'll never see it when I return the favor. My main concern is that he would even consider double-crossing me. If it happens again, he eats lead."

"There's one other thing, boss. All night I've been picking up weird interference on the field strength meter."

He pulled the debugging device from the briefcase he was holding, and handed it to Costellini.

292

"It's not a standard bug, and it's not very strong. But something's transmitting."

Conroy immediately shut down the recorder built into her belt. *An FS meter,* she thought. *Pretty high-tech for a bunch of thugs. I'll have to be more careful.*

"How'd it go?" Fred Billings heard Kelly Mitchell ask Skip Sanders.

"Pretty good. I was ahead fifty grand until the last hand. But then I lost eighty, so I ended up a little behind," he chuckled.

"Eighty in one hand?" she responded. "And you can still smile?"

"Costellini lost eight hundred fifty thousand in the same game."

"Where's a person get that kind of money?"

"It's better for you not to know."

"I can keep a secret, you should know that by now."

A few moments of relative silence interrupted the exchange, during which it was clear to Billings that Kelly and her client were getting reacquainted.

"Like I said," she said, after the long embrace. "You know me well enough to know you can trust me."

"True enough," he replied, trying to catch his breath.

"So . . . where does a person get that kind of money?"

"Organized crime. This guy's pretty high up. Like I said, it's better for you not to know."

"Know what?" she asked, playfully. "But why in God's name would he come to Raptor?"

"Not in God's name, that's for sure. Just the opposite. He's the one who chased God out of Raptor."

"You mean he bought the church after it went bankrupt?"

"Yes and no. He bought the church. It never went bankrupt. It just seemed to go bankrupt. But it never was actually in any danger of defaulting on the loan."

"I don't understand financial things."

"Neither did Nathan Freeman. He made the mistake of leaving them to me."

"Why shouldn't he? Weren't you the church treasurer at the time?"

"And president of the bank. The smartest thing I ever did was to buy that mortgage through my own corporation, because I knew that sooner or later somebody was going to want that building real bad. So when Stanley Hawkins showed up with a blank check, I was in the driver's seat. Three million down, and two million when it opened sounded pretty reasonable, I thought. So all of a sudden, the church books looked bad enough to call the loan. The rest is history.

"On top of that, I get ten percent of the net for the next twenty years. My retirement policy. But if you ever tell a soul, I could end up in jail instead of Acapulco.

"By the way," he continued. "When are you going to come down there and make this relationship permanent?"

"I don't know, dear," she replied. "When I'm with you, I can't imagine being with anybody else. That's all that matters tonight."

The transmission ended abruptly.

She must have turned it off, Billings said to himself. *But that was good, Kelly. Very good. Now if we can just get this guy into court, maybe Freeman will get his wish.*

ello, Judy?" Bruce Davidson said into the pay phone at the Hope Center. "It's Bruce. How are you?"

"Great," Judy Billings said. "And Sandy's great, too. But she misses you, especially at night. She just wanders around trying to find somebody to sleep with."

"Yeah," he laughed. "I'm not surprised. She sleeps in my big double bed with me every night. Guess I spoiled her rotten."

"How are you, Bruce? I mean, how are you, really?"

"It's been the most difficult couple weeks in my whole life," he replied. "But also the best. I was calling to thank Fred for bringing me here."

"He's not home," Judy replied.

"Then I'll call back later. When do you expect him?"

She hesitated. "I don't. I mean, I don't expect him any-time soon. He left Friday on a case. Said he was going to help Clare."

"Did he say why she needed help?"

"Not really," she replied. "He never tells me any details.

But at supper he sat and flexed his right hand during the whole meal. I don't even think he knew he was doing it. That's what worries me. When he does that, it usually means he's thinking about the guys that broke his fingers."

Perelli! Bruce recoiled at the thought. *Why would he be in Raptor? Because organized crime would like to own a Colorado gambling town. I threw Clare into the lion's den, and now Fred's trying to get her out.*

"Don't worry, Judy. It'll be okay. Just have Fred call me when he gets back, please."

Davidson slammed the phone down, his mind reeling from the news. *I have to go. I have to get out of here!*

He rushed back to his room, changed into loose-fitting jeans and a flannel top, grabbed his FBI badge and his wallet, and walked to the receptionist's desk. "Miss Wellesley," he said. "Dr. Oberly gave me an assignment I can't complete unless I leave campus. A certain friend I've wronged over the years is not available by phone, but I know where he is. So I'm going to go find him, ask his forgiveness, and be back here by dark. I need a twelve-hour pass."

Allison Wellesley studied Bruce's face for a moment, then nodded, and handed him a slip of paper. "If Doris said to do it, it must be important," she said. "But it's highly irregular. I'm in big trouble if you don't get back by nine tonight."

"I'll be here," he said, "with bells on."

Now I have to find some wheels, he said to himself. *Hitchhike? Might take all day. Hot-wire a vehicle from the lot? Not a good idea.*

As he stood on the sidewalk, trying to figure out what to do next, Harold drove up and stopped right in front of him. "What's up, Bruce?" he asked. "You look like your best friend just died."

"He might, if I don't get there to help him soon enough."

"You're leaving campus?"

Bruce fished out the pass and showed it to Harold. "Doris's orders," he said. "I'll give you anything you name to drive me to Raptor, that mining town where they legalized gambling."

"All I want from you is your promise to stay on the wagon. I'd drive you to China and back if you would stay sober."

Bruce looked into Harold's eyes. "You have my word."

"Deal," Harold said. "It's on my way, anyhow. But how are you going to get back?"

"By hook or by crook," Bruce said. "But I'll get back, I promise."

All Sunday morning, from her perch in the confessional booth, Clare Conroy watched the caterers prepare for the football party in the Upper Room. A six-foot-wide TV screen was set up in the corner to her right, out of her view. A banquet table, loaded with a variety of fruits, snacks, and finger sandwiches was set up in the corner opposite the screen, with a huge punch bowl at the bottom of a Rocky Mountain waterfall providing a backdrop. Beer, beer nuts, pretzels, crackers, and cheese were stacked a foot high along the wall to her left, and the aroma of fresh-baked pizza filled the room from somewhere down below.

If lunch is this good, what will dinner be like? she wondered, trying to control her hunger. But there was no getting around the fact that she was famished. Since hiding in the stairwell connected to her room in the early evening on Saturday, she hadn't had anything to eat. In fact, the only time she had risked visiting her hotel room had been at three in the morning, to use the bathroom and freshen up a bit. There was simply too much at stake, with only a few hours to go before her plan went into effect.

At ten-thirty, when *The NFL Today* came on, Vincent Costellini showed up, obviously anxious to hear the latest news that might affect his bets. Connie, his red-haired, amply-endowed but very young escort, never left his arm as he ate up every word the prognosticators had to say.

"Hey, Connie," he said. "Do you like football? I mean do you really like football?"

"I like anything you like," she said.

"How about anchovy pizza? You like anchovy pizza?"

"Never had it, but I'm sure I'll like it, Vincent."

He snapped his fingers, and immediately a waiter stood by his side. "Medium pizza, everything on it, including anchovies," Costellini said. "And Miller Genuine Draft for me. What do you want, babe?"

"The same sounds good."

"Make that two."

Costellini draped his arm around the young woman's shoulder. "What is a beautiful girl like you doing in a little backwoods town like this?"

"I don't know, Vincent," she started to answer.

"Call me Vince."

"I don't know, *Vince*," Connie answered. "Maybe because nobody's taken me anyplace else."

"Ever been to New York?"

"Never been out of Colorado," she replied. "When the casinos opened, I had just graduated from high school, with nothing to do. So I answered Charlotte's ad, and the rest is history."

"How much do you make a year?" he asked, toying with her.

"It all depends on gratuities." She suddenly covered her mouth with a hand. "I'm sorry. I shouldn't have mentioned that."

"No problem," he said, reaching out to touch her cheek. "I'm the one who asked. How much?"

"Fifteen, maybe twenty thousand."

"So five hundred is a pretty good day?"

"A pretty good *week*."

Costellini reached in his pocket, and fished out a wad of bills. The outside greenbacks were twenties, but after peeling away ten or fifteen of those, he got to the Ben Franklins.

"Here," he said, "just for being you," sticking five one-hundred-dollar bills down the front of her dress.

"Oh, Vince," she said. "Nobody ever did that to me before."

"All I ask," he responded, "is for you to stick to me like glue. I'm kind of nervous because—you might find this hard to believe—I've bet ten thousand dollars on every NFL game today."

"Ten thousand?" she said. "You mean for every game, you might win ten thousand dollars or lose ten thousand dollars?"

"Exactly. But it doesn't really matter who wins or loses. All that matters is the point spread."

"I don't know what you mean."

"No problem, babe. Take Indianapolis at Denver. The Broncos are favored by three. So if I bet on Indianapolis and they lose by two or less, I win, even if they lose. Tell you what, if that happens, you can have the money."

"Ten thousand dollars?" she said, her mouth wide with surprise. "You're fooling."

"Not at all. It's just pocket change."

"I like you, Vince," she said, kissing him passionately. "I never met anyone like you before."

"I like you, too, pet," he said. "Most of the women I know are leeches. But you're different. Very different. In fact, I bet you don't even know my last name, do you?"

She shook her head. "Is that important?"

You bet your life, sister, Conroy wanted to scream. *In three hours, you'll wish you worked at Pick 'n Save.*

At noon, Nathan and Annie Freeman stopped for lunch at Fool's Gold State Recreation Area. In the middle of a peanut-butter-and-jelly sandwich, Nate happened to glance at the driver dozing in the Winnebago camper parked next to his pickup.

After staring a minute to be sure his impression was correct, he turned to Annie and said, "I'll be back in a second." He walked nonchalantly to the open passenger window of the other vehicle, and said, "Excuse me, sir. But I was wondering if you believe that conspiracy theory about the new Cathedral Casino?"

The old man behind the wheel sat bolt upright and reached for the keys as he turned to face the intruder. "Reverend Freeman!" Billings said. "How did you recognize me?"

"Your right hand," Freeman said, staring at the gnarled fingers of the agent's right hand. "I noticed it in Boulder, and when you were napping just now, you had your hand on the steering wheel."

Billings looked past the minister and noticed Annie watching.

"That's Annie, Fred," Freeman said. "My wife." He waved her over to the camper.

"You brought *her* up here for this? Didn't Conroy explain who we're dealing with?"

Instead of answering, Freeman unbuttoned his shirt and peeled it off his shoulders. He turned around so Billings could see the stripes on his back.

"I heard about it," Billings said, as Annie stepped up to Nathan's side. "In fact, I've seen it."

He paused, scanning the parking lot to see if anyone else had noted their conversation. "Come on in. We have an hour to kill, so we might as well do it comfortably."

Once they were settled in the camper, Nate picked up on the comment Billings had made. "What do you mean, you've seen it?" he asked.

"The video they made at the cemetery," Billings replied. "Friday night Conroy found it in a safe at the Kingsford mansion."

"Can we see it?" Nate asked.

"Why, Nate?" Annie asked. "I've already seen the result."

"But you need to see something else—actually, someone else."

Billings cued the tape and handed Nate the control. The minister watched intently, as did his wife, at least until the first crack of the witch's whip. Nate froze the frame a moment later. "Look, Annie," he said.

"I can't. I can't even listen. The hatred is overwhelming."

"The witch's?"

"My own. I want to kill her, and I've never felt that way before about anyone."

"Just look at the screen for a minute," he said, gently, "and then I'll turn it off. There," he pointed. "Ellie and Sarah Smith. I couldn't believe it. And see . . . everybody's wearing choir robes from the church."

Annie stared at the evidence, her mouth open in surprise. "What possesses people to act this way?" she asked.

"*Who* possesses these people would be a better question," he replied. "I saw it in the witch's eyes. I heard it in her voice, just like I heard it from Stephanie."

"Speaking of Stephanie," Billings interjected. "Conroy also found this tape in the safe. It's pretty gruesome, but at least we finally know what happened to her." He paused for a moment, then said. "She committed suicide, apparently in a drug-induced trance, or maybe hypnotized."

"She did it in front of a camera?" the minister asked, looking at the packaging and the printed label, which proclaimed: *The Ultimate Sacrifice.* "You're positive it wasn't trick photography, like in the movies?"

"We found her body buried in the mine," Billings said, as Nate looked away, his fists clenched tightly, tears in his eyes. "I'm sorry."

"I hate them with perfect hatred," Freeman murmured. "I count them mine enemies." Then he turned to the FBI man and asked, "Who's behind it?"

"Organized crime," Billings replied. "It's become a multi-billion-dollar business, in just the past five years. Porno fans need increasingly gory stuff to feed their addictions; these guys are only too happy to provide it."

"The outlaws we're after today?"

Billings nodded. "Especially Costellini. But we want Perelli, too. You might know him as Stanley Hawkins."

"Are they the guys who stole my church?"

"Actually, Skip Sanders stole your church and then sold it to them. I got it on tape last night. If we can get him into court, we'll have a case."

"I want to help," Annie said.

"Ever use a camcorder?" Billings asked. "We want this whole deal taped, but I'll have my hands full monitoring a bug."

"She won't be in danger?" Nate asked.

"Not parked in this with me at the south end of Main Street," Billings said.

"Just show me how it works," Annie answered. "I'll give it my best shot."

35

At one o'clock, Eddie Hazard rode into Raptor on Nate Freeman's horse, and tied it to the hitching post at the North Star Tavern. He went inside, bought five hundred dollars worth of tokens and started to play the one-dollar slots. At 1:30, having lost half the coins, he climbed up on the stool where all the people in the casino could see him, and began shouting.

"This machine is rigged!" he yelled. "This whole town is rigged. See the cameras in the ceilings?" He pointed, and the curious gamblers who had gathered around him stared upward to see the button-sized holes above them, spaced about ten feet apart throughout the hall.

"They've been watching every move you make, controlling every dollar you win. They call it gaming, but it ain't no game—it's a giant rip-off!"

As he said this, several of the men closest to him chimed in. "Yeah, it ain't no game!" one yelled. "It's highway robbery."

"It's crooked," another shouted, pounding on the

machine in front of him. "They're all crooked, and the people who run them are crooks."

A third man joined in, kicking one machine after another. "It should be against the law," he shouted. "But it ain't. Legal larceny! That's what it is."

As the men continued shouting, the casino emptied, until only Hazard and his cronies and the North Star's staff were left.

"Thanks, guys," he whispered, handing each of the men a hundred-dollar bill. "Now get out of here and stay out of the way."

Leonard Price was watching the Bronco's pre-game show in the Upper Room, with Perelli, Costellini, Sanders, and their dates when the radio on his belt squawked.

"Chief Price. Chief Price," the North Star's lone security officer said. "There's a riot downstairs."

He plugged in the earphone, and replied, "Say again? Hazard? He must've gone over the edge. I'll be right there."

"What's up?" Perelli asked.

"Eddie Hazard's back in town, losing money and carrying on as usual. Only this time he took it too far. Made such a scene, all the North Star customers walked out. I guess it's time to teach him a lesson he won't forget. I'll be back in a few minutes."

When Eddie Hazard saw the police cruiser pull away from the curb and head north, he dashed out the door of the tavern and jumped on the horse.

Price flipped on the siren and lights, and put the pedal to the metal, just as the suspect galloped around the corner and headed east on Bank Street. At the next corner, the horse turned south, with the police car in hot pursuit, siren screaming.

He really is nuts, Price figured, *if he thinks he's going to get away in the middle of town. But at least he's saving me some work . . . leading me right to the ja . . .*

Without warning, a camper pulled out of the driveway next to the jail and across Nugget Street, directly in Price's path, just after the horse and rider galloped past. The policeman slammed on the brakes, barely in time, and skidded to a stop a foot from the vehicle's right rear tire.

Stupid tourists, he muttered, turning to look out the back window so he could back away and get on with the chase. But when his eyes passed the open passenger-side window, he found himself looking into the barrel of a service revolver.

"Good afternoon, Mr. Price," Agent Billings said, showing the chief his FBI badge. "You are under arrest for suspicion of murder, conspiracy to commit murder, kidnapping, obstruction of justice, and interstate trafficking in pornographic materials. You have the right to remain silent. Anything you say can and will be used against you in a court of law."

Billings opened the passenger door slowly, and slid in. "Now pull the vehicle behind the jail," he said.

As they reached the back door, Eddie Hazard rode up and dismounted. "Give your keys to Mr. Hazard, my special deputy for today," Billings commanded Price. "Isn't it strange how what goes around comes around?"

The agent took Price's gun, badge, and hat, climbed into the police cruiser, and followed the camper, which Annie Freeman was driving, to the south end of town.

At 1:50, Annie pulled the Winnebago across both lanes of Main Street, blocking off access to the town from the south.

Billings, in Price's police car, turned on the cruiser's lights and slowly made his way north, following north-bound vehicles out of town, until he reached the North Star Tavern, where Nate Freeman's pickup was now blocking access from the north. The minister, himself, was standing in the road, stapler in one hand and a stack of handbills in the other. Black Bart, his .45-caliber six-gun, was strapped to his right leg.

Billings pulled the cruiser across both lanes, left the lights flashing, and then slid behind the wheel of Freeman's truck. "So far, so good," he said. "Just give me time to get back to the camper. I need to know what's going on in the Upper Room. Good luck."

Freeman watched Billings drive to the camper. Then he counted backwards from twenty before he strode down the street and ascended the front porch of Settler's Bank. He stapled a poster to the front door. He repeated the pro-cedure every two feet in both directions, on the building's walls, windowsills, and railings. In ten minutes, he had effectively papered the front of the building with eleven-by-seventeen mug shots of the bank's manager, Stanley Hawkins.

"Here's Stanley Hawkins, the manager of this bank," he announced to the crowd of curious onlookers. "But read the fine print. Notice that his real name is George Perelli, and that he's been on the FBI's most-wanted list for suspicion of murder, manufacturing of explosives, and interstate transportation of stolen goods. Just the sort of fellow you always wanted to come into your beautiful, sleepy little town!"

"Where's Price?" Vincent Costellini yelled over the crowd noise coming from the TV. "He said he'd be back in a couple minutes. They're kicking off right now. He's gonna miss it, after all the money we spent on this party."

George Perelli walked to the window and looked out. At the north end of the street, the police car was blocking traffic, its lights rotating. Looking south, he saw no traffic at all, except where there seemed to be some sort of accident involving a camper.

"I don't like this," he muttered. But when he looked directly across the street, he liked it even less. For there was Nathan Freeman, standing on the bank steps, surrounded by posters bearing an unflattering photo of George Perelli.

"Excuse me, boss," he said, quickly spinning the cylinder of the snub-nosed .357 he always carried, concealed in a holster in the small of his back. "I think I'll go see if Leonard needs any help. If you're still taking bets, I'll take Denver for twenty thou and give you six points."

"You're on," Costellini replied, pulling Connie a little closer on the couch that had been set up right in front of the screen. "There's another twenty for you, babe, if Indianapolis wins or even if they lose by less than six."

Perelli turned on his heel and went down the steps.

Two down, one to go, Conroy said to herself, from her hiding place. *So far, so good.*

Suddenly, however, Costellini's bodyguard turned off the TV's sound. "Sorry, boss," he said, "but this field

308

strength meter is picking up a very strong signal today. This room is bugged, I'm sure of it."

"How is that possible?" Costellini said.

"I don't know," the fellow replied. "I'm just doing my job." With that, he started walking around the room, pointing the antenna of the meter at the walls, ceiling, and floors. At one point, he came within eighteen inches of Conroy's hiding place. But she had long since switched off her recorder.

Shut your mike off, Kelly. Turn it off, now, the agent tried to communicate telepathically. But Kelly was sitting on the lap of Skip Sanders, eating potato chips and sipping champagne, oblivious to the fact that her transmissions were being picked up.

After one especially crunchy chip, the bodyguard followed the signal to Kelly, and stood in front of her, the end of the antenna nearly touching her necklace. He glanced at Costellini, who leaped to his feet.

"What's the meaning of this?" he demanded, walking over and glaring menacingly at the woman.

"The meaning of what?" Sanders intervened.

"Nobody bugs Vincent Costellini!" the mafia man shouted, ripping the necklace from Kelly's neck.

She screamed, and Skip Sanders jumped to his feet to defend her.

Costellini carefully examined the necklace, then shoved it in Kelly's face. "Who you working for, babe?" he growled, grabbing her by the throat. The other girls in the room pressed back as far as they could into corners.

"Who?" he repeated, producing a switchblade. "You

have five seconds to start talking, or your lips will be in the wrong place. Five, four, three, two, *one*."

As he moved his hand to cut the woman, Skip Sanders dove between them. In the melee that ensued, Costellini knifed the former banker in the gut. He slumped to the floor, as Kelly knelt to help him.

Costellini grabbed her by the hair, pulled her to her feet, and asked the same question again. "Who you working for? Don't make me kill you, too."

That was all the carnage Clare Conroy was willing to endure.

In one motion, the agent kicked out the panel between her and the party, even as she shouted, "Freeze! FBI."

Costellini, totally surprised by the intrusion, released his grip just enough for Kelly to escape. But in that split second, the bodyguard had pulled his weapon. As he swung it toward Conroy, she fired three quick shots from her automatic, striking the man twice in the chest, and once between the eyes. He fell backward with a crash, and never moved again.

"Drop it, Costellini," she said, pointing to the knife.

He did.

"The answer to your question is, she *was* working for me."

"Figures, Conroy."

"You know me? Well, then, I won't waste time on introductions, except to read you your rights."

"Don't bother," he replied. "You'll never get me into court."

"Don't try anything foolish," she replied. "Or I'll save the taxpayers a lot of money, like I just did with your friend over there."

Then Conroy turned and addressed the people still left in the room. "Girls," she said, "just sit down and relax for a few minutes. Have a pizza or something. You've wandered into a major arrest, but when it's over you can wander back down to Alice's."

"I won't leave Skip," Kelly said. "He saved my life."

Conroy picked up the necklace and talked to Billings. "I have Costellini in custody. His bodyguard is dead. Skip Sanders is going to need a hospital real soon or he will be, too."

She walked over to the window, keeping the gun on Costellini. Outside, she could see Perelli and Freeman facing each other across the street.

"Hold on, Skip," she said to Sanders. "Five minutes and this is over."

Sanders, looking up at her from the floor, nodded weakly.

"Thanks, Harold," Bruce Davidson said. "It looks like this is as close as we'll get. I'll walk from here."

In front of them, a mile-long line of vehicles snaked its way up the canyon north toward Raptor. Horns were sounding, but nothing was moving either way on the narrow two-lane road.

Bruce walked briskly toward the town, his anxiety increasing with every step as he pondered what might be happening there. About halfway up the slope, he noticed a rough-looking fellow sitting in an open Jeep, talking into the microphone of his CB radio, an open beer in his left hand.

"Excuse me," Bruce said, displaying his FBI badge. "Do you know why traffic is stopped?"

The man's mouth dropped open, and he placed the beer can in a cup holder between the seats. "Ain't sure," the driver replied. "Sounds like one of them monthly shoot-outs, but I thought they only happened on Fridays."

"I have to get there, now!" Bruce shouted. "You can take me, or you can let me have this vehicle."

"Hop in," the driver responded, "and hold on!" He yanked the steering wheel left, gunned the vehicle into the southbound lane, and raced north toward Raptor.

Two minutes later, Bruce Davidson stood at the south end of Main Street, next to the camper that was blocking the street.

Perelli heard what sounded like small-caliber gunfire coming from the building he had just left. But then the words being hurled at him by the preacher across the street and the sight of the posters on the bank building so inflamed him that his only thought was to eradicate Freeman.

"There he is, ladies and gentlemen," Freeman announced, pointing to Perelli. "Fine, upstanding Stanley Hawkins, bank manager who knows nothing about managing banks, but a lot about killing innocent people. You know why he's here? Because this bank is owned by organized crime. The Cathedral Casino is a front for organized crime. And before long, every square inch of this town will belong to organized crime and the good, honest citizens who built it will be gone forever."

"Freeman!" Perelli yelled across the street. "Freeman, you're a liar." He started walking toward the preacher, who stepped out to meet him. "I'll see you put away for this."

312

"First you have to live through the afternoon," Freeman said, as he pulled his shirt away from Black Bart. "You stole my church, skinned my dog alive, and killed my horse. And Thursday night, your people did this to me."

He unbuttoned his shirt and let it slide down his back; the bystanders behind him gawked at the sight of his wounds.

"That's what you're about, Perelli," the preacher continued, rebuttoning the shirt. "And that's what these people need to know. But that ain't the half of it, folks. He's producing snuff videos—you know what that is? It's films where people get their lives snuffed out . . . that's right, killed. Mr. Perelli here has been killing people right off our streets, and you could be next."

"You're crazy, Freeman," Perelli said. "Everybody knows that."

"That so? How about Stephanie Lockwood? You made her star in *The Ultimate Sacrifice.* How much money did you make on that, huh?"

Now the two men stood in the middle of the street, face-to-face, thirty feet from each other. Perelli eyed Nate's sidearm.

"She killed herself!" he yelled.

When the hit man realized he had implicated himself simply by admitting he knew about it, he pulled his gun. But as he leveled it at Freeman, it was torn from his grip by the first of four shots launched his way by the preacher. The first spun the handgun skyward. The second, third, and fourth shots kept it spinning. When it hit the ground at Perelli's feet, he started to reach for what had been reduced to a piece of worthless metal.

Freeman grinned and said, "Go ahead, make my day."

Perelli froze, conscious of his disadvantage. Freeman strode toward him.

"Now take 'er easy," Freeman warned. "Just walk in front of me to the police cruiser over there and get in the backseat, nice and slow."

The crowd clapped. "These get better every month," one bystander said.

36

Bruce Davidson could hardly believe his eyes as he watched Freeman accomplish in three minutes what the FBI had been trying to do for over a decade. Davidson started walking toward the cruiser, anxious to make sure Perelli stayed put, now that the hit man was finally in custody.

But as the bureau chief passed the open driver's side window of the Winnebago, a familiar voice stopped him in his tracks. "Bruce," Fred Billings exclaimed. "What are you doing here?"

Davidson stepped back, and looked more carefully at the old man who had just spoken his name.

"I tried to call you this morning, and Judy told me where you were. I thought you might need an extra hand, so I checked out for twelve hours. But it looks like you didn't need my help as much as I needed your forgiveness."

Billings looked into his friend's eyes. "You got it, Bruce. But can we talk when this thing is wrapped? At the moment, there's too much going on." He patted the earphones he

315

was wearing for emphasis, and turned the key to start the vehicle's engine.

"Hold on, Annie!" Billings called to the woman videotaping through the camper's open side door. "They're almost to the street."

"Oh," Billings added, as Bruce opened the passenger-side door to climb in. "This is Annie, Nate Freeman's wife. Annie . . . my boss, Bruce Davidson."

"Pleased to meet you," Annie said to Bruce. Then, looking at Billings, she asked, "Sanders is still alive, then?"

"So far," Billings replied. "Costellini knifed him," he informed Davidson. "Annie's had some medical training. She'll try to keep Sanders alive until we get to the hospital."

"Costellini?" Davidson said. "You got him too?"

At that moment, Vincent Costellini stepped out the front door of the Cathedral Casino, followed by Clare Conroy, who marched him, at gunpoint, to the waiting cruiser. She locked him in the backseat next to Perelli, then slid into the vehicle's front seat, separated from her captives by a thick wire mesh. The car had a gun rack on the driver's side, which held the police chief's shotgun and rifle.

When the casino door opened again, Kelly Mitchell could be seen helping Skip Sanders toward the steps. Billings shoved the camper into gear, pulled the wheel hard left, and headed for the middle of town.

Before they had gone fifty feet, however, Sanders stumbled and pitched, headlong, down the stairs and onto the sidewalk, pulling the prostitute with him as he fell. Freeman and Conroy rushed toward the casino steps to help.

In the distraction of the moment, Connie, Vincent Costellini's escort, slipped behind the wheel of the cruiser,

316

threw it into reverse, whipped the vehicle around, and careened north, out of town, burning rubber all the way.

"What the—" Billings exclaimed, slamming on the brakes. "We'll never catch them in this," he said to Bruce. "Nate's pickup is our only chance." He tossed the keys at Bruce, and pointed back to the red 4x4 still parked next to where the camper had been.

Davidson jumped from the camper, ran to the 4x4, and tore after the fugitives, with Billings following close behind. As he passed the church, Bruce slowed down just enough for Clare to hop in next to him. Freeman leaped into the truck bed as Davidson hit the accelerator again.

"Surprise!" he said to Conroy as they sped northward. "The Lone Ranger has returned." *Unmasked,* he added silently.

"I should've taken the keys," she chastised herself. "I was so stupid, so careless!"

"Can't think of everything," he replied, calmly. "Don't whip yourself."

She looked at him, puzzled. "But *Perelli.* I wanted him, *for you.* I know how much you hate him. I'm sorry."

"In Yogi Berra's immortal words, It ain't over till it's over," Bruce replied.

"Connie," Vincent Costellini said, when the town was out of sight behind them. "Stop the car. We'll take it from here."

Both men leaped out as the vehicle skidded to a stop and their liberator unlocked the doors. Perelli jumped behind the wheel. Costellini pulled the young woman from the car and kissed her. "Thanks, babe. Here's my number and a few bucks for your trouble. He handed her the whole roll from his pocket. Come see me in New York and I'll take care of you. Real good care."

"We better cut the chatter, boss. Somebody's coming!"

Costellini looked back down the switchback cut into Hawk Mountain Pass, where a red pickup could be seen racing up the grade. "Run back behind those trees, Connie," he told her. "After that truck goes by, flag down a ride and get yourself out of here."

"There they are," Conroy shouted, as the cruiser disappeared over the canyon rim, about a mile ahead in a straight line, but at least three miles by road.

"Take 'er right up the face," Nate yelled through the little sliding window between him and the cab. "See the power line? There's a jeep trail underneath it."

"Hold on," Davidson shouted. He swerved off the road and onto the trail. He nudged the vehicle into four-wheel high and took it up the slope as fast as he dared. When they topped the hill, they had gained about a mile on the cruiser, still visible in the distance.

"Hello, Rockies Air Rescue?" Perelli said, using the police radio. "This is Leonard Price. Just got a report of a climbing accident, possible fatality, at Elk Creek Canyon. How soon can you meet me there?"

"ETA twelve minutes, sir," the dispatcher replied.

"Okay," Perelli said. "Pick me up at the overlook. I'll clear a spot for you."

"Ten-four. We'll be there."

Perelli took the next left turn. "We'll never get out of here on the ground," he explained to Costellini. "Especially in a cruiser. But we might outrun 'em by air. All they have is a made-over Huey from Vietnam, but it'll have to do."

Annie Freeman leaned over, trying to hear what Skip Sanders was saying as Billings took the switchbacks as fast as he could in the Winnebago.

"I'm dying," Sanders whispered again. "I want to make a confession."

"My husband's the clergyman, not me," she replied.

"I know," he said. "And I'm real sorry I put him, and you, through all this. I want to tell how I stole the church. I can't take this to my grave, and I can't let Costellini keep it."

Annie grabbed the camcorder and taped, as Sanders talked. "It was all too tempting," he began. "So much money, after so many years just barely getting by. Millions started pouring in, but I couldn't get my hands on any of it until the million-dollar offer on the church started me thinking: If I owned that building, I could name my price. So I convinced Nate to redecorate, loaned the money through the bank, and bought the mortgage through a corporation I set up. After that, it was just a matter of time until the right offer came along, which it did, fairly soon.

"So I falsified the records, and called the loan. All the papers are in the steeple, right above the bell.

"But let me add something else, just in case Costellini and his friends fight to keep the church. Call this my last will and testament, which supercedes and renders null and void any other wills I have previously drawn up. I, Cyrus Robert Sanders, otherwise known as Skip Sanders, do hereby bequeath my entire estate, including my home in Acapulco, any and all cash in my accounts, domestic and foreign, and my ten-percent interest in the net profits of the Cathedral Casino, should it ever open, to Nathan and Annie Freeman, of . . . where do you live, Annie?"

"Pueblo," she replied. "But we don't want your money, Skip."

"Of Pueblo, Colorado," he said to the camera. "Because they'll make better use of it than I ever would have," he added, straining to stay conscious.

From the front seat, Fred Billings interrupted, as he slowed to a stop. "Open the door, Kelly."

When she did so, in stepped Connie Baker. "Thanks," she said. "I just need a ride to . . ." She stopped at the sight of Kelly's face.

"Jail," Billings said from the front, pointing his handgun toward the young woman, who made no effort to escape.

"You are under arrest. You have the right to remain silent. Anything you say can and will be used against you in a court of law."

"But Vincent was so nice to me. He gave me twelve thousand dollars!" She showed them the money.

"Money isn't everything, Connie," Skip Sanders whispered. "Take my word . . . for . . . it." His eyes fluttered one last time and then fixed on the ceiling.

The helicopter appeared right on schedule, fluttering to a stop about twenty feet from the cruiser. As soon as it landed, the copilot jumped out and ran to the side of the police car.

George Perelli rolled down his window and greeted the fellow with the muzzle of Price's shotgun. "Don't make me use this, pal," he said, stepping out of the car. "Just walk in front of me back to that copter and tell your friends to climb out."

Costellini locked the cruiser doors and stuck the keys in his pocket before following Perelli to the aircraft. By the time he arrived, all four members of the rescue team were backing away from it, their hands in the air.

Perelli stashed the shotgun under the pilot's seat and started the engine. The helicopter pulled up from the ground just as Freeman's truck barreled up next to the cruiser in a cloud of dust.

"No!" Davidson protested, as he vaulted from the cab and ran to the canyon's edge. "Not again!"

Clare arrived at his side a moment later.

"Give me your gun," Davidson commanded.

"But they're already out of range."

"Not if I can get to that rifle," Davidson replied, pointing to the gun rack in the locked cruiser.

"No problem," she said. One shot from the Beretta turned the vehicle's closed window into a shower of glass.

Bruce grabbed the Remington seven-millimeter Magnum rifle and leaned across the cruiser's hood for support as he aimed. *Be on!* he urged it, as he swung it toward the copter, now two hundred yards away, at eye level. The aircraft was headed slightly left, exposing Perelli for a few seconds to a shot from Davidson's position.

Davidson laid the crosshairs of the rifle's scope on the hit man's chest and started to squeeze. A thousand times during the past eleven years he had dreamed of this moment, when all the hatred of all the years could be released, and Ellen's death finally avenged.

But suddenly, uninvited, her voice came into his brain. "Do not be overcome by evil, but overcome evil with good."

321

Okay, he shouted internally. He raised the crosshairs and fired at the engine cowling instead.

In the Huey, George Perelli stared at the instrument panel as the engine sputtered, then quit.

"What happened?" Costellini yelled, from the copilot's seat.

"Hydraulics. Line busted. We're autorotating. Brace yourself!"

"You brace *yourself!*" Costellini yelled back, driving his switchblade into Perelli, just below his rib cage.

Perelli looked down incredulously at the knife, and then at his boss. "Why?" he asked.

"One, you cheated last night," Costellini said. "Two, you didn't tell me about the gold table in the mine. Now this. Three strikes and you're . . ."

"Out!" Perelli roared, as he lowered his right shoulder and drove Costellini through the open door. The mafia chief hit the ground five seconds before the helicopter crashed on top of him.

Bruce ran to the canyon rim and peered through the rifle's scope at the wreckage five hundred feet below. In the cockpit, George Perelli sat motionless for nearly a minute before he stirred. "He's still alive," Davidson said to Conroy, who was standing next to him. "But he seems to be injured pretty badly."

The rescue crew's chief took one look down, then dashed back to the cruiser. "I'll call Stevensville for backup," he said. "They can be here in twenty minutes."

The copilot, standing next to Bruce, asked in a quavering voice, "What's this all about, anyway?"

"FBI," Davidson replied, producing his badge. "You just helped us capture two of the most wanted criminals in the country."

"I hate to say this," Conroy reminded Davidson. "But Perelli's down there and we're up here, so he's not captured quite yet. We need to get these on him," she added, holding out the handcuffs she had grabbed from the cruiser. "Cover me," she said, hanging the cuffs on her belt loop.

She started over the edge, but stopped short when Bruce said, "It's too dangerous, Clare. I'll go."

"I messed it up," she said. "I want to clean it up."

"I'll go with her," Nate Freeman said. "Then we'll have him surrounded." He patted his six-shooter, for emphasis. "Besides, I'm an EMT. He may need medical attention."

"Okay," Davidson nodded.

George Perelli shook his head to clear the fog. He glanced groggily upward, toward the sounds the climbers were making. Then he looked down at the body of Vincent Costellini, crushed under the helicopter's landing gear. The shotgun was pinned under his own collapsed seat.

When Clare Conroy saw Perelli move, she yelled, "Freeze, Perelli. This is the FBI. You're under arrest."

"Come and get me," Perelli muttered. Then he fell forward against the instrument panel as if unconscious.

Nate Freeman reached the crash scene first. Approaching cautiously from the right rear of the aircraft, he could see that Perelli was still breathing, his right hand clutching the handle of a knife imbedded in his side. The minister leaned into the cockpit for a closer look.

Suddenly, Freeman found himself face-to-face with the point of the switchblade, which Perelli had pulled out of his own wound. With his left hand the hit man pinned the preacher against the instrument panel, grasping him by the hair.

"Your gun," Perelli said. "Hand it over, slowly. No funny business or you're dead meat."

"Okay," Freeman said, pulling out Black Bart. He glanced at the bleeding gash in Perelli's gut. "But if we don't plug that hole right soon, you'll be dead, yourself."

"As if you'd be concerned."

"I hate to see a man die without confessin' his sins," Freeman said.

Perelli looked down at the wound, cocked the hammer of the Colt .45, and pointed it at Freeman. "You can fix it . . . after Agent Conroy joins our little party."

Perelli grinned at Clare, who had taken cover behind a nearby boulder, her pistol aimed at the hit man. "Drop it and come here," he said, putting the gun's muzzle against Freeman's head, "or the preacher is history."

"Don't, please," she yelled. She dropped the Beretta and stepped into the open with her hands in the air. "He's suffered enough already. Take me and let him go," she said as she walked slowly toward the others.

"Suffered?" Perelli laughed. "You don't know the meaning of the word. But you will, I promise."

When Conroy reached the wreck, Perelli relaxed his grip on the minister and grabbed Clare by the blouse. He pulled her face up to his and said, "We have some unfinished business, don't we, dear?"

"If you're up to it," she replied.

He shoved her back to arm's length and tightened his grip. "You'll find out soon enough," he said.

Freeman interrupted. "There's some gauze and tape here. I think I can help you."

"Do it," Perelli said, training the gun on Conroy as the minister bandaged the wound.

"This'll hold it for awhile," Freeman said, when he had finished. "But you need a doctor real soon, or you'll bleed to death inside."

"I'll take my chances," Perelli replied. "And you can take yours. You fixed me up, so I'll give you until the count of ten before I shoot. See how far you can get."

Freeman stared at Perelli, then at Conroy, then back at Perelli, who said, impassively, "One."

"He means it, Nate," Clare said. "He's a murderer."

"That's not very nice," Perelli said, slapping Clare's face. "Two," he said, pulling her close again.

"I ain't runnin'," Freeman said.

"Three," Perelli continued.

"Cowards run," Freeman said, looking Perelli in the eyes.

"Four."

"And I ain't one. You should know that by now."

"All I know is that you're stupid. Five."

"Smart enough to get my church back."

"Little good it'll do you dead. Six."

"I ain't afraid of dyin'."

"Time to say your prayers. Seven."

As Freeman slowly raised his eyes toward the sky, he saw Bruce Davidson taking aim with the rifle.

"Eight."

The minister fell to his knees and Perelli moved his head

slightly, adjusting his aim, at the exact moment that Davidson fired. The rifle's bullet grazed Perelli's scalp and ricocheted off the rocks behind him. At the sound, Perelli flinched, discharging the pistol in his hand. The Colt's bullet struck Nate Freeman in the upper right quadrant of his chest. He glanced at the wound, and then stared at Clare for a split second, his face a mixture of surprise and pain. Then he fell over on the ground, unconscious.

Perelli yanked Conroy down behind the copter. With his left arm locked around her throat and the pistol to her head, he said, "Who is that up there?"

"Davidson," she replied, gasping for breath.

"Figures," Perelli said. "Tell him he just killed the preacher."

"You pulled the trigger," she said, studying Freeman for a moment, relieved to see he was still breathing.

"Maybe I wouldn't have, but you'll never know. Tell Deadeye Davidson to throw his rifle over the edge."

"Bruce!" she yelled. "Throw the rifle into the canyon. Nate's hit in the chest. He needs . . ."

"Shut up," Perelli said. He tore the handcuffs off her belt loop and cuffed her hands in front of her. "Now, get moving."

"Where?"

"Up the hill. We're gonna take a ride in the Reverend's truck. He won't mind, I'm sure."

"You'll never get away."

"Never say never to me," he replied. "Now march, and don't try anything funny or your brains are mincemeat." He stooped and picked up the switchblade, folded it, and slipped it in his pocket. Then he stuck the gun's muzzle into her back, prodding her up the steep slope.

37

B
ruce Davidson watched helplessly as George Perelli marched Clare Conroy up the incline. *His head was square in the crosshairs. No wind. A good rest.* He replayed the incident in his mind. *When Freeman moved, it was my only chance. Perelli should have missed, not me.*

Perelli shoved his hostage through the passenger side door of the truck, and locked it. Then he turned and grinned at Davidson, who was standing fifty feet away, hands at his side. "If you follow us," Perelli said, "she dies. Another dead woman on your conscience."

"So, you *did* kill my wife. Finally, you admit it!"

"*You* killed her when you gave her the keys."

"Who hired you?"

"Costellini." Perelli nodded toward the canyon. "Looks like you're even," he said. Then he climbed into the truck and started the engine.

Davidson dashed toward the vehicle as Perelli backed it up to turn around. The agent grabbed the truck's open tailgate just as the hit man floored the accelerator. For a moment, Bruce clung to the pickup, one foot on the trailer hitch and the other on the bumper as the 4x4 picked up speed. Perelli, watching in the rearview mirror, laughed as Davidson struggled to climb into the truck bed. He swerved hard left, then right, trying to shake Bruce off.

When this didn't work, however, Perelli pulled out Freeman's gun, pointed it through the open rear window, and cocked it.

"Bruce, jump!" Clare Conroy yelled.

Davidson dove to his right, and tumbled to a stop in the soft leaves along the edge of the road.

As Perelli reached through the window to get a better shot, Conroy twisted and kicked his wrist as hard as she could against the window frame. Perelli's hand opened involuntarily for a split second, and the Colt .45 fell into the truck bed. It discharged skyward on the first bounce, then spun out of the truck and landed a few feet from Davidson, who rushed toward it.

Perelli slammed on the brakes and punched Conroy flush in the face. Her head snapped back hard against the window. Then she fell sideways onto the seat, out cold.

Davidson picked up the gun and fired, as Perelli ducked and hit the accelerator again. The first shot took out the truck's rear window. The second shot shattered the windshield. The third hit the rearview mirror a few inches to Perelli's left. The fourth struck the dash, just right of the steering wheel, behind which Perelli was crouched. Bruce steadied the gun and fired again, just as the vehicle disappeared from view. The hammer fell on an empty chamber.

Davidson stood in the road and prayed, out loud, "God,

if you can rescue a little fawn, you can rescue Clare Conroy. Please, Lord, I beg you. Don't let her die."

Suddenly, in the distance behind him, he heard, "Rescue One, this is Rescue Two. Come in."

Hot-wire the cruiser! Davidson dashed back toward the police car, where the first crew's chief was responding to the radio's message.

"What's their ETA?" he yelled as he ran.

"Five minutes."

"Which direction are they coming from?"

"East."

Davidson grabbed the microphone. "Rescue Two," he said. "This is Bruce Davidson, FBI. We have a hostage situation in an eastbound red pickup. Can you see it?"

"Affirmative," the voice replied. "They just turned south, toward Hawk Mountain Pass. Should we pursue?"

Davidson hesitated, torn between Conroy's predicament and Freeman's. "Negative," he said. "Priority one is a gunshot wound in the canyon, next to the crash."

"Roger."

Bruce leaned under the cruiser's dash and ripped out the wires to the ignition. *Okay,* he commanded himself. *Calm down. You can do this.*

With his Swiss army knife, Davidson scraped the edge of two wires, then laid one across the other.

The engine kicked over, then started. "Perelli," Bruce vowed. "If she dies, I'll kill you with my bare hands." He wheeled the vehicle around and headed east, as fast as possible, the cruiser's lights flashing and siren blaring.

When he had gone about a mile, the helicopter passed overhead, a rescue basket in its open doorway, ready to be lowered.

***

Clare Conroy woke with a start. Instinctively, she reached for her aching face, remembering the handcuffs as she tried to move her hands.

"Where are we?" she demanded, pushing herself upright.

"A place where your worst nightmares can come true," Perelli replied.

"The Kingsford estate," she said, immediately recognizing the mansion.

"Specifically, the Kingsford Mine," Perelli said. "A guy could really hole up there, don't you think?" He then walked around to her side of the truck and pulled her out.

"Especially if his best girlfriend is with him," he added.

He pushed her toward the mine entrance. When they reached it, Perelli unlocked the lock, pulled off the chain, and opened the latch. The huge doors creaked open, wide enough for them to step through. He pulled Conroy and the chain inside, then closed the doors behind them and secured them from within with the chain and lock. For a moment, Perelli and Conroy were in total darkness, except for a thin shaft of light coming through the crack between the doors.

"If I'd planned ahead," he said, "I would've brought a lantern. But we'll have to make do with my little lighter." He flicked the Bic, and they were instantly standing in a small circle of light.

"How far do you expect to get with that?" she said.

"As far as I need to, dear. I don't need any light to do what I have in mind for you. Now, walk slowly down the shaft ahead of me. No tricks or this knife carves you into pretty little pieces."

Conroy, trying to fight her growing fear, counted the steps as she walked. But no matter how hard she tried, she couldn't block out her last terrifying experience in this cavern.

God, she prayed, trembling. *Will I be just another corpse in this giant tomb? How can I get away this time?*

Suddenly, a psalm she had memorized during her Inter-Varsity days at Yale burst into her mind: "I love you, O Lord, my strength," it began.

With each step, she recited another verse.

"The Lord is my rock, my fortress and my deliverer; my God is my rock, in whom I take refuge.

"He is my shield and the horn of my salvation, my stronghold.

"I call to the Lord, who is worthy of praise, and I am saved from my enemies. . . ."

A peace she'd never felt flooded her soul. On the fourteenth step of the recitation, an idea jumped at her from the text: "He shot his arrows and scattered the enemies, great bolts of lightning routed them."

When they reached the gold altar, Perelli picked her up, as if she weighed nothing, and laid her upon it. She looked up at him, without blinking, then started to unbutton her blouse, from the top down.

"What are you doing?" he said.

"It's my favorite blouse," she replied, without moving her hands. "I didn't want you to rip it."

"I'll say what gets ripped and what doesn't," he yelled. He folded the switchblade and tucked it into his pocket. Then, holding the lighter above her, he grabbed the fabric with his left hand.

"Suit yourself," she said. Then the room filled with light from the wings of the eagle pin, which Conroy had discharged directly into Perelli's eyes.

He cursed, dropped the lighter on the floor, grabbed his

temporarily blinded eyes, and then reached for Conroy. But she was already gone.

"You can't get away in here," he yelled. "And when I find you, I promise, you'll wish you'd never been born."

At the top of Hawk Mountain Pass, Bruce Davidson pulled the cruiser to the side of the road. He flipped off the lights and siren, and picked up the microphone.

"Rescue Two," he asked. "How's your patient?"

"Alive," a voice replied, "though he should have died before we got here. He's going to make it."

"The Reverend has good connections," Bruce said, relieved.

"Evidently," the pilot said. "We're lifting off now. Heading for Mountain View Hospital."

"Good. That'll take you right over my position," Davidson replied. "Let me know if you see that truck anywhere. I've lost them."

"Roger that. We'll take it up to two thousand feet."

Conroy stood in the pitch blackness with her back against the rock wall. To her right, up the incline, she could hear Perelli coming.

My only hope is Kingsford's tunnel, she urged herself. *But I have no idea how deep I've gone, and I can't see a thing.*

She continued reciting the same psalm: "You, O Lord, keep my lamp burning; my God turns my darkness into light."

Clare closed her eyes, and stepped gingerly toward the center of the shaft until she reached the trackless railroad ties.

"With your help I can advance against a troop; with my God I can scale a wall," she whispered, taking a step down the slope. With each verse, she moved forward, one tie at a time, confident that as long as she stayed on them, she would remain somewhere near the middle of the mine.

"As for God, his way is perfect . . . He is a shield for all who take refuge in him. . . .

"He makes my feet like the feet of a deer; he enables me to stand on the heights."

She turned left and walked slowly toward the wall until she collided with an uneven surface. *The stairs! Maybe there's still time.* She clambered up and into the tunnel.

Less than a minute after the helicopter passed overhead, the pilot's voice came over the radio. "I see the truck. It's parked at the Kingsford Mine. Take the left at the bottom of the pass. Over and out."

"Thanks," Davidson replied. He threw the cruiser into gear and tore down the switchbacks. As he drove, he tuned the radio to the State Police frequency. "Anyone listening," he said, "this is FBI agent Bruce Davidson requesting backup. Hostage situation in progress at the Kingsford Mine, near Raptor. Do you copy?"

"Roger, Mr. Davidson," a voice replied. "This is Cold River dispatch. We have two officers south of Raptor. Major traffic problem caused some fender benders."

"Get them here, ASAP," Davidson replied. "And as many others as you can muster."

With no railroad ties to guide her, Clare Conroy crawled through the tunnel leading to the Kingsford estate, until she bumped her head against the door she knew led into what had been Dr. Bradley's office. Then she stood and examined the wood surface with her hands. The door had some etchings, but there was no handle.

There must be a switch, she thought, *just like the other side. But I'll never find it, handcuffed, in the dark.*

Each second's delay increased the likelihood that Perelli would catch up. *Was that a noise in the tunnel?* Conroy wondered. *He's just around the corner!*

The knowledge that she was only a door's thickness from freedom added to Conroy's panic, until she remembered the eagle still pinned to her blouse. *A microsecond's better than nothing,* she assured herself. She stepped backward to get a better view, then activated the flash unit.

For a thousandth of a second the cavern was illuminated, long enough for Conroy to see a button recessed into the wall to her right. She punched it, just as Perelli appeared at the bend, still carrying his lighter.

The heavy door pivoted, revealing Bradley's extensive library, part of which lined the panel's exterior. Conroy's first thought was to try to outrun her pursuer. At that moment, however, she remembered that the door would close itself in five seconds. She also thought of her watch.

Maybe I can keep it closed, she hoped as she armed the mechanism and fired the first .22-caliber bullet at the switch. Although it missed, the sound halted Perelli, momentarily, ten feet from Clare.

"A .44 Magnum couldn't stop me now," he snickered.

"Maybe not," Clare replied, backing into the doorway, counting silently. "But four inches of solid oak will."

When the door started to swivel shut, she fired again. This time, the button blew apart. She collapsed backwards onto the floor of the room, safe at last.

"No!" Perelli yelled.

When he reached the panel, the opening was still eight inches wide. The hit man reached through, grabbed one of the books off the shelf, and jammed it into the crack. Then

334

he reached through with both hands and tried to force the unit open. It groaned against his brute strength, but held fast.

"Sorry to leave you stuck like this, George," Clare said. "Stay right there and I'll go and get some help."

Conroy turned and ran out of the room and through the house. She burst out the mansion's front door just as the squad car driven by Bruce Davidson skidded to a stop in the driveway.

Bruce bolted from the vehicle and met Clare halfway. He took one look at her battered face and then said, "Where is he? I'll teach him to . . ."

"He's trapped," she replied. "But don't go after him alone, Bruce, please. He's . . . *they're* too strong." Then she started to cry.

Davidson took her in his arms. "Backup's on the way," he said. "But what do you mean, *they?* Isn't he alone?"

"Physically, he's alone," she replied. "Metaphysically, he's not. Otherwise he'd be dead. But then again, if God weren't stronger, I'd be dead myself."

In the distance, two police sirens could be heard approaching the estate.

"I know what you mean," he said. "Without his help, I'd still be a slave to my past, not to mention demon rum."

She stepped back, studying his face. "And now?" she asked.

"Now I've been released from their grip, like you need to be released from those handcuffs. But I still have to learn to manage my freedom."

"The key's in my back pocket," she said. As he unlocked the cuffs, she added, "Obviously, you've made a lot of progress."

"Thanks to you," he replied. "You were the only one who told me the truth."

"About?"

"About the hole I wanted you to fill. The hole I wanted *everyone* to fill, but no one ever could. I'm sorry, Clare. I hope you will forgive me."

"Of course," she replied. "I love you, Bruce. I have for a long time. But I just couldn't get inside, where I have to be if it's going to be real."

She reached out and took his hands, then pulled him close, leaning her head against his shoulder.

"I love you, too, Clare," he said. "But not the way I did when I asked you to marry me. Then, I wanted what I thought you could give me. Now, I'd rather give you something, instead."

"How about *yourself?*" she answered. "I think I'm ready now."

"But am I?" he said. "There's so much unfinished business."

He paused, pulled back, and looked deeply into her blue eyes, as he continued, "With my past. With my present. With the program." *Not to mention Doris,* he thought.

"When Perelli drove away with you a few minutes ago," he continued, "and I started shooting at him, the rage returned. Hatred gripped me, just like before. For that moment, I was right back where I started."

"I can help, if you'll let me," she replied.

"How?"

"By loving you so much there wouldn't be any room for hate."

"Could you do that, Clare? Can anybody actually do that?"